Spider and Jeanne Robinson

# Stardance

QUANTUM SCIENCE FICTION

Futura Publications Limited
An Orbit Book

An Orbit Book

First published in Great Britain by
Futura Publications Limited in 1979

A Quantum Science Fiction Novel

Portions of this work first appeared in *Analog*
magazine in different form.

ISBN 0 7088 8049 5

Printed in Great Britain by
Hazell Watson & Viney Ltd
Aylesbury, Bucks

Futura Publications Limited
110 Warner Road
Camberwell, London SE5

This one's for Luanna Mountainborne,
who may well make prophets of us one day . . .

"In order to find one's place in the infinity of being, one must be able both to separate and unite."

—*I Ching*

# Acknowledgments

What we'd like to do here is thank all the people without whom this book could not have been finished, as opposed to, but not excluding, that general gang of friends and relatives who kept us alive during its writing; they would have done so anyway, book or no book, and should be thanked in different ways.

Among the former and sometimes the latter are: Ben Bova, Gordon R. Dickson, our agent Kirby McCauley, our editor and friend Jim Frenkel, Joe W. Haldeman, Jerry Pournelle, Ph.D., and Laurence Janifer, all of whom donated information, advice, and assistance above and beyond the call of friendship, all at the cost of working time or leisure or both. It should be clearly understood that none of the above people are to blame for what we have done with their information and aid: any errors are ours.

On a less personal but just as basic level, this book could also never have become what it is without *A House In Space*, Henry S.F. Cooper's fascinating account of zero-gee life in Skylab; G. Harry Stine's *The Third Industrial Revolution*, which built Skyfac in our minds; the recent works of John Varley and Frank Herbert, who roughly simultaneously pioneered (at least as far as we know) the concept on which the ending of this book depends;

Murray Louis's exquisite and moving columns in *Dance-Magazine*; the books, past advice and present love of Stephen Gaskin; the inspirational dance of Toronto Dance Theatre, Murray Louis, Pilobolus, the Contact Improv Movement, and all of our dancing buddies in Nova Scotia; the lifework of Robert Heinlein, Theodore Sturgeon, Edgar Pangborn, and John D. MacDonald; the whiskey of Mr. Jameson, the coffee of Jamaica, and the music of Frank Zappa, Paul Simon, and Yes.

# 1

# Stardance

## Chapter 1

I can't really say that I knew her, certainly not the way Seroff knew Isadora. All I know of her childhood and adolescence are the anecdotes she chanced to relate in my hearing—just enough to make me certain that all three of the contradictory biographies on the current best-seller list are fictional. All I know of her adult life are the relatively few hours she spent in my presence and on my monitors—more than enough to tell me that every newspaper account I've seen is fictional. Carrington probably believed he knew her better than I, and in a limited sense he was correct—but he would never have written about it, and now he is dead.

But I was her video man, since the days when you touched the camera with your hands, and I knew her backstage: a type of relationship like no other on Earth or off it. I don't believe it can be described to anyone not of the profession—you might think of it as somewhere between co-workers and combat buddies. I was with her the day she came to Skyfac, terrified and determined, to stake her life upon a dream. I watched her work and worked with her for that whole two months, through endless rehearsals, and I have saved every tape and they are not for sale.

And, of course, I saw the Stardance. I was there. I taped it.

I guess I can tell you some things about her.

To begin with, it was not, as Cahill's *Shara* and Von Derski's *Dance Unbound: The Creation of New Modern* suggest, a lifelong fascination with space and space travel that led her to become her race's first zero-gravity dancer. Space was a means to her, not an end, and its vast empty immensity scared her at first. Nor was it, as Melberg's hardcover tabloid *The Real Shara Drummond* claims, because she lacked the talent to make it as a dancer on Earth. If you think free-fall dancing is easier than conventional dance, you try it. Don't forget your dropsickness bag.

But there is a grain of truth in Melberg's slander, as there is in all the best slanders. She could *not* make it on Earth—but not through lack of talent.

I first saw her in Toronto in July of 1989. I headed Toronto Dance Theater's video department at that time, and I hated every minute of it. I hated everything in those days. The schedule that day called for spending the entire afternoon taping students, a waste of time and tape that I hated more than anything except the phone company. I hadn't seen the new year's crop yet, and was not eager to. I love to watch dance done well—the efforts of a tyro are usually as pleasing to me as a first-year violin student in the next apartment is to you.

My leg was bothering me more than usual as I walked into the studio. Norrey saw my face and left a group of young hopefuls to come over. "Charlie . . . ?"

"I know, I know. They're tender fledglings, Charlie, with egos as fragile as an Easter egg in December. Don't bite them, Charlie. Don't even bark at them if you can help it, Charlie."

She smiled. "Something like that. Leg?"

"Leg."

Norrey Drummond is a dancer who gets away with looking like a woman because she's small. There's about a hundred and fifteen pounds of her, and most of it is heart. She stands about five-four, and is perfectly capable of seeming to tower over the tallest student. She has more energy than the North American Grid, and uses it as efficiently as a vane pump (do you know the principle of a standard piston-type pump? Go look up the principle of a vane pump). There's a signaturelike uniqueness to her dance, the only reason I can see why she got so few of the really juicy parts in company productions until Modern gave way to New Modern. I liked her because she didn't pity me.

"It's not only the leg," I admitted. "I hate to see the tender fledglings butcher your choreography."

"Then you needn't worry. The piece you're taping today is by . . . one of the students."

"Oh fine. I knew I should have called in sick." She made a face. "What's the catch?"

"Eh?"

"Why did the funny thing happen to your voice just as you got to 'one of my students'?"

She blushed. "Dammit, she's my sister."

Norrey and I go back a *long* way together, but I'd never met a sister—not unusual these days, I suppose. My eyebrows rose. "She must be good then."

"Why, thank you, Charlie."

"Bullshit. I give compliments right-handed or not at all—I'm not talking about heredity. I mean that you're so hopelessly ethical you'd bend over backward to avoid nepotism. For you to give your own sister a feature like that, she must be *terrific*."

"Charlie, she is," Norrey said simply.

"We'll see. What's her name again?"

"Shara." Norrey pointed her out, and I understood the rest of the catch. Shara Drummond was ten years younger than her sister—and a good eighteen centimeters taller, with fifteen or eighteen more kilos. I noted absently that she was stunningly beautiful, but it didn't lessen my dismay—in her best years, Sophia Loren could never have become a Modern dancer. Where Norrey was small, Shara was big, and where Norrey was big, Shara was bigger. If I'd seen her on the street I might have whistled appreciatively—but in the studio I frowned.

"My God, Norrey, she's enormous."

"Mother's second husband was a football player," she said mournfully. "She's awfully good."

"If she *is* good, that *is* awful. Poor girl. Well, what do you want me to do?"

"What makes you think I want you to do anything?"

"You're still standing here."

"Oh. I guess I am. Well . . . have lunch with us, Charlie?"

"Why?" I knew perfectly well why, but I expected a polite lie.

Not from Norrey Drummond. "Because you two have something in common, I think."

I paid her honesty the compliment of not wincing. "I suppose we do."

"Then you will?"

"Right after the session."

She twinkled and was gone. In a remarkably short time she had organized the studio full of wandering, chattering young people into something that resembled a dance ensemble if you squinted. They warmed up during the twenty minutes it took me to set up and check out my equipment. I positioned one camera in front of them, one behind, and kept one in my hands for walk-around closeup work. I never triggered it.

There's a game that you play in your mind. Every time someone catches or is brought to your attention, you begin making guesses about them. You try to extrapolate their character and habits from their appearance. Him? Surly, disorganized—leaves the cap off the toothpaste and drinks boilermakers. Her? Art-student type, probably uses a diaphragm and writes letters in a stylized calligraphy of her own invention. Them? They look like schoolteachers from Miami, probably here to see what snow looks like, attend a convention. Sometimes I come pretty close. I don't know how I typecast Shara Drummond, in those first twenty minutes. The moment she began to dance, all preconceptions left my mind. She became something elemental, something unknowable, a living bridge between our world and the one the Muses live in.

I know, on an intellectual and academic level, just about all there is to know about dance, and I could not categorize or classify or even really comprehend the dance she danced that afternoon. I saw it, I even appreciated it, but I was not equipped to understand it. My camera dangled from the end of my arm, next to my jaw. Dancers speak of their "center," the place their motion centers around, often quite near the physical center of gravity. You strive to "dance from your center," and the "contraction-and-release" idea which underlies so much of Modern dance depends on the center for its focus of energy. Shara's center seemed to move about the room under its own power, trailing limbs that attached to it by choice rather than necessity. What's the word for the outermost part of the sun, the part that still shows in an eclipse? Corona? That's what her limbs were: four lengthy tongues of flame that followed the center in its eccentric, whirling orbit, writhing fluidly around its surface. That the lower two frequently contacted the floor seemed coincidental—indeed the other two touched the floor nearly as regularly.

There were other students dancing. I know this because the two automatic videocameras, unlike me, did their job and recorded the piece as a whole. It was called *Birthing*, and depicted the formation of a galaxy that ended up resembling Andromeda. It was not an accurate literal portrayal, but it wasn't intended to be. Symbolically, it felt like the birth of a galaxy.

In retrospect. At the time I was aware only of the galaxy's heart: Shara. Students occluded her from time to time, and I simply never noticed. It hurt to watch her.

If you know anything about dance, this must all sound horrid to you. A dance about a *nebula*? I know, I know. It's a ridiculous notion. And it worked. In the most gut-level, cellular way it worked—save only that Shara was too good for those around her. She did not belong in that eager crew of awkward, half-trained apprentices. It was like listening to the late Stephen Wonder trying to work with a pickup band in a Montreal bar.

But that wasn't what hurt.

Le Maintenant was shabby, but the food was good and the house brand of grass was excellent. Show a Diner's Club card in there and Fat Humphrey'd show you a galley full of dirty dishes. It's gone now. Norrey and Shara declined a toke, but in my line of work it helps. Besides, I needed a few hits. How to tell a lovely lady her dearest dream is hopeless?

I didn't need to ask Shara to know that her dearest dream was to dance. More: to dance professionally. I have often speculated on the motives of the professional artist. Some seek the narcissistic assurance that others will actually pay cash to watch or hear them. Some are so incompetent or disorganized that they can support themselves in no other way. Some have a message which they feel needs expressing. I suppose most artists combine aspects of all three. This is not complaint—what they do for us is necessary. We should be grateful that there *are* motives.

But Shara was one of the rare ones. She danced because she simply needed to. She needed to say things which could be said in no other way, and she needed to take her meaning and her living from the saying of them. Anything else would have demeaned and devalued the essential statement of her dance. I knew this, from watching that one dance.

Between toking up and keeping my mouth full and then toking again (a mild amount to offset the slight down that eating brings), it was over half an hour before I was required to say anything beyond an occasional grunted response to the luncheon chatter of the ladies. As the coffee arrived, Shara looked me square in the eye and said, "Do you talk, Charlie?"

She was Norrey's sister, all right.

"Only inanitites."

"No such thing. Inane people, maybe."

"Do you enjoy dancing, Ms. Drummond?"

She answered seriously. "Define 'enjoy.' "

I opened my mouth and closed it, perhaps three times. You try it.

"And for God's sake tell me why you're so intent on not talking to me. You've got me worried."

"Shara!" Norrey looked dismayed.

"Hush. I want to know."

I took a crack at it. "Shara, before he died I had the privilege of meeting Bertram Ross. I had just seen him dance. A producer who knew and liked me took me backstage, the way you take a kid to see Santa Claus. I had expected him to look older offstage, at rest. He looked younger, as if that incredible motion of his was barely in check. He talked to me. After a while I stopped opening my mouth, because nothing ever came out."

She waited, expecting more. Only gradually did she comprehend the compliment and its dimension. I had assumed it would be obvious. Most artists *expect* to be complimented. When she did twig, she did not blush or simper. She did not cock her head and say, "Oh, come on." She did not say, "You flatter me." She did not look away,

She nodded slowly and said, "Thank you, Charlie.

That's worth a lot more than idle chatter." There was a suggestion of sadness in her smile, as if we shared a bitter joke.

"You're welcome."

"For heaven's sake, Norrey, what are you looking so upset about?"

The cat now had Norrey's tongue.

"She's disappointed in me," I said. "I said the wrong thing."

"That was the wrong thing?"

"It should have been, 'Ms. Drummond, I think you ought to give up dancing.'"

"It should have been '*Shara*, I think you ought' . . . *what?*"

"Charlie—" Norrey began.

"I was supposed to tell you that we can't all be professional dancers, that they also surf who only sand and wade. Shara, I was supposed to tell you to dump the dance—before it dumps you."

In my need to be honest with her, I had been more brutal than was necessary, I thought. I was to learn that bluntness never dismayed Shara Drummond. She demanded it.

"Why you?" was all she said.

"We're inhabiting the same vessel, you and I. We've both got an itch that our bodies just won't let us scratch."

Her eyes softened. "What's your itch?"

"The same as yours."

"Eh?"

"The man was supposed to come and fix the phone on Thursday. My roommate Karen and I had an all-day rehearsal. We left a note. Mister telephone man, we had to go out, and we sure couldn't call you, heh heh. Please get the key from the concierge and come on in; the phone's in the bedroom. The phone man never showed up. They never do." My hands seemed to be shaking. "We came up the back stairs from the alley. The phone was still dead, but I never thought to take down the note on the front door. I got sick the next morning. Cramps. Vomiting. Karen and I were just friends, but she stayed home to take care of me. I suppose on a Friday night the note seemed even more plausible. He slipped the lock with a piece of plastic, and Karen came out of the kitchen as he was unplugging the stereo. He was so indignant he shot her. Twice. The noise scared him; by the time I got there he was halfway out the door. He just had time to put a slug through my hip joint, and then he was gone. They never got him. They never even came to fix the phone." My hands were under control now. "Karen was a damned good dancer, but I was better. In my head I still am."

Her eyes were round. "You're not Charlie . . . Charles *Armstead*."

I nodded.

"Oh my God. So *that's* where you went."

I was shocked by how shocked she looked. It brought me back from the cold and windy border of self-pity. I began a little to pity her again. I should have guessed the depth of her empathy. And in the way that really mattered, we were too damned alike—we *did* share the same bitter joke. I wondered why I had wanted to shock her.

"They couldn't repair the joint?" she asked softly.

"I can walk splendidly if asymmetrically. Given a strong enough motivation, I can even run short distances. I can't dance worth a damn."

"So you became a video man."

"Three years ago. People who know both video and dance are about as common as garter belts these days. Oh, they've been taping dance since the '70s—usually with the imagination of a network news cameraman. If you film a stage play with two cameras in the orchestra pit, is it a movie?"

"You try to do for dance what the movie camera did for drama?"

"It's a pretty fair analogy. Where it breaks down is that dance is more analogous to music than to drama. You can't stop and start it easily, or go back and retake a scene that didn't go in the can right, or reverse the chronology to get a tidy shooting schedule. The event happens and you record it. What I am is what the record industry pays top dollar for: a mix-man with savvy enough to know which ax is wailing at the moment and mike it high—and the sense to have given the heaviest dudes the best mikes. There are a few others like me. I'm the best."

She took it the way she had the compliment to herself —at face value. Usually when I say things like that, I don't give a damn what reaction I get, or I'm being salty and hoping for outrage. But I was pleased at her acceptance, pleased enough to bother me. A faint irritation made me go brutal again, *knowing* it wouldn't work. "So what all this leads to is that Norrey was hoping I'd suggest some similar form of sublimation for you. Because I'll make it in dance before you will."

She stubborned up. "I don't buy that, Charlie. I know what you're talking about, I'm not a fool, but I think I can beat it."

"Sure you will. *You're too damned big, lady*. You've got tits like both halves of a prize honeydew melon and an ass that any actress in Hollywood would sell her parents for and in Modern dance that makes you d-e-d dead, you haven't got a chance. Beat it? You'll beat your head in first, how'm I doing, Norrey?"

"For Christ's sake, Charlie!"

I softened. I can't work Norrey into a tantrum—I like her too much. It almost kept us living together, once. "I'm sorry, hon. My leg's giving me the mischief, and I'm stinkin' mad. She *ought* to make it—and she won't. She's your sister, and so it saddens you. Well, I'm a total stranger, and it enrages me."

"How do you think it makes me feel?" Shara blazed,

startling us both. I hadn't known she had so much voice. "So you want me to pack it in and rent me a camera, huh, Charlie? Or maybe sell apples outside the studio?" A ripple ran up her jaw. "Well I will be damned by all the gods in southern California before I'll pack it in. God gave me the large economy size, but there is not a surplus pound on it and it fits me like a glove and I can by Jesus *dance* it and I will. You may be right—I may beat my head in first. But I will get it done." She took a deep breath. "Now I thank you for your kind intentions, Char . . . Mister Armst . . . oh shit." The tears came and she left hastily, spilling a quarter-cup of cold coffee on Norrey's lap.

"Charlie," Norrey said through clenched teeth, "why do I like you so much?"

"Dancers are dumb." I gave her my handkerchief.

"Oh." She patted at her lap awhile. "How come you like me?"

"Video men are smart."

"Oh."

I spent the afternoon in my apartment, reviewing the footage I'd shot that morning, and the more I watched, the madder I got.

Dance requires intense motivation at an extraordinarily early age—a blind devotion, a gamble on the as-yet-unrealized potentials of heredity and nutrition. The risk used to be higher in ballet, but by the late '80s Modern had gotten just as bad. You can begin, say, classical ballet training at age six—and at fourteen find yourself broad-shouldered, the years of total effort utterly wasted. Shara had set her childhood sights on Modern dance—and found out too late that God had dealt her the body of a woman.

She was not fat—you have seen her. She was tall, big-boned tall, and on that great frame was built a rich, ripely female body. As I ran and reran the tapes of *Birthing*, the pain grew in me until I even forgot the ever present aching of my own leg. It was like watching a supremely gifted basketball player who stood four feet tall.

To make it in Modern dance nowadays, it is essential to get into a big company. You cannot be seen unless you are visible. (Government subsidy operates on the principle that Big Is Better—a sadly self-fulfilling prophecy. The smaller companies and independents have always had to knife each other for pennies—but since the early '80s there haven't *been* any pennies.)

"Merce *Cunningham* saw her dance, Charlie. Martha Graham saw her dance, just before she died. Both of them praised her warmly, for her choreography as much as for her technique. Neither offered her a position. I'm not even sure I blame them—I can sort of understand, is the hell of it."

Norrey could understand all right. It was her own defect magnified a hundredfold: uniqueness. A company member must be capable of excellent solo work—but she must also be able to blend into group effort, in ensemble work. Shara's very uniqueness made her virtually useless as a company member. She could not help but draw the eye.

And once drawn, the male eye at least would never leave. Modern dancers must sometimes work nude these days, and it is therefore meet that they have the bodies of four-teen-year-old boys. We may have ladies dancing with few or no clothes on up here, but by God it is Art. An actress or a musician or a singer or a painter may be lushly endowed, deliciously rounded—but a dancer must be nearly as sexless as a high fashion model. Perhaps God knows why. Shara could not have purged her dance of her sexuality even if she had been interested in trying, and as I watched her dance on my monitor and in my mind's eye, I knew she was not.

Why did her genius have to lie in the only occupation

besides model and nun in which sexiness is a liability? It broke my heart, by empathic analogy.

"It's no good at all, is it?"

I whirled and barked. "Dammit, you made me bite my tongue."

"I'm sorry." She came from the doorway into my living room. "Norrey told me how to find the place. The door was ajar."

"I forgot to shut it when I came home."

"You leave it open?"

"I've learned the lesson of history. No junkie, no matter how strung out he is, will enter an apartment with the door ajar and the radio on. Obviously there's someone home. And you're right, it's no damn good at all. Sit down."

She sat on the couch. Her hair was down, now, and I liked it better that way. I shut off the monitor and popped the tape, tossing it on a shelf.

"I came to apologize. I shouldn't have blown up at you at lunch. You were trying to help me."

"You had it coming. I imagine by now you've built up quite a head of steam."

"Five years worth. I figured I'd start in the States instead of Canada. Go farther faster. Now I'm back in Toronto and I don't think I'm going to make it here either. You're right, Mr. Armstead—I'm too damned big. Amazons don't dance."

"It's still Charlie. Listen, something I want to ask you. That last gesture, at the end of *Birthing*—what was that? I thought it was a beckoning, Norrey says it was a farewell, and now that I've run the tape it looks like a yearning, a reaching out."

"Then it worked."

"Pardon?"

"It seemed to me that the birth of a galaxy called for all three. They're so close together in spirit it seemed silly to give each a separate movement."

"Mmm." Worse and worse. Suppose Einstein had had aphasia? "Why couldn't you have been a rotten dancer? That'd just be irony. This"—I pointed to the tape—"is high tragedy."

"Aren't you going to tell me I can still dance for myself?"

"No. For you that'd be worse than not dancing at all."

"My God, you're perceptive. Or am I that easy to read?"

I shrugged.

"Oh Charlie," she burst out, "what am I going to do?"

"You'd better not ask me that." My voice sounded funny.

"Why not?"

"Because I'm already two-thirds in love with you. And because you're not in love with me and never will be. And so that is the sort of question you shouldn't ask me."

It jolted her a little, but she recovered quickly. Her eyes softened, and she shook her head slowly. "You even know why I'm not, don't you?"

"And why you won't be."

I was terribly afraid she was going to say, "Charlie, I'm sorry," but she surprised me again. What she said was, "I can count on the fingers of one foot the number of grown-up men I've ever met. I'm grateful for you. I guess ironic tragedies come in pairs?"

"Sometimes."

"Well, now all I have to do is figure out what to do with my life. That should kill the weekend."

"Will you continue your classes?"

"Might as well. It's never a waste of time to study. Norrey's teaching me things."

All of a sudden my mind started to percolate. Man is a rational animal, right? Right? "What if I had a better idea?"

"If you've got another idea, it's better. Speak."

"Do you have to have an audience? I mean, does it have to be *live*?"

"What do you mean?"

"Maybe there's a back way in. Look, they're building tape facilities into all the TVs nowadays, right? And by now everybody has collected all the old movies and Ernie Kovacs programs and such that they always wanted, and now they're looking for new stuff. Exotic stuff, too esoteric for network or local broadcast, stuff that—"

"The independent video companies, you're talking about."

"Right. TDT is thinking of entering the market, and the Graham company already has."

"So?"

"So suppose we go freelance? You and me? You dance it and I'll tape it: a straight business deal. I've got a few connections, and I can get more. I could name you ten acts in the music business right now that never go on tour— just record and record. Why don't you bypass the structure of the dance companies and take a chance on the public? Maybe word of mouth could—"

Her face was beginning to light up like a jack-o'-lantern. "Charlie, do you think it could work? Do you really think so?"

"I don't think it has a snowball's chance." I crossed the room, opened up the beer fridge, took out the snowball I keep there in the summer, and tossed it at her. She caught it, but just barely, and when she realized what it was, she burst out laughing. "I've got just enough faith in the idea to quit working for TDT and put my time into it. I'll invest my time, my tape, my equipment and my savings. Ante up."

She tried to get sober, but the snowball froze her fingers and she broke up again. "A snowball in July. You madman. Count me in. I've got a little money saved. And . . . and I guess I don't have much choice, do I?"

"I guess not."

# Chapter 2

The next three years were some of the most exciting years of my life, of both our lives. While I watched and taped, Shara transformed herself from a potentially great dancer into something truly awesome. She did something I'm not sure I can explain.

She became dance's analogue of the jazzman.

Dance was, for Shara, self-expression, pure and simple, first, last, and always. Once she freed herself from the attempt to fit into the world of company dance, she came to regard choreography per se as an *obstacle* to her self-expression, as a preprogrammed rut, inexorable as a script and as limiting. And so she devalued it.

A jazzman may blow *Night in Tunisia* for a dozen consecutive nights, and each evening will be a different experience, as he interprets and reinterprets the melody according to his mood of the moment. Total unity of artist and his art: spontaneous creation. The melodic starting point distinguishes the result from pure anarchy.

In just this way Shara devalued preperformance choreography to a starting point, a framework on which to build whatever the moment demanded, and then jammed around it. She learned in those three busy years to dis-

18

mantle the interface between herself and her dance. Dancers have always tended to sneer at improv dancing, even while they practiced it, in the studio, for the looseness it gave. They failed to see that *planned* improv, improv around a theme fully thought out in advance, was the natural next step in dance. Shara took the step. You must be very, very good to get away with that much freedom. She was good enough.

There's no point in detailing the professional fortunes of Drumstead Enterprises over those three years. We worked hard, we made some magnificent tapes, and we couldn't sell them for paperweights. A home videocassette industry indeed grew—and they knew as much about Modern dance as the record industry knew about the blues when *they* started. The big outfits wanted credentials, and the little outfits wanted cheap talent. Finally we even got desperate enough to try the schlock houses—and learned what we already knew. They didn't have the distribution, the prestige, or the technical specs for the critics to pay any attention to them. Word-of-mouth advertising is like a gene pool—if it isn't a certain minimum size to start with, it doesn't get anywhere. "Spider" John Koerner is an incredibly talented musician and songwriter who has been making and selling his own records since 1972. How many of you have ever heard of him?

In May of 1992 I opened my mailbox in the lobby and found the letter from VisuEnt Inc., terminating our option with deepest sorrow and no severance. I went straight over to Shara's apartment, and my leg felt like the bone marrow had been replaced with thermite and ignited. It was a very long walk.

She was working on *Weight Is A Verb* when I got there. Converting her big living room into a studio had cost time, energy, skullsweat, and a fat bribe to the landlord, but it was cheaper than renting time in a studio, considering the sets we wanted. It looked like high mountain country that day, and I hung my hat on a fake alder when I entered.

She flashed me a smile and kept moving, building up to greater and greater leaps. She looked like the most beautiful mountain goat I ever saw. I was in a foul mood and I wanted to kill the music (McLaughlin and Miles together, leaping some themselves), but I never could interrupt Shara when she was dancing. She built it gradually, with directional counterpoint, until she seemed to hurl herself into the air, stay there until she was damned good and ready, and then hurl herself down again. Sometimes she rolled when she hit and sometimes she landed on her hands, and always the energy of falling was transmuted into some new movement instead of being absorbed. It was total energy output, and by the time she was done I had calmed down enough to be almost philosophical about our mutual professional ruin.

She ended up collapsed in upon herself, head bowed, exquisitely humbled in her attempt to defy gravity. I couldn't help applauding. It felt corny, but I couldn't help it.

"Thank you, Charlie."

"I'll be damned. Weight *is* a verb. I thought you were crazy when you told me the title."

"It's one of the strongest verbs in dance—the strongest, I guess—and you can make it do *anything*."

"Almost anything."

"Eh?"

"VisuEnt gave us our contract back."

"Oh." Nothing showed in her eyes, but I knew what was behind them. "Well, who's next on the list?"

"There is no one left on the list."

"*Oh*." This time it showed. "Oh."

"We should have remembered. Great artists are never honored in their own lifetime. What we ought to do is drop dead—then we'd be all set."

In my way I was trying to be strong for her, and she knew it and tried to be strong for me.

"Maybe what we should do is go into death insurance, for artists," she said. "We pay the client premiums against a controlling interest in his estate, and we guarantee that he'll die."

"We can't lose. And if he becomes famous in his life-time he can buy out."

"Terrific. Let's stop this before I laugh myself to death."

"Yeah."

She was silent for a long time. My own mind was racing efficiently, but the transmission seemed to be blown—it wouldn't *go* anywhere. Finally she got up and turned off the music machine, which had been whining softly ever since the tape ended. It made a loud *click*.

"Norrey's got some land in Prince Edward Island," she said, not meeting my eyes. "There's a house."

I tried to head her off with the punchline from the old joke about the kid shoveling out the elephant cage in the circus whose father offers to take him back and set him up with a decent job. "What? And leave show business?"

"Screw show business," she said softly. "If I went to PEI now, maybe I could get the land cleared and plowed in time to get a garden in." Her expression changed. "How about you?"

"Me? I'll be okay. TDT asked me to come back."

"That was six months ago."

"They asked again. Last week."

"And you said no. Moron."

"Maybe so, maybe so."

"The whole damn thing was a waste of time. All that time. All that energy. All that work. I might as well have been farming in PEI—by now the soil'd be starting to bear well. What a waste, Charlie, what a stinking waste."

"No, I don't think so, Shara. It sounds glib to say that 'nothing is wasted,' but—well, it's like that dance you just did. Maybe you can't beat gravity—but it surely is a beautiful thing to *try*."

"Yeah, I know. Remember the Light Brigade. Remember the Alamo. They tried." She laughed bitterly.

"Yes, and so did Jesus of Nazareth. Did you do it for material reward, or because it needed doing? If nothing else we now have several hundred thousand meters of the most magnificent dance recordings on tape, commercial value zero, real value incalculable, and by me that is no waste. It's over now, and we'll both go do the next thing, but it was *not a waste*." I discovered that I was shouting, and stopped.

She closed her mouth. After a while she tried a smile. "You're right, Charlie. It wasn't a waste. I'm a better dancer than I ever was."

"Damn right. You've transcended choreography."

She smiled ruefully. "Yeah. Even Norrey thinks it's a dead end."

"It is *not* a dead end. There's more to poetry than haiku and sonnets. Dancers don't *have* to be robots, delivering memorized lines with their bodies."

"They do if they want to make a living."

"We'll try it again in a few years. Maybe they'll be ready then."

"Sure. Let me get us some drinks."

I slept with her that night, for the first and last time. In the morning I broke down the set in the living room while she packed. I promised to write. I promised to come and visit when I could. I carried her bags down to the car, and stowed them inside. I kissed her and waved goodbye. I went looking for a drink, and at four o'clock the next morning a mugger decided I looked drunk enough and I broke his jaw, his nose and two ribs, and then sat down on him and cried. On Monday morning I showed up at the studio with my hat in my hand and a mouth like a bus-station ashtray and crawled back into my old job. Norrey didn't ask any questions. What with rising food prices, I gave up eating anything but bourbon, and in six months I was fired. It went like that for a long time.

I never did write to her. I kept getting bogged down after "Dear Shara. . . ."

When I got to the point of selling my video equipment for booze, a relay clicked somewhere and I took stock of myself. The stuff was all the life I had left, and so I went to the local AlAnon instead of the pawnshop and got sober. After a while my soul got numb, and I stopped flinching when I woke up. A hundred times I began to wipe the tapes I still had of Shara—she had copies of her own—but in the end I could not. From time to time I wondered how *she* was doing, and I could not bear to find out. If Norrey heard anything, she didn't tell me about it. She even tried to get me my job back a third time, but it was hopeless. Reputation can be a terrible thing once you've blown it. I was lucky to land a job with an educational TV station in New Brunswick.

It was a long couple of years.

Vidphones were coming out by 1995, and I had breadboarded one of my own without the knowledge or consent of the phone company, which I still hated more than anything. When the peanut bulb I had replaced the damned bell with started glowing softly off and on one evening in June, I put the receiver on the audio pickup and energized the tube, in case the caller was also equipped. "Hello?"

She was. When Shara's face appeared, I got a cold cube of fear in the pit of my stomach, because I had quit seeing her face everywhere when I quit drinking, and I had been thinking lately of hitting the sauce again. When I blinked and she was still there, I felt a very little better and tried to speak. It didn't work.

"Hello, Charlie. It's been a long time."

The second time it worked. "Seems like yesterday. Somebody else's yesterday."

"Yes, it does. It took me *days* to find you. Norrey's in Paris, and no one else knew where you'd gone."

"Yeah. How's farming?"

"I . . . I've put that away, Charlie. It's even more creative than dancing, but it's not the same."

"Then what *are* you doing?"

"Working."

"*Dancing?*"

"Yes. Charlie, I need you. I mean, I have a job for you. I need your cameras and your eye."

"Never mind the qualifications. Any kind of need will do. *Where are you?* When's the next plane there? Which cameras do I pack?"

"New York, an hour from now, and none of them. I didn't mean 'your cameras' literally—unless you're using GLX-5000s and a Hamilton Board lately."

I whistled. It hurt my mouth. "Not on my budget. Besides, I'm old-fashioned—I like to hold 'em with my hands."

"For this job you'll use a Hamilton, and it'll be a twenty-input Masterchrome, brand new."

"You grew poppies on that farm? Or just struck diamonds with the roto-tiller?"

"You'll be getting paid by Bryce Carrington."

I blinked.

"Now will you catch that plane so I can tell you about it? The New Age, ask for the Presidential Suite."

"The hell with the plane, I'll walk. Quicker." I hung up.

According to the *Time* magazine in my dentist's waiting room, Bryce Carrington was the genius who had become a multibillionaire by convincing a number of giants of industry to underwrite Skyfac, the great orbiting complex that kicked the bottom out of the crystals market—and seventy-'leven other markets besides. As I recalled the story, some rare poliolike disease had wasted both his legs and put him in a wheelchair. But the legs had lost strength, not function—in lessened gravity they worked well enough. So he created Skyfac, establishing mining crews on Luna to supply it with cheap raw materials, and spent most of his time in orbit under reduced gravity. His picture made him look like a reasonably successful author (as opposed to writer). Other than that I knew nothing about him. I paid little attention to news and none at all to space news.

The New Age was *the* hotel in New York in those days, built on the ruins of the Sheraton. Ultraefficient security, bulletproof windows, carpet thicker than the outside air, and a lobby of an architectural persuasion that John D. MacDonald once called "Early Dental Plate." It stank of money. I was glad I'd made the effort to locate a necktie, and I wished I'd shined my shoes. An incredible man blocked my way as I came in through the airlock. He moved and was built like the toughest, fastest bouncer I ever saw, and he dressed and acted like God's butler. He said his name was Perry, as if he didn't expect me to believe it. He asked if he could help me, as though he didn't think so.

"Yes, Perry. Would you mind lifting up one of your feet?"

"Why?"

"I'll bet twenty dollars you've shined your soles."

Half his mouth smiled, and he didn't move an inch. "Whom did you wish to see?"

"Shara Drummond."

"Not registered."

"The Presidential Suite."

"Oh." Light dawned. "Mister Carrington's lady. You should have said so. Wait here, please." While he phoned to verify that I was expected, keeping his eye on me and his hand near his pocket, I swallowed my heart and rearranged my face. So that was how it was. All right then. That was how it was.

Perry came back and gave me the little button-transmitter that would let me walk the corridors of the New

Age without being cut down by automatic laser-fire, and explained carefully that it would blow a largish hole in me if I attempted to leave the building without returning it. From his manner I gathered that I had just skipped four grades in social standing. I thanked him, though I'm damned if I know why.

I followed the green fluorescent arrows that appeared on the bulbless ceiling, and came after a long and scenic walk to the Presidential Suite. Shara was waiting at the door, in something like an angel's pajamas. It made all that big body look delicate. "Hello, Charlie."

I was jovial and hearty. "Hi, babe. Swell joint. How've you been keeping yourself?"

"I haven't been."

"Well, how's Carrington been keeping you, then?" Steady, boy.

"Come in, Charlie."

I went in. It looked like where the Queen stayed when she was in town, and I'm sure she enjoyed it. You could have landed an airplane in the living room without waking anyone in the bedroom. It had two pianos. Only one fireplace, barely big enough to barbecue a buffalo—you have to scrimp somewhere, I guess. Roger Kellaway was on the quadio, and for a wild moment I thought he was actually in the suite, playing some unseen third piano. So this was how it was.

"Can I get you something, Charlie?"

"Oh, sure. Hash Oil, Citrolli Supreme. Dom Perignon for the pipe."

Without cracking a smile she went to a cabinet that looked like a midget cathedral, and produced precisely what I had ordered. I kept my own features impressive and lit up. The bubbles tickled my throat, and the rush was exquisite. I felt myself relaxing, and when we had passed the narghile's mouthpiece a few times I felt her relax. We looked at each other then—really looked at each other—then at the room around us and then at each other again. Simultaneously we roared with laughter, a laughter that blew all the wealth out of the room and let in richness. Her laugh was the same whooping, braying belly laugh I remembered so well, an unselfconscious and lusty laugh, and it reassured me tremendously. I was so relieved I couldn't stop laughing myself, and that kept *her* going, and just as we might have stopped she pursed her lips and blew a stuttered arpeggio. There's an old audio recording called the *Spike Jones Laughing Record*, where the tuba player tries to play "The Flight Of The Bumblebee" and falls down laughing, and the whole band breaks up and horselaughs for a full two minutes, and evey time they run out of air the tuba player tries another flutter and roars and they all break up again, and once when Shara was blue I bet her ten dollars that she couldn't listen to that record without at least giggling and I won. When I understood now that she was quoting it, I shuddered and dissolved into great whoops of new laughter, and a minute later we had reached the stage where we literally laughed ourselves out of our chairs and lay on the floor in agonies of mirth, weakly pounding the floor and howling. I take that laugh out of my memory now and then and rerun it—but not often, for such records deteriorate drastically with play.

At last we dopplered back down to panting grins, and I helped her to her feet.

"What a perfectly dreadful place," I said, still chuckling.

She glanced around and shuddered. "Oh God, it *is*, Charlie. It must be awful to need this much front."

"For a horrid while I thought *you* did."

She sobered, and met my eyes. "Charlie, I wish I could resent that. In a way I do need it."

My eyes narrowed. "Just what do you mean?"

"I need Bryce Carrington."

"This time you can trot out the qualifiers. *How* do you need him?"

"I need his money," she cried.

How can you relax and tense up at the same time? "Oh, *damn* it, Shara! Is *that* how you're going to get to dance? Buy your way in? What does a critic go for, these days?"

"Charlie, stop it. I need Carrington to get seen. He's going to rent me a hall, that's all."

"If that's all, let's get out of this dump right now. I can bor— get enough cash to rent you any hall in the world, and I'm just as willing to risk my money."

"Can you get me Skyfac?"

"*Uh?*"

I couldn't for the life of me imagine why she proposed to go to Skyfac to dance. Why not Antarctica?

"Shara, you know even less about space than I do, but you must know that a satellite broadcast doesn't have to be made from a satellite?"

"Idiot. It's the setting I want."

I thought about it. "Moon'd be better, visually. Mountains. Light. Contrast."

"The visual aspect is secondary. I don't want one-sixth gee, Charlie. I want zero gravity."

My mouth hung open.

"And I want you to be my video man."

God, she was a rare one. What I needed then was to sit there with my mouth open and think for several minutes. She let me do just that, waiting patiently for me to work it all out.

"Weight isn't a verb anymore, Charlie," she said finally. "That dance ended on the assertion that you can't beat gravity—you said so yourself. Well, that statement is incorrect—obsolete. The dance of the twenty-first century will have to acknowledge that."

"And it's just what you need to make it. A new kind of dance for a new kind of dancer. Unique. It'll catch the public eye, and you should have the field entirely to yourself for years. I like it, Shara. I like it. But can you pull it off?"

"I thought about what you said: that you can't beat gravity but it's beautiful to try. It stayed in my head for months, and then one day I was visiting a neighbor with a TV and I saw newsreels of the crew working on Skyfac Two. I was up all night thinking, and the next morning I came up to the States and got a job in Skyfac One. I've been up there for nearly a year, getting next to Carrington. I can do it, Charlie, I can make it work." There was a ripple in her jaw that I had seen before—when she'd told me off in Le Maintenant. It was a ripple of determination.

Still I frowned. "With Carrington's backing."

Her eyes left mine. "There's no such thing as a free lunch."

"What does he charge?"

She failed to answer, for long enough to answer me. In that instant I began believing in God again, for the first time in years, just to be able to hate Him.

But I kept my mouth shut. She was old enough to manage her own finances. The price of a dream gets higher every year. Hell, I'd half expected it from the moment she'd called me.

But only half.

"Charlie, don't just sit there with your face all knotted up. Say something. Cuss me out, call me a whore, *something*."

"Nuts. You be your own conscience; I have trouble enough being my own. You want to dance, you've got a patron. So now you've got a video man."

I hadn't intended to say that last sentence at all.

Strangely, it almost seemed to disappoint her at first. But then she relaxed, and smiled. "Thank you, Charlie. Can you get out of whatever you're doing right away?"

"I'm working for an educational station in Shediac. I even got to shoot some dance footage. A dancing bear from the London Zoo. The amazing thing was how well he danced." She grinned. "I can get free."

"I'm glad. I don't think I could pull this off without you."

"I'm working for you. Not for Carrington."

"All right."

"Where is the great man, anyway? Scuba diving in the bathtub?"

"No," came a quiet voice from the doorway. "I've been sky diving in the lobby."

His wheelchair was a mobile throne. He wore a five-hundred-dollar suit the color of strawberry ice cream, a powder-blue turtleneck and one gold earring. The shoes were genuine leather. The watch was the newfangled bandless kind that literally tells you the time. He wasn't tall enough for her, and his shoulders were absurdly broad, although the suit tried hard to deny both. His eyes were like twin blueberries. His smile was that of a shark wondering which part will taste best. I wanted to crush his head between two boulders.

Shara was on her feet. "Bryce, this is Charles Armstead. I told you. . . ."

"Oh yes. The video chap." He rolled forward and extended an impeccably manicured hand. "I'm Bryce Carrington, Armstead."

I remained in my seat, hands in my lap. "Ah yes. The rich chap."

One eyebrow rose an urbane quarter inch. "Oh my. Another rude one. Well, if you're as good as Shara says you are, you're entitled."

"I'm rotten."

The smile faded. "Let's stop fencing, Armstead. I don't expect manners from creative people, but I have far more significant contempt than yours available if I need any. Now I'm tired of this damned gravity and I've had a rotten day testifying for a friend and it looks like they're going to recall me tomorrow. Do you want the job or don't you?"

He had me there. I did. "Yeah."

"All right, then. Your room is 2772. We'll be going up to Skyfac in two days. Be here at eight A.M."

"I'll want to talk with you about what you'll be needing, Charlie," Shara said. "Give me a call tomorrow."

I whirled to face her, and she flinched from my eyes.

Carrington failed to notice. "Yes, make a list of your requirements by tonight, so it can go up with us. Don't scrimp—if you don't fetch it, you'll do without. Good night, Armstead."

I faced him. "Good night, Mr. Carrington." Suh.

He turned toward the narghile, and Shara hurried to refill the chamber and bowl. I turned away hastily and made for the door. My leg hurt so much I nearly fell on the way, but I set my jaw and made it. When I reached the door I said to myself, you will now open the door and go through it, and then I spun on my heel. "Carrington!"

He blinked, surprised to discover I still existed. "Yes?"

"Are you *aware* that she doesn't love you in the slightest? Does that matter to you in any way?" My voice was high, and my fists were surely clenched.

"Oh," he said, and then again, "Oh. So that's what it is. I didn't *think* success alone merited that much contempt." He put down the mouthpiece and folded his fingers together. "Let me tell you something, Armstead. No one has ever loved me, to my knowledge. This suite does not love me." His voice took on human feeling for the first time. "But it is *mine*. Now get out."

I opened my mouth to tell him where to put his job, and then I saw Shara's face, and the pain in it suddenly made me deeply ashamed. I left at once, and when the door closed behind me I vomited on a rug that was worth slightly less than a Hamilton Masterchrome board. I was sorry then that I'd worn a necktie.

The trip to Pike's Peak Spaceport, at least, was aesthetically pleasurable. I enjoy air travel, gliding among stately clouds, watching the rolling procession of mountains and plains, vast jigsaws of farmland, and intricate mosaics of suburbia unfolding below.

But the jump to Skyfac in Carrington's personal shuttle, *That First Step*, might as well have been an old Space Commando rerun. I *know* they can't put portholes in space ships—but dammit, a shipboard video relay conveys no better resolution, color values, or presence than you get on your living room tube. The only differences are that the stars don't "move" to give the illusion of travel, and there's no director editing the POV to give you dramatically interesting shots.

Aesthetically speaking. The *experiential* difference is that they do not, while you are watching the Space Commando, sell hemorrhoid remedies, strap you into a couch, batter you with thunders, make you weigh better than half a megagram for an unreasonably long time, and then drop you off the edge of the world into weightlessness. Body fluids began rising into my upper half: my ears sang, my nose flooded, and I "blushed" deep red. I had been prepared for nausea, but what I got was even more shocking: the sudden, unprecedented, total absence of pain in my leg. Shara got the nausea for both of us, barely managing to deploy her dropsickness bag in time. Carrington unstrapped and administered an antinausea injection with sure movements. It seemed to take forever to hit her, but when it did there was an enormous change—color and strength returned rapidly, and she was apparently fully recovered by the time the pilot announced that we were commencing docking and would everyone please strap in and shut up? I half expected Carrington to bark manners into him, but apparently the industrial magnate was not that sort of fool. He shut up and strapped himself down.

My leg didn't hurt in the slightest. Not at all.

The Skyfac complex looked like a disorderly heap of bicycle tires and beach balls of various sizes. The one our pilot made for was more like a tractor tire. We matched course, became its axle, and matched spin, and the damned thing grew a spoke that caught us square in the airlock. The airlock was "overhead" of our couches, but we entered and left it feet first. A few yards into the spoke, the direction we traveled became "down," and handholds became a ladder. Weight increased with every step, but even when we had emerged into a rather large cubical compartment it was far less than Earth normal. Nonetheless my leg resumed nibbling at me.

The room tried to be a classic reception room, high-level ("Please be seated. His Majesty will see you shortly"), but the low gee and the p-suits racked along two walls spoiled the effect. Unlike the Space Commando's armor, a real pressure suit looks like nothing so much as a people-shaped baggie, and they look particularly silly in repose. A young dark-haired man in tweed rose from behind a splendidly gadgeted desk and smiled. "Good to see you, Mr. Carrington. I hope you had a pleasant jump."

"Fine thanks, Tom. You remember Shara, of course. This is Charles Armstead. Tom McGillicuddy." We both displayed our teeth and said we were delighted to meet one another. I could see that beneath the pleasantries, McGillicuddy was upset about something.

"Nils and Mr. Longmire are waiting in your office, sir. There's . . . there's been another sighting."

"God *damn* it," Carrington began, and cut himself off. I stared at him. The full force of my best sarcasm had failed to anger this man. "All right. Take care of my guests while I go hear what Longmire has to say." He started for the door, moving like a beach ball in slow motion but under his own power. "Oh yes—the *Step* is loaded to the gun'ls with bulky equipment, Tom. Have her brought round to the cargo bays. Store the equipment in Six." He left, looking worried. McGillicuddy activated his desk and gave the necessary orders.

"What's going on, Tom?" Shara asked when he was through.

He looked at me before replying. "Pardon my asking, Mr. Armstead, but—are you a newsman?"

"Charlie. No, I'm not. I am a video man, but I work for Shara."

"Mmmm. Well, you'll hear about it sooner or later. About two weeks ago an object appeared within the orbit of Neptune, just appeared out of nowhere. There were . . . certain other anomalies. It stayed put for half a day and then vanished again. The Space Command slapped a hush on it, but it's common knowledge on board Skyfac."

"And the thing has appeared again?" Shara asked.

"Just beyond the orbit of Saturn."

I was only mildly interested. No doubt there was an explanation for the phenomenon, and since Isaac Asimov wasn't around I would doubtless never understand a word of it. Most of us gave up on intelligent nonhuman life when Project Ozma came up empty. "Little green men, I suppose. Can you show us the Lounge, Tom? I understand it's just like the one we'll be working in."

He seemed to welcome the change of subject. "Sure thing."

McGillicuddy led us through a p-door opposite the one Carrington had used, through long halls whose floors curved up ahead of and behind us. Each was outfitted differently, each was full of busy, purposeful people, and each reminded me somehow of the lobby of the New Age, or perhaps of the old movie *2001*. Futuristic Opulence, so understated as to fairly shriek. Wall Street lifted bodily into orbit—the *clocks* were on Wall Street time. I tried to make myself believe that cold, empty space lay a short distance away in any direction, but it was impossible. I decided it was a good thing spacecraft didn't have portholes—once he got used to the low gravity, a man might forget and open one to throw out a cigar.

I studied McGillicuddy as we walked. He was immaculate in every respect, from necktie knot to nail polish, and he wore no jewelry at all. His hair was short and black, his beard inhibited, and his eyes surprisingly warm in a professionally sterile face. I wondered what he had sold his soul for. I hoped he had gotten his price.

We had to descend two levels to get to the Lounge. The gravity on the upper level was kept at one-sixth normal, partly for the convenience of the Lunar personnel who were Skyfac's only regular commuters, and mostly (of course) for the convenience of Carrington. But descending brought a subtle increase in weight, to perhaps a fifth or a quarter normal. My leg complained bitterly, but I found to my surprise that I preferred the pain to its absence. It's a little scary when an old friend goes away like that.

The Lounge was a larger room than I had expected, quite big enough for our purposes. It encompassed all three levels, and one whole wall was an immense video screen, across which stars wheeled dizzily, joined with occasional regularity by a slice of mother Terra. The floor was crowded with chairs and tables in various groupings, but I could see that, stripped, it would provide Shara with entirely adequate room to dance. From long habit my feet began to report on the suitability of the floor as a dancing surface. Then I remembered how little use the floor was liable to get.

"Well," Shara said to me with a smile, "this is what home will look like for the next six months. The Ring Two Lounge is identical to this one."

"Six?" McGillicuddy said. "Not a chance."

"*What do you mean?*" Shara and I said together.

He blinked at our combined volume. "Well, *you'll* probably be good for that long, Charlie. But Shara's already had a year of low gee, while she was in the typing pool."

"So what?"

"Look, you expect to be in free fall for long periods of time, if I understand this correctly?"

"Twelve hours a day," Shara agreed.

He grimaced. "Shara, I hate to say this . . . but I'll be surprised if you last a month. A body designed for a one-gee environment doesn't work properly in zero gee."

"But it will adapt, won't it?"

He laughed mirthlessly. "Sure. That's why we rotate all personnel Earthside every fourteen months. Your body will adapt. One way. No return. Once you've fully adapted, returning to Earth will stop your heart—if some other major systemic failure doesn't occur first. Look, you were just Earthside for three days—did you have any chest pains? Dizziness? Bowel trouble? Dropsickness on the way up?"

"All of the above," she admitted.

"There you go. You were close to the nominal fourteen-month limit when you left. And your body will adapt even faster under no gravity at all. The successful free-fall endurance record of about eight months was set by a Skyfac construction gang with bad deadline problems—and they hadn't spent a year in one-sixth gee first, *and* they weren't straining their hearts the way you will be. Hell, there are four men in Luna now, from the original mining team, who will never see Earth again. Eight of their teammates tried. Don't you two know *any*thing about space? *Didn't Carrington tell you?*"

I had *wondered* why Carrington had gone to the trouble of having our preflight physicals waived.

"But I've got to have at least four months. Four months of solid work, every day. I *must*." She was dismayed, but fighting hard for control.

McGillicuddy started to shake his head, and then thought better of it. His warm eyes were studying Shara's face. I knew exactly what he 'was thinking, and I liked him for it.

He was thinking, *How to tell a lovely lady her dearest dream is hopeless?*

He didn't know the half of it. I *knew* how much Shara had already—irrevocably—invested in this dream, and something in me screamed.

And then I saw her jaw ripple and I dared to hope.

Doctor Panzella was a wiry old man with eyebrows like two fuzzy caterpillars. He wore a tight-fitting jumpsuit which would not foul a p-suit's seals should he have to get into one in a hurry. His shoulder-length hair, which should have been a mane on that great skull, was clipped securely back against a sudden absence of gravity. A cautious man. To employ an obsolete metaphor, he was a suspenders-*and*-belt type. He looked Shara over, ran tests on the spot, and gave her just under a month and a half. Shara said some things. I said some things. McGillicuddy said some things. Panzella shrugged, made further, very careful tests, and reluctantly cut loose of the suspenders. Two months. Not a day over. Possibly less, depending on subsequent monitoring of her body's reactions to extended weightlessness. Then a year Earthside before risking it again. Shara seemed satisfied.

I didn't see how we could do it.

McGillicuddy had assured us that it would take Shara at least a month simply to learn to handle herself competently in zero gee, much less dance. Her familiarity with one-sixth gee would, he predicted, be a liability rather than an asset. Then figure three weeks of choreography and rehearsal, a week of taping and just maybe we could broadcast one dance before Shara had to return to Earth. Not good enough. She and I had calculated that we would need three successive shows, each well received, to make a big enough dent in the dance world for Shara to squeeze into it. A year was far too big a spacing to be effective— and *who knew how soon Carrington might tire of her?* So I hollered at Panzella.

"Mister Armstead," he said hotly, "I am specifically

contractually forbidden to allow this young lady to commit suicide." He grimaced sourly. "I'm told it's terrible public relations."

"Charlie, it's okay," Shara insisted. "I can fit in three dances. We may lose some sleep, but we can do it."

"I once told a man nothing was impossible. He asked me if I could ski through a revolving door. You haven't got . . ."

My brain slammed into hyperdrive, thought about things, kicked itself in the ass a few times, and returned to realtime in time to hear my mouth finish without a break: ". . . much choice, though. Okay Tom, have that damned Ring Two Lounge cleaned out, I want it naked and spotless and have somebody paint over that damned video wall, the same shade as the other three and I mean *the same*. Shara, get out of those clothes and into your leotard. Doctor, we'll be seeing you in twelve hours; quit gaping and *move*, Tom—we'll be going over there at once; *where the hell are my cameras?*"

McGillicuddy spluttered.

"Get me a torch crew—I'll want holes cut through the walls, cameras behind them, one-way glass, six locations, a room adjacent to the Lounge for a mixer console the size of a jetliner cockpit, and bolt a Norelco coffee machine next to the chair. I'll need another room for editing, complete privacy and total darkness, size of any efficiency kitchen, another Norelco."

McGillicuddy finally drowned me out. "Mister *Armstead*, this is the Main Ring of the Skyfac One complex, the administrative offices of one of the wealthiest corporations in existence. If you think this whole Ring is going to stand on its head for you. . . ."

So we brought the problem to Carrington. He told McGillicudddy that henceforth Ring Two was *ours*, as well as any assistance whatsoever that we requested. He looked rather distracted. McGillicuddy started to tell him by how many weeks all this would put off the opening of the Skyfac Two complex. Carrington replied very quietly that he could add and subtract quite well, thank you, and McGillicuddy got white and quiet.

I'll give Carrington that much. He gave us a free hand.

Panzella ferried over to Skyfac Two with us. We were chauffeured by lean-jawed astronaut types, on vehicles looking for all the world like pregnant broomsticks. It was as well that we had the doctor with us—Shara fainted on the way over. I nearly did myself, and I'm sure that broomstick has my thigh-prints on it yet. Falling through space is a scary experience the first time. Some people never get used to it. Most people. Shara responded splendidly once we had her inboard again, and fortunately her dropsickness did not return. Nausea can be a nuisance in free fall, a disaster in a p-suit. By the time my cameras and mixer had arrived, she was on her feet and sheepish. And while I browbeat a sweating crew of borrowed techs into installing them faster than was humanly possible, Shara began learning how to move in zero gee.

We were ready for the first taping in three weeks.

# Chapter 3

Living quarters and minimal life support were rigged for us in Ring Two so that we could work around the clock if we chose, but we spent nearly half of our nominal "off-hours" in Skyfac One. Shara was required to spend half of three days a week there with Carrington, and spent a sizable portion of her remaining nominal sack time out in space, in a p-suit. At first it was a conscious attempt to overcome her gut-level fear of all that emptiness. Soon it became her meditation, her retreat, her artistic reverie—an attempt to gain from contemplation of the cold black depths enough insight into the meaning of extraterrestrial existence to dance of it.

I spent my own time arguing with engineers and electricians and technicians and a damn fool union legate who insisted that the second lounge, finished or not, belonged to the hypothetical future crew and administrative personnel. Securing his permission to work there wore the lining off my throat and the insulation off my nerves. Far too many nights I spent slugging instead of sleeping. Minor example: Every interior wall in the whole damned second Ring was painted the identical shade of turquoise—and they couldn't duplicate it to cover that godforsaken video wall in the Lounge. It was McGillicuddy who saved me from gibbering apoplexy—at his suggestion I washed off the third latex job, unshipped the outboard camera that fed the wall-screen, brought the camera inboard and fixed it to scan an interior wall in an adjoining room. That made us friends again.

It was all like that: jury-rig, improvise, file to fit and paint to cover. If a camera broke down, I spent sleep time talking with off-shift engineers, finding out what parts in stock could be adapted. It was simply too expensive to have anything shipped up from Earth's immense gravity well, and Luna didn't have what I needed.

At that, Shara worked harder than I did. A body must totally recoordinate itself to function in the absence of weight—she literally had to forget everything she had ever known or learned about dance and acquire a whole new set of skills. This turned out to be even harder than we had expected. McGillicuddy had been right: what Shara had learned in her year of one-sixth gee was an exaggerated attempt to *retain* terrestrial patterns of coordination. Rejecting them altogether was actually easier for *me*.

But I couldn't keep up with her—I had to abandon any thought of handheld camera work and base my plans solely on the six fixed cameras. Fortunately GLX-5000s have a ball-and-socket mount: even behind that damned one-way glass I had about forty degrees of traverse on each one. Learning to coordinate all six simultaneously on the Hamilton Board did a truly extraordinary thing to me: It lifted me that one last step to unity with my art. I found that I could learn to be aware of all six monitors with my mind's eye, to perceive almost spherically, to—not share my attention among the six—to *encompass* them all, seeing like a six-eyed creature from many angles at once. My mind's eye became holographic; my awareness multilayered. I began to really understand, for the first time, three-dimensionality.

It was that fourth dimension that was the kicker. It took Shara two days to decide that she could not possibly become proficient enough in free-fall maneuvering to sustain a half-hour piece in the time required. So she rethought her work plan too, adapting her choreography to the demands of her situation. She put in six hard days under normal Earth weight.

And for her, too, the effort was that one last step toward apotheosis.

On Monday of the fourth week we began taping *Liberation*.

Establishing shot:

A great turquoise box, seen from within. Dimensions unknown, but the color somehow lends an impression of immensity, of vast distances. Against the far wall a swinging pendulum attests that this is a standard-gravity environment; but the pendulum swings so slowly and is so featureless in construction that it is impossible to estimate its size and so extrapolate that of the room.

Because of this trompe-l'oeil effect, the room seems rather smaller than it really is when the camera pulls back and we are wrenched into proper perspective by the appearance of Shara, inert, face down on the floor, her head toward us.

She wears beige leotard and tights. Hair the color of fine mahogany is pulled back into a loose ponytail which fans across one shoulder blade. She does not appear to breathe. She does not appear to be alive.

Music begins. The aging Mahavishnu, on obsolete nylon acoustic, establishes a minor E in no hurry at all. A pair of small candles in simple brass holders appear inset on either side of the room. They are larger than life, though small beside Shara. Both are unlit.

Her body . . . there is no word. It does not move, in the sense of motor activity. One might say that a ripple passes through it, save that the motion is clearly all outward from her center. She *swells*, as if the first breath of life were being taken by her whole body at once. She lives.

The twin wicks begin to glow, oh, softly. The music takes on quiet urgency.

Shara raises her head to us. Her eyes focus somewhere beyond the camera yet short of infinity. Her body writhes, undulates, and the glowing wicks are coals (that this brightening takes place in slow motion is not apparent).

A violent contraction raises her to a crouch, spilling the ponytail across her shoulder. Mahavishnu begins a cyclical cascade of runs, in increasing tempo. Long, questing tongues of yellow-orange flame begin to blossom *downward* from the twin wicks, whose coals are turning to blue.

The contraction's release flings her to her feet. The twin skirts of flame about the wicks curl up over themselves, writhing furiously, to become conventional candle-flames, flickering now in normal time. Tablas, tambouras, and a bowed string bass join the guitar, and they segue into an energetic interplay around a minor seventh that keeps trying, fruitlessly, to find resolution in the sixth. The candles stay in perspective, but dwindle in size until they vanish.

Shara begins to explore the possibilities of motion. First she moves only perpendicular to the camera's line of sight, exploring that dimension. Every motion of arms or legs or head is clearly seen to be a defiance of gravity—of a force as inexorable as radioactive decay, as entropy itself. The most violent surges of energy succeed only for a time—the outflung leg falls, the outthrust arm drops. She must struggle or fall. She pauses in thought.

Her hands and arms reach out toward the camera, and at the instant they do we cut to a view from the left-hand wall. Seen from the right side, she reaches out into this new dimension, and soon begins to move in it. (As she moves backward out of the camera's field, its entire image shifts right on our screen, butted out of the way by the incoming image of a second camera, which picks her up as the first loses her without a visible seam.)

The new dimension too fails to fulfill Shara's desire for freedom from gravity. Combining the two, however, presents so many permutations of movement that for a while, intoxicated, she flings herself into experimentation. In the next fifteen minutes Shara's entire background and history in dance are recapitulated, in a blinding tour de force that incorporates elements of jazz, Modern, and the more graceful aspects of Olympic-level mat gymnastics. Five cameras come into play, singly and in pairs on splitscreen, as the "bag of tricks" amassed in a lifetime of study and improvisation are rediscovered and performed by a superbly trained and versatile body, in a pyrotechnic display that would shout of joy if her expression did not remain aloof, almost arrogant. *This is the offering*, she seems to say, *which you would not accept. This, by itself, was not good enough.*

And it is not. Even in its raging energy and total control, her body returns again and again to the final compromise of mere erectness, that last simple refusal to fall.

Clamping her jaw, she works into a series of leaps, ever longer, ever higher. She seems at last to hang suspended for full seconds, straining to fly. When, inevitably, she falls, she falls reluctantly, only at the last possible instant tucking and rolling back onto her feet. The musicians are in a crescendoing frenzy. We see her now only with the single original camera, and the twin candles have returned, small but burning fiercely.

The leaps begin to diminish in intensity and height, and she takes longer to build to each one. She has been dancing flat out for nearly twenty minutes; as the candle flames begin to wane, so does her strength. At last she retreats to a place beneath the indifferent pendulum, gathers herself with a final desperation, and races forward toward us. She reaches incredible speed in a short space, hurls herself into a double roll and bounds up into the air off one foot, seeming a full second later to push off against empty air for a few more centimeters of height. Her body goes rigid, her eyes and mouth gape wide, the flames reach maximum brilliance, the music peaks with the tortured wail of an electric guitar and—she falls, barely snapping into a roll in time, rising only as far as a crouch. She holds there for a long moment, and gradually her head and shoulders slump, defeated, toward the floor. The candle flames draw in upon themselves in a curious way and appear to go out. The string bass saws on alone, modulating down to D.

Muscle by muscle, Shara's body gives up the struggle. The air seems to tremble around the wicks of the candles, which have now grown nearly as tall as her crouching form.

Shara lifts her face to the camera with evident effort. Her face is anguished, her eyes nearly shut. A long beat.

All at once she opens her eyes wide, squares her shoulders, and contracts. It is the most exquisite and total contraction ever dreamed of, filmed in realtime but seeming almost to be in slow motion. She holds it. Mahavishnu comes back in on guitar, building in increasing tempo from a downtuned bass string to a D chord with a flatted fourth. Shara holds.

We shift for the first time to an overhead camera, looking down on her from a great height. As Mahavishnu's picking speed increases to the point where the chord seems a sustained drone, Shara slowly lifts her head, still holding the contraction, until she is staring directly up at us. She poises there for an eternity, like a spring wound to the bursting point . . .

. . . and explodes upward toward us, rising higher and faster than she possibly can in a soaring flight that *is* slow motion now, coming closer and closer until her hands disappear to either side and her face fills the screen, flanked by two candles which have bloomed into gouts of yellow flame in an instant. The guitar and bass are submerged in an orchestra.

Almost at once she whirls away from us, and the POV

switches to the original camera, on which we see her fling herself down ten meters to the floor, reversing her attitude in mid-flight and twisting. She comes out of her roll in an absolutely flat trajectory that takes her the length of the room. She hits the far wall with a crash audible even over the music, shattering the still pendulum. Her thighs soak up the kinetic energy and then release it, and once again she is racing toward us, hair streaming straight out behind her, a broad smile of triumph growing larger in the screen.

In the next five minutes all six cameras vainly try to track her as she caroms around the immense room like a hummingbird trying to batter its way out of a cage, using the walls, floor and ceiling the way a jai-alai master does, *existing in three dimensions*. Gravity is defeated. The basic assumption of all dance is transcended.

Shara is transformed.

She comes to rest at last at vertical center in the fore-front of the cube, arms-legs-fingers-toes-face straining *outward*, her body turning gently end over end. All four cameras that bear on her join in a four-way splitscreen, the orchestra resolves into its final E major, and—fade out.

I had neither the time nor the equipment to create the special effects that Shara wanted. So I found ways to warp reality to my need. The first candle segment was a twinned shot of a candle being blown out from above—in ultraslow motion, and in reverse. The second segment was a simple recording of linear reality. I had lit the candle, started taping—and had the Ring's spin killed. A candle behaves oddly in zero gee. The low-density combustion gases do not rise up from the flame, allowing air to reach it from beneath. The flame does not go out: it becomes dormant. Restore gravity within a minute or so, and it blooms back to life again. All I did was monkey with speeds a bit to match in with the music and Shara's dance. I got the idea from Harry Stein, Skyfac's construction foreman, who was helping me design things Shara would need for the next dance.

I piped it to the video wall in the Ring One Lounge, and everyone in Skyfac who could cut work crowded in for the broadcast. They saw exactly what was being sent out over worldwide satellite hookup—(Carrington had arranged twenty-five minutes without commercial interruption)—almost a full half second before the world did.

I spent the broadcast in the Communications Room, chewing my fingernails. But it went without a hitch, and I slapped my board dead and made it to the Lounge in time to see the last half of the standing ovation. Shara stood before the screen, Carrington sitting beside her, and I found the difference in their expressions instructive. Her face showed no embarrassment or modesty. She had had faith in herself throughout, had approved this tape for broadcast—she was aware, with that incredible detachment of which so few artists are capable, that the wild applause was only what she deserved. But her face showed that she was deeply surprised—and deeply grateful—to be given what she deserved.

Carrington, on the other hand, registered a triumph strangely admixed with relief. He too had had faith in Shara, and had backed it with a large investment—but his faith was that of a businessman in a gamble he believes will pay off, and as I watched his eyes and the glisten of sweat on his forehead, I realized that no businessman ever takes an expensive gamble without worrying that it may be the fiasco that will begin the loss of his only essential commodity: face.

Seeing his kind of triumph next to hers spoiled the moment for me, and instead of thrilling for Shara I found myself almost hating her. She spotted me, and waved me to join her before the cheering crowd, but I turned and literally flung myself from the room. I borrowed a bottle from Harry Stein and got stinking.

The next morning my head felt like a fifteen-amp fuse

on a forty-amp circuit, and I seemed to be held together only by surface tension. Sudden movements frightened me. It's a long fall off that wagon, even at one-sixth gee.

The phone chimed—I hadn't had time to rewire it—and a young man I didn't know politely announced that Mr. Carrington wished to see me in his office. At once. I spoke of a barbed-wire suppository, and what Mr. Carrington might do with it, at once. Without changing expression he repeated his message and disconnected.

So I crawled into my clothes, decided to grow a beard, and left. Along the way I wondered what I had traded my independence for, and why?

Carrington's office was oppressively tasteful, but at least the lighting was subdued. Best of all, its filter system would handle smoke—the sweet musk of pot lay on the air. I accepted a macrojoint of "Maoi-Zowie" from Carrington with something approaching gratitude, and began melting my hangover.

Shara sat next to his desk, wearing a leotard and a layer of sweat. She had obviously spent the morning rehearsing for the next dance. I felt ashamed, and consequently snappish, avoiding her eyes and her hello. Panzella and McGillicuddy came in on my heels, chattering about the latest sighting of the mysterious object from deep space, which had appeared this time in the Asteroid Belt. They were arguing over whether or not it displayed signs of sentience, and I wished they'd shut up.

Carrington waited until we had all seated ourselves and lit up, then rested a hip on his desk and smiled. "Well, Tom?"

McGillicuddy beamed. "Better than we expected, sir. All the ratings agree we had about 74 per cent of the world audience. . . ."

"The hell with the nielsens," I snapped. *What did the critics say?*"

McGillicuddy blinked. "Well, the general reaction so far is that Shara was a smash. The *Times*. . . ."

I cut him off again. "What was the less-than-general reaction?"

"Well, nothing is ever unanimous."

"Specifics. The dance press? Liz Zimmer? Migdalski?"

"Uh. Not as good. Praise, yes—only a blind man could've panned that show. But guarded praise. Uh, Zimmer called it a magnificent dance spoiled by a gimmicky ending."

"And Migdalski?" I insisted.

"He headed his review, 'But What Do You Do For An Encore?'" McGillicuddy admitted. "His basic thesis was that it was a charming one-shot. But the *Times*. . . ."

"Thank you, Tom," Carrington said quietly. "About what we expected, isn't it, my dear? A big splash, but no one's willing to call it a tidal wave yet."

She nodded. "But they will, Bryce. The next two dances will sew it up."

Panzella spoke up. "Ms. Drummond, may I ask you why you played it the way you did? Using the null-gee interlude only as a brief adjunct to conventional dance—surely you must have expected the critics to call it gimmickry."

Shara smiled and answered. "To be honest, Doctor, I had no choice. I'm learning to use my body in free fall, but it's still a conscious effort, almost a pantomime. I need another few weeks to make it second nature, and it *has* to be if I'm to sustain a whole piece in it. So I dug a conventional dance out of the trunk, tacked on a five-minute ending that used every zero-gee move I knew, and found to my extreme relief that they made thematic sense together. I told Charlie my notion, and he made it work visually and dramatically—the whole business of the candles was his, and it underlined what I was trying to say better than any set we could have built."

"So you have not yet completed what you came here to do?" Panzella asked her.

"Oh, no. Not by any means. The next dance will show the world that dance is more than controlled falling. And

the third . . . the third will be what this has all been for."
Her face lit, became animated. "The third dance will be
the one I have wanted to dance all my life. I can't entirely
picture it, yet—but I know that when I become capable
of dancing it, I will create it, and it will be my greatest
dance."

Panzella cleared his throat. "How long will it take
you?"

"Not long," she said. "I'll be ready to tape the next
dance in two weeks, and I can start on the last one almost at once. With luck, I'll have it in the can before my
month is up."

"Ms. Drummond," Panzella said gravely, "I'm afraid
you don't have another month."

Shara went white as snow, and I half rose from my seat.
Carrington looked intrigued.

"How much time?" Shara asked.

"Your latest tests have not been encouraging. I had
assumed that the sustained exercise of rehearsal and practice would tend to slow your system's adaptation. But most
of your work has been in total weightlessness, and I failed
to realize the extent to which your body is accustomed to
sustained exertion—in a terrestrial environment. There
are already signs of Davis's Syndrome in—"

"*How much time?*"

"Two weeks. Possibly three, if you spend three separate hours a day at hard exercise in two gravities. We can
arrange that by—"

"That's ridiculous," I burst out. "Don't you understand
about dancers' spines? She could ruin herself in two gees."

"I've got to have four weeks," Shara said.

"Ms. Drummond, I am very sorry."

"I've got to have four weeks."

Panzella had that same look of helpless sorrow that
McGillicuddy and I had had in our turn, and I was suddenly sick to death of a universe in which people had to

keep looking at Shara that way. "Dammit," I roared, "she needs four weeks."

Panzella shook his shaggy head. "If she stays in zero gee for four working weeks, she may die."

Shara sprang from her chair. "Then I'll die," she cried. "I'll take that chance. I *have* to."

Carrington coughed. "I'm afraid I can't permit you to, darling."

She whirled on him furiously.

"This dance of yours is excellent PR for Skyfac," he said calmly, "but if it were to kill you it might boomerang, don't you think?"

Her mouth worked, and she fought desperately for control. My own head whirled. Die? Shara?

"Besides," he added, "I've grown quite fond of you."

"Then I'll stay up here in space," she burst out.

"Where? The only areas of sustained weightlessness are factories, and you're not qualified to work in one."

"Then for God's sake give me one of the new pods, the smaller spheres. Bryce, I'll give you a higher return on your investment than a factory pod, and I'll. . . ." Her voice changed. "I'll be available to you always."

He smiled lazily. "Yes, but I might not *want* you always, darling. My mother warned me strongly against making irrevocable decisions about women. Especially informal ones. Besides, I find zero-gee sex rather too exhausting as a steady diet."

I had almost found my voice, and now I lost it again. I was glad Carrington was turning her down—but the way he did it made me yearn to drink his blood.

Shara too was speechless for a time. When she spoke, her voice was low, intense, almost pleading. "Bryce, it's a matter of timing. If I broadcast two more dances in the next four weeks, I'll have a world to return to. If I have to go Earthside and wait a year or two, that third dance will sink without a trace—no one'll be looking, and they won't have the memory of the first two. This is my only option, Bryce—*let me take the chance.* Panzella can't guarantee four weeks will kill me."

"I can't guarantee your survival," the doctor said.

"You can't guarantee that any of us will live out the day," she snapped. She whirled back to Carrington, held him with her eyes. "Bryce, *let me risk it.*" Her face underwent a massive effort, produced a smile that put a knife through my heart. "I'll make it worth your while."

Carrington savored that smile and the utter surrender in her voice like a man enjoying a fine claret. I wanted to slay him with my hands and teeth, and I prayed that he would add the final cruelty of turning her down. But I had underestimated his true capacity for cruelty.

"Go ahead with your rehearsal, my dear," he said at last. "We'll make a final decision when the time comes. I shall have to think about it."

I don't think I've ever felt so hopeless, so . . . impotent in my life. Knowing it was futile, I said, "Shara, I can't let you risk your life—"

"I'm going to do this, Charlie," she cut me off, "with or without you. No one else knows my work well enough to tape it properly, but if you want out I can't stop you." Carrington watched me with a detached interest. "Well?" she prodded.

I said a filthy word. "You know the answer."

"Then let's get to work."

Tyros are transported on the pregnant broomsticks. Old hands hang outside the airlock, dangling from handholds on the outer surface of the spinning Ring (not hard in less than half a gee). They face in the direction of their spin, and when their destination comes under the horizon, they just drop off. Thruster units built into gloves and boots supply the necessary course corrections. The distances involved are small. Still, there are very few old hands.

Shara and I were old hands, having spent more hours in weightlessness than some technicians who'd been working in Skyfac for years. We made scant and efficient use of our thrusters, chiefly in canceling the energy imparted to us by the spin of the Ring we left. We had throat mikes and hearing-aid-sized receivers, but there was no conversation on the way across the void. Being without a local vertical—a defined "up" and "down"—is more confusing and distressing than can possibly be imagined by anyone who has never left Earth. For that very reason, all Skyfac structures are aligned to the same imaginary "ecliptic," but it doesn't help very much. I wondered if I would ever get used to it—and even more I wondered whether I should ever get used to the cessation of pain in my leg. It even seemed to hurt less under spin these days.

We grounded, with much less force than a skydiver does, on the surface of the new studio. It was an enormous steel globe, studded with sunpower screens and heat losers, tethered to three more spheres in various stages of construction on which Harry Stein's boys were even now working. McGillicuddy had told me that the complex when completed would be used for "controlled density processing," and when I said, "How nice," he added, "Dispersion foaming and variable density casting," as if that explained everything. Perhaps it did. Right at the moment, it was Shara's studio.

The airlock led to a rather small working space around a smaller interior sphere some fifty meters in diameter. It too was pressurized, intended to contain a vacuum, but its locks stood open. We removed our p-suits, and Shara unstrapped her thruster bracelets from a bracing strut and put them on, hanging by her ankles from the strut while she did so. The anklets went on next. As jewelry they were a shade bulky—but they had twenty minutes' continuous use each, and their operation was not visible in normal atmosphere and lighting. Zero-gee dance without them would have been enormously more difficult.

As she was fastening the last strap I drifted over in front of her and grabbed the strut. "Shara . . . ."

"Charlie, I can beat it. I'll exercise in *three* gravities, and I'll sleep in two, and I'll make this body last. I know I can."

"You could skip *Mass Is A Verb* and go right to the *Stardance*."

She shook her head. "I'm not ready yet—and neither is the audience. I've got to lead myself and them through dance in a sphere first—in a contained space—before I'll be ready to dance in empty space, or they to appreciate it. I have to free my mind, and theirs, from just about every preconception of dance, change all the postulates. Even two stages is too few—but it's the irreducible minimum." Her eyes softened. "Charlie—I must."

"I know," I said gruffly and turned away. Tears are a nuisance in free fall—they don't *go* anywhere, just form silly-looking expanding spherical contact lenses, in which the world swims. I began hauling myself around the surface of the inner sphere toward the camera emplacement I was working on, and Shara entered the inner sphere to begin rehearsal.

I prayed as I worked on my equipment, snaking cables among the bracing struts and connecting them to drifting terminals. For the first time in years I prayed, prayed that Shara would make it. That we both would.

The next twelve days were the toughest of my life. Shara worked as hard as I did. She spent half of every day working in the studio, half of the rest in exercise under two and a quarter gravities (the most Dr. Panzella would permit), and half of the rest in Carrington's bed, trying to make him contented enough to let her stretch her time limit. Perhaps she slept in the few hours left over. I only know that she never looked tired, never lost her composure or her dogged determination. Stubbornly, reluctantly, her body lost its awkwardness, took on grace even in an environment where grace required enormous concentration. Like a child learning how to walk, Shara learned how to fly.

I even began to get used to the absence of pain in my leg.

What can I tell you of *Mass*, if you have not seen it? It cannot be described, even badly, in mechanistic terms, the way a symphony could be written out in words. Conventional dance terminology is, by its built-in assumptions, worse than useless, and if you are at all familiar with the new nomenclature you *must* be familiar with *Mass Is A Verb*, from which it draws *its* built-in assumptions.

Nor is there much I can say about the technical aspects of *Mass*. There were no special effects; not even music. Raoul Brindle's superb score was composed *from the dance*, and added to the tape with my permission two years later, but it was for the original, silent version that I was given the Emmy. My entire contribution, aside from editing and installing the two trampolines, was to camouflage batteries of wide-dispersion light sources in clusters around each camera eye, and wire them so that they energized only when they were out-of-frame with respect to whichever camera was on at the time—ensuring that Shara was always lit from the front, presenting two (not always congruent) shadows. I made no attempt to employ flashy camera work; I simply recorded what Shara danced, changing POV only as she did.

No, *Mass Is A Verb* can be decribed only in symbolic terms, and then poorly. I can say that Shara demonstrated that mass and inertia are as able as gravity to supply the dynamic conflict essential to dance. I can tell you that from them she distilled a kind of dance that could only have been imagined by a group-head consisting of an acrobat, a stunt-diver, a skywriter and an underwater ballerina. I can tell you that she dismantled the last interface between herself and utter freedom of motion, subduing her body to her will and space itself to her need.

And still I will have told you less than nothing. For Shara sought more than freedom—she sought meaning. *Mass* was, above all, a spiritual event—its title pun reflecting its thematic ambiguity between the technological and the theological. Shara made the human confrontation with existence a transitive act, literally meeting God halfway. I do not mean to imply that her dance at any time addressed an exterior God, a discrete entity with or without white beard. Her dance addressed reality, gave successive expression to the Three Eternal Questions asked by every human being who ever lived.

Her dance observed her *self*, and asked, *"How have I come to be here?"*

Her dance observed the universe in which self existed, and asked, *"How did all this come to be here with me?"*

And at last, observing her self in relation to its universe, *"Why am I so alone?"*

And having asked these questions with every muscle and sinew she possessed, she paused, hung suspended in the center of the sphere, her body and soul open to the universe, and when no answer came, she contracted. Not in a dramatic, coiling-spring sense as she had in *Liberation*, a compressing of energy and tension. This was physically similar, but an utterly different phenomenon. It was an act of introspection, a turning of the mind's (soul's?) eye in upon itself, to seek answers that lay nowhere else. Her body too, therefore, seemed to fold in upon itself, compacting her mass, so evenly that her position in space was not disturbed.

And reaching within herself, she closed on emptiness.

The camera faded out, leaving her alone, rigid, encapsulated, yearning. The dance ended, leaving her three questions unanswered, the tension of their asking unresolved. Only the expression of patient waiting on her face blunted the shocking edge of the non-ending, made it bearable, a small, blessed sign whispering, "To be continued."

By the eighteenth day we had it in the can, in rough form. Shara put it immediately out of her mind and began choreographing *Stardance*, but I spent two hard days of editing before I was ready to release the tape for broadcast. I had four days until the half-hour of prime time Carrington had purchased—but that wasn't the deadline I felt breathing down the back of my neck.

McGillicuddy came into my workroom while I was editing, and although he saw the tears running down my face he said no word. I let the tape run, and he watched in silence, and soon his face was wet too. When the tape had been over for a long time he said, very softly, "One of these days I'm going to have to quit this stinking job."

I said nothing.

"I used to be a karate instructor. I was pretty good. I could teach again, maybe do some exhibition work, make ten percent of what I do now."

I said nothing.

"The whole damned Ring's bugged, Charlie. The desk in my office can activate and tap any vidphone in Skyfac. Four at a time, actually."

I said nothing.

"I saw you both in the airlock, when you came back the last time. I saw her collapse. I saw you bringing her around. I heard her make you promise not to tell Dr. Panzella."

I waited. Hope stirred.

He dried his face. "I came in here to tell you I was going to Panzella, to tell him what I saw. He'd bully Carrington into sending her home right away."

"And now?" I said.

"I've seen that tape."

"And you know that the *Stardance* will probably kill her?"

"Yes."

"And you know we have to let her do it?"

"Yes."

Hope died. I nodded. "Then get out of here and let me work."

He left.

On Wall Street and aboard Skyfac it was late afternoon when I finally had the tape edited to my satisfaction. I called Carrington, told him to expect me in half an hour, showered, shaved, dressed, and left.

A major of the Space Command was there with him when I arrived, but he was not introduced and so I ignored him. Shara was there too, wearing a thing made of orange smoke that left her breasts bare. Carrington had obviously made her wear it, as an urchin writes filthy words on an altar, but she wore it with a perverse and curious dignity that I sensed annoyed him. I looked her in the eye and smiled. "Hi, kid. It's a good tape."

"Let's see," Carrington said. He and the major took seats behind the desk, and Shara sat beside it.

I fed the tape into the video rig built into the office wall, dimmed the lights, and sat across from Shara. It ran twenty minutes, uninterrupted, no soundtrack, stark naked.

It was terrific.

"Aghast" is a funny word. To make you aghast, a thing must hit you in a place you haven't armored over with cynicism yet. I seem to have been born cynical; I have been aghast three times that I can remember. The first was when I learned, at the age of three, that there were people who could deliberately hurt kittens. The second was when I learned, at age seventeen, that there were people who could actually take LSD and then hurt other people for fun. The third was when *Mass Is A Verb* ended and Carrington said in perfectly conversational tones, "Very pleasant; very graceful. I like it," when I learned, at age forty-five, that there were men, not fools or cretins but intelligent men, who could watch Shara Drummond dance and fail to *see*. We all, even the most cynical of us, always have some illusion which we cherish.

Shara simply let it bounce off her somehow, but I could see that the major was as aghast as I, controlling his features with a visible effort.

Suddenly welcoming a distraction from my horror and dismay, I studied him more closely, wondering for the first time what he was doing here. He was my age, lean and more hard-bitten than I am, with silver fuzz on top of his skull and an extremely tidy mustache on the front. I'd taken him for a crony of Carrington's, but three things changed my mind. Something indefinable about his eyes told me that he was a military man of long combat experience. Something equally indefinable about his carriage told me that he was on duty at the moment. And something quite definable about the line his mouth made told me that he was disgusted with the duty he had drawn.

When Carrington went on, "What do you think, Major?" in polite tones, the man paused for a moment, gathering his thoughts and choosing his words. When he did speak, it was not to Carrington.

"Ms. Drummond," he said quietly, "I am Major William Cox, commander of S.C. *Champion*, and I am honored to meet you. That was the most profoundly moving thing I have ever seen."

Shara thanked him most gravely. "This is Charles Armstead, Major Cox. He made the tape."

Cox regarded me with new respect. "A magnificent job, Mister Armstead." He stuck out his hand and I shook it.

Carrington was beginning to understand that we three shared a thing which excluded him. "I'm glad you enjoyed it, Major," he said with no visible trace of sincerity. "You can see it again on your television tomorrow night, if you chance to be off duty. And eventually, of course, cassettes will be made available. Now perhaps we can get to the matter at hand."

Cox's face closed as if it had been zippered up, became stiffly formal. "As you wish, sir."

Puzzled, I began what I thought was the matter at hand. "I'd like your own Comm Chief to supervise the actual transmission this time, Mr. Carrington. Shara and I will be too busy to—"

"My Comm Chief will supervise the broadcast, Armstead," Carrington interrupted, "but I don't think you'll be particularly busy."

I was groggy from lack of sleep; my uptake was slow.

He touched his desk delicately. "McGillicuddy, report at once," he said, and released it. "You see, Armstead, you and Shara are both returning to Earth. At once."

"*What?*"

"Bryce, you *can't*," Shara cried. "You *promised*."

"Did I? My dear, there were no witnesses present last night. Altogether for the best, don't you agree?"

I was speechless with rage.

McGillicuddy entered. "Hello, Tom," Carrington said pleasantly. "You're fired. You'll be returning to Earth at once, with Ms. Drummond and Mr. Armstead, aboard Major Cox's vessel. Departure in one hour, and don't leave anything you're fond of." He glanced from McGillicuddy to me. "From Tom's desk you can tap any vidphone in Skyfac. From my desk you can tap Tom's desk."

Shara's voice was low. "Bryce, two days. God damn you, name your price."

He smiled slightly. "I'm sorry, darling. When informed of your collapse, Dr. Panzella became most specific. Not even one more day. Alive you are a distinct plus for Skyfac's image—you are my gift to the world. Dead you are an albatross around my neck. I cannot allow you to die on my property. I anticipated that you might resist leaving, and so I spoke to a friend in the," he glanced at Cox, "*higher* echelons of the Space Command, who was good enough to send the Major here to escort you home. You are not under arrest in the legal sense—but, I assure you that you have no choice. Something like protective custody applies. Good-bye, Shara." He reached for a stack of reports on his desk, and I surprised myself considerably.

I cleared the desk entirely, tucked head catching him squarely in the sternum. His chair was bolted to the deck and so it snapped clean. I recovered so well that I had time for one glorious right. Do you know how, if you punch a basketball squarely, it will bounce up from the floor? That's what his head did, in low-gee slow motion.

Then Cox had hauled me to my feet and shoved me into the far corner of the room. "Don't," he said to me, and his voice must have held a lot of that "habit of command" they talk about because it stopped me cold. I stood breathing in great gasps while Cox helped Carrington to his feet.

The multibillionaire felt his smashed nose, examined the blood on his fingers, and looked at me with raw hatred. "You'll never work in video again, Armstead. You're through. Finished. Un-em-ployed, you got that?"

Cox tapped him on the shoulder, and Carrington spun on him. "What the hell do you want?" he barked.

Cox smiled. "Carrington, my late father once said, 'Bill, make your enemies by choice, not by accident.' Over the years I have found that to be excellent advice. You suck."

"And not particularly well," Shara agreed.

Carrington blinked. Then his absurdly broad shoulders swelled and he roared, "Out, all of you! *Off my property at once!*"

By unspoken consent, we waited for Tom, who knew his cue. "Mister Carrington, it is a rare privilege and a great honor to have been fired by you. I shall think of it always as a Pyrrhic defeat." And he half-bowed and we left, each buoyed by a juvenile feeling of triumph that must have lasted ten seconds.

# Chapter 4

The sensation of falling that you get when you first enter zero gee is literal truth—but it fades rapidly as your body learns to treat it as illusion. Now, in zero gee for the last time, for the half hour or so before I would be back in Earth's gravitational field, I felt like I was falling. Plummeting into some bottomless gravity well, dragged down by the anvil that was my heart, the scraps of a dream that should have held me aloft fluttering overhead.

The *Champion* was three times the size of Carrington's yacht, which childishly pleased me until I recalled that he had summoned it here without paying for either fuel or crew. A guard at the airlock saluted as we entered. Cox led us aft to the compartment where we were to strap in. He noticed along the way that I used only my left hand to pull myself along, and when we stopped, he said, "Mr. Armstead, my late father also told me, 'Hit the soft parts with your hand. Hit the hard parts with a utensil.' Otherwise I can find no fault with your technique. I wish I could shake your hand."

I tried to smile, but I didn't have it in me. "I admire your taste in enemies, Major."

"A man can't ask for more. I'm afraid I can't spare

time to have your hand looked at until we've grounded. We begin reentry immediately."

"Forget it. Get Shara down, fast and easy."

He bowed to Shara, did *not* tell her how deeply he was to et cetera, wished us all a comfortable journey, and left. We strapped into our acceleration couches to await ignition. There ensued a long and heavy silence, compounded of a mutual sadness that bravado could only have underlined. We did not look at each other, as though our combined sorrow might achieve some kind of critical mass. Grief struck us dumb, and I believe that remarkably little of it was self-pity.

But then a whole lot of time seemed to have gone by. Quite a bit of intercom chatter came faintly from the next compartment, but ours was not in circuit. At last we began to talk, desultorily, discussing the probable critical reaction to *Mass Is A Verb*, whether analysis was worthwhile or the theater really dead, anything at all except future plans. Eventually there was nothing else to talk about, so we shut up again. I guess I'd say we were in shock.

For some reason I came out of it first. "What the hell is taking them so long?" I barked irritably.

Tom started to say something soothing, then glanced at his watch and yelped. "You're right. It's been over an hour."

I looked at the wall clock, got hopelessly confused until I realized it was on Greenwich time rather than Wall Street, and realized he was correct. "Chrissakes," I shouted, "the whole bloody *point* of this exercise is to protect Shara from overexposure to free fall! I'm going forward."

"Charlie, hold it." Tom, with two good hands, unstrapped faster than I. "Dammit, stay right there and cool off. I'll go find out what the holdup is."

He was back in a few minutes, and his face was slack. "We're not going anywhere. Cox has orders to sit tight."

"What? Tom, what the *hell* are you talking about?"

His voice was all funny. "Red fireflies. More like bees, actually. In a balloon."

He simply *could not* be joking, which meant he flat out *had* to have gone completely round the bend, which meant that somehow I had blundered into my favorite nightmare, where everyone but me goes crazy and begins gibbering at me. So I lowered my head like an enraged bull and charged out of the room so fast the door barely had time to get out of my way.

It just got worse. When I reached the door to the bridge I was going much too fast to be stopped by anything short of a body block, and the crewmen present were caught flatfooted. There was a brief flurry at the door, and then I was on the bridge, and then I decided that I had gone crazy too, which somehow made everything all right.

The forward wall of the bridge was one enormous video tank—and just enough off center to faintly irritate me, standing out against the black deep as clearly as cigarettes in a darkroom, there truly did swarm a multitude of red fireflies.

The conviction of unreality made it okay. But then Cox snapped me back to reality with a bellowed, "*Off this bridge, Mister.*" If I'd been in a normal frame of mind it would have blown me out the door and into the farthest corner of the ship; in my current state it managed to jolt me into acceptance of the impossible situation. I shivered like a wet dog and turned to him.

"Major," I said desperately, "what is going on?"

As a king may be amused by an insolent varlet who refuses to kneel, he was bemused by the phenomenon of someone failing to obey him. It bought me an answer. "We are confronting intelligent alien life," he said concisely. "I believe them to be sentient plasmoids."

I had never for a moment believed that the mysterious object which had been leap-frogging around the solar system since I came to Skyfac was *alive*. I tried to take it in, then abandoned the task and went back to my main priority. "I don't care if they're eight tiny reindeer; you've got to get this can back to Earth *now*."

"Sir, this vessel is on Emergency Red Alert and on Combat Standby. At this moment the suppers of everyone in North America are getting cold unnoticed. I will consider myself fortunate if I ever see Earth again. Now get off my bridge."

"But you don't *understand*. Shara's right on the edge: farting around like this'll kill her. That's what you came up here to prevent, dammit—"

"MISTER ARMSTEAD! This is a military vessel. We are facing more than fifty intelligent beings who appeared out of hyperspace near here twenty minutes ago, beings who therefore use a drive beyond my conception with no visible parts. If it makes you feel any better I am aware that I have a passenger aboard of greater intrinsic value to my species than this ship and everyone else aboard her, and if it is any comfort to you this knowledge already provides a distraction I need like an auxiliary anus, and I can no more leave this orbit than I can grow horns. Now will you get off this bridge or will you be dragged?"

I didn't get a chance to decide; they dragged me.

On the other hand, by the time I got back to our compartment, Cox had put our vidphone screen in circuit with the tank on the bridge. Shara and Tom were studying it with rapt attention. Having nothing better to do, I did too.

Tom had been right. They *did* act more like bees, in the swarming rapidity of their movement. I couldn't get an accurate count: about fifty. And they *were* in a balloon—a faint, barely visible thing on the fine line between transparency and translucence. Though they darted like furious red gnats, it was only within the confines of the spheroid balloon—they never left it or seemed to touch its inner surface.

As I watched, the last of the adrenalin rinsed out of my kidneys, but it left a sense of frustrated urgency. I tried to grapple with the fact that these Space Commando special effects represented something that was—more important than Shara. It was a primevally disturbing notion, but I could not reject it.

In my mind were two voices, each hollering questions at the top of their lungs, each ignoring the other's questions. One yelled: *Are those things friendly? Or hostile? Or do they even use those concepts? How big are they? How far away? From where?* The other voice was less ambitious, but just as loud; all it said, over and over again, was: *How much longer can Shara remain in free fall without dooming herself?*

Shara's voice was full of wonder. "They're . . . they're *dancing*."

I looked closer. If there was a pattern to the flies-on-garbage swarm they made, I couldn't detect it. "Looks random to me."

"Charlie, look. All that furious activity, and they never bump into each other or the walls of that envelope they're in. They must be in orbits as carefully choreographed as those of electrons."

"Do atoms dance?"

She gave me an odd look. "Don't they, Charlie?"

"Laser beam," Tom said.

We looked at him.

"Those things have to be plasmoids—the man I talked to said they show on deepspace radar. That means they're ionized gases of some kind—the kind of thing that used to cause UFO reports." He giggled, then caught himself. "If you could slice through that envelope with a laser, I'll bet you could deionize them pretty good—besides, that envelope has to hold their life support, whatever it is they metabolize."

I was dizzy. "Then we're not defenseless?"

"You're both talking like soldiers," Shara burst out. "I tell you, they're dancing. Dancers aren't fighters."

"Come on, Shara," I barked. "Even if those things happen to be remotely like us, that's not true. T'ai chi, karate, kung fu—they're dance." I nodded to the screen. "All we know about these animated embers is that they travel interstellar space. That's enough to scare me."

"Charlie, *look* at them," she commanded.

I did.

By God, they didn't look threatening. And they did, the more I watched, seem to move in a dancelike way, whirling in mad adagios just too fast for the eye to follow. Not at all like conventional dance—more analogous to what Shara had begun with *Mass Is A Verb*. I found myself wanting to switch to another camera for contrast of perspective, and that made my mind start to wake up at last. Two ideas surfaced, the second one necessary in order to sell Cox the first.

"How far do you suppose we are from Skyfac?" I asked Tom.

He pursed his lips. "Not far. There hasn't been much more than maneuvering acceleration. The damned things were probably attracted to Skyfac in the first place—it must be the most easily visible sign of intelligent life in this system." He grimaced. "Maybe they don't *use* planets."

I reached forward and punched the audio circuit. "Major Cox."

"*Get off this circuit.*"

"How would you like a closer view of those things?"

"We're staying put. Now stop jiggling my elbow and get off this circuit or I'll—"

"Will you listen to me? I have four mobile cameras in space, remote control, self-contained power and light, and better resolution than you've got. They were set up to tape Shara's next dance."

He shifted gears at once. "Can you patch them into my ship?"

"I think so. But I'll have to get back to the master board in Ring One."

"No good, then. I can't tie myself to a top—what if I have to fight or run?"

"Major—how far a walk is it?"

It startled him a bit. "A couple of klicks, as the crow flies. But you're a groundlubber."

"I've been in free fall for most of two months. Give me a portable radar and I can ground on Phobos."

"Mmmm. You're a civilian—but dammit, I need better video. Permission granted."

Now for the first idea. "Wait—one thing more. Shara and Tom must come with me."

"Nuts. This isn't a field trip."

"Major Cox—Shara *must* return to a gravity field as quickly as possible. Ring One'll do—in fact, it'd be ideal, if we enter through the 'spoke' in the center. She can descend very slowly and acclimatize gradually, the way a diver decompresses in stages, but in reverse. Tom will have to come along and stay with her—if she passes out and falls down the tube, she could break a leg even in one-sixth gee. Besides, he's better at EVA than either of us."

He thought it over. "Go."

We went.

The trip back to Ring One was longer than any Shara or I had ever made, but under Tom's guidance we made it with minimal maneuvering. Ring, *Champion* and aliens formed an equiangular triangle about five or six klicks on a side. Seen in perspective, the aliens took up about twice as much volume as a sphere the diameter of Ring One— one hell of a big balloon. They did not pause or slacken in their mad gyration, but somehow they seemed to watch us cross the gap to Skyfac. I got the impression of a biologist studying the strange antics of a new species. We kept our suit radios off to avoid distraction, and it made me just a little bit more susceptible to suggestion.

I failed to even notice the absence of a local vertical. I was too busy.

I left Tom with Shara and dropped down the tube six rungs at a time. Carrington was waiting for me in the reception room, with two flunkies. It was plain to see that he was scared silly, and trying to cover it with anger. "God damn it, Armstead, those are my bloody cameras."

"Shut up, Carrington. If you put those cameras in the hands of the best technician available—me—and if I put their data in the hands of the best strategic mind in space —Cox—we *might* be able to save your damned factory for you. And the human race for the rest of us." I moved forward, and he got out of my way. It figured. Putting all humanity in danger might just be bad PR.

After all the practicing I'd done it wasn't hard to direct four mobile cameras through space simultaneously by eye. The aliens ignored their approach. The Skyfac comm crew fed my signals to the *Champion*, and patched me in to Cox on audio. At his direction I bracketed the balloon with the cameras, shifting POV at his command. Space Command Headquarters must have recorded the video, but I couldn't hear their conversation with Cox, for which I was grateful. I gave him slow-motion replay, close-ups, splitscreens—everything at my disposal. The movements of individual fireflies did not appear particularly symmetrical, but patterns began to repeat. In slow motion they looked more than ever as though they were dancing, and although I couldn't be sure, it seemed to me that they were increasing their tempo. Somehow the dramatic tension of their dance began to build.

And then I shifted POV to the camera which included Skyfac in the background, and my heart turned to hard vacuum and I screamed in pure primal terror—halfway between Ring One and the swarm of aliens, coming up on them slowly but inexorably, was a p-suited figure that had to be Shara.

With theatrical timing, Tom appeared in the doorway beside me, leaning heavily on Harry Stein, his face drawn with pain. He stood on one foot, the other plainly broken.

"Guess I can't . . . go back to exhibition work . . . after all," he gasped. "Said . . . 'I'm sorry, Tom' . . . knew she was going to swing on me . . . wiped me out anyhow. Oh dammit, Charlie, I'm sorry." He sank into an empty chair.

Cox's voice came urgently. "What the hell is going on? Who is that?"

She *had* to be on our frequency. "Shara!" I screamed. "Get your ass back in here!"

"I can't, Charlie." Her voice was startlingly loud, and very calm. "Halfway down the tube my chest started to hurt like hell."

"Ms. Drummond," Cox rapped, "if you approach any closer to the aliens I will destroy you."

She laughed, a merry sound that froze my blood. "Bullshit, Major. You aren't about to get gay with laser beams near those things. Besides, you need me as much as you do Charlie."

"What do you mean?"

"These creatures communicate by dance. It's their equivalent of speech, a sophisticated kind of sign language, like hula."

"You can't know that."

"I *feel* it. I know it. Hell, how else do you communicate in airless space? Major Cox, I am the only qualified interpreter the human race has at the moment. Now will you kindly shut up so I can try to learn their language?"

"I have no authority to . . . ."

I said an extraordinary thing. I should have been gibbering, pleading with Shara to come back, even racing for a p-suit to *bring* her back. Instead I said, "She's right. Shut up, Cox."

"But—"

"Damn you, *don't waste her last effort.*"

He shut up.

Panzella came in, shot Tom full of painkiller, and set his ankle right there in the room, but I was oblivious. For over an hour I watched Shara watch the aliens. I watched them myself, in the silence of utter despair, and for the life of me I could not follow their dance. I strained my mind, trying to suck meaning from their crazy whirling, and failed. The best I could do to aid Shara was to record everything that happened, for a hypothetical posterity. Several times she cried out softly, small muffled exclamations, and I ached to call out to her in reply, but did not. With the last exclamation, she used her thrusters to bring her closer to the alien swarm, and hung there for a long time.

At last her voice came over the speaker, thick and slurred at first, as though she were talking in her sleep. "God, Charlie. Strange. So strange. I'm beginning to read them."

"How?"

"Every time I begin to understand a part of the dance, it . . . it brings us closer. Not telepathy, exactly. I just . . . know them better. Maybe it is telepathy, I don't know. By dancing what they feel, they give it enough intensity to make me understand. I'm getting about one concept in three. It's stronger up close."

Cox's voice was gentle but firm. "What have you learned, Shara?"

"That Tom and Charlie were right. They are warlike. At least, there's a flavor of arrogance to them—a conviction of superiority. Their dance is a challenging, a dare. Tell Tom I think they *do* use planets."

"What?"

"I think at one stage of their development they're corporeal, planet-bound. Then when they have matured sufficiently, they . . . become these fireflies, like caterpillars becoming butterflies, and head out into space."

"Why?" from Cox.

"To find spawning grounds. They want Earth."

There was a silence lasting perhaps ten seconds. Then Cox spoke up quietly. "Back away, Shara. I'm going to see what lasers will do to them."

"No!" she cried, loud enough to make a really first-rate speaker distort.

"Shara, as Charlie pointed out to me, you are not only expendable, you are for all practical purposes expended."

"No!" This time it was me shouting.

"Major," Shara said urgently, "that's not the way. Believe me, they can dodge or withstand anything you or Earth can throw at them. I *know*."

"Hell and damnation, woman," Cox said. "What do you want me to do? Let them have the first shot? There are vessels from four countries on their way right now, but they won't—"

"Major, wait. Give me time."

He began to swear, then cut off. "How much time?"

She made no direct reply. "If only this telepathy thing works in reverse . . . it must. I'm no more strange to them than they are to me. Probably less so; I get the idea they've been around. Charlie?"

"Yeah."

"This is a take."

I knew. I had known since I first saw her in open space on my monitor. And I knew what she needed now, from the faint trembling of her voice. It took everything I had, and I was only glad I had it to give. With extremely realistic good cheer, I said, "Break a leg, kid," and killed my mike before she could hear the sob that followed.

And she danced.

It began slowly, the equivalent of one-finger exercises, as she sought to establish a vocabulary of motion that the creatures could comprehend. *Can you see*, she seemed to say, *that* this *movement is a reaching, a yearning? Do you see that* this *is a spurning*, this *an unfolding*, that *a graduated elision of energy? Do you feel the ambiguity in the way I distort this arabesque, or that the tension can be resolved* so?

And it seemed that Shara was right, that they had infinitely more experience with disparate cultures than we, for they were superb linguists of motion. It occurred to me later that perhaps they had selected motion for communication because of its very universality. Man danced before he spoke. At any rate, as Shara's dance began to build, their own began to slow down perceptibly in speed and intensity, until at last they hung motionless in space, watching her.

Soon after that, Shara must have decided that she had sufficiently defined her terms, at least well enough for pidgin communication—for now she began to dance in earnest. Before she had used only her own muscles and the shifting masses of her limbs. Now she added thrusters, singly and in combination, moving within as well as in space. Her dance became a true dance: more than a collection of motions, a thing of substance and meaning. It was unquestionably the *Stardance*, just as she had prechoreographed it, as she had always intended to dance it. That it had something to say to utterly alien creatures, of man and his nature, was not at all a coincidence: it was the essential and ultimate statement of the greatest artist of her age, and it had something to say to God himself.

The camera lights struck silver from her p-suit, gold from the twin air tanks on her shoulders. To and fro against the black backdrop of space, she wove the intricacies of her dance, a leisurely movement that seemed somehow to leave echoes behind it. And the meaning of those great loops and whirls became clear, drying my throat and clamping my teeth.

For her dance spoke of nothing more and nothing less than the tragedy of being alive, and being human. It spoke, most eloquently, of despair. It spoke of the cruel humor of limitless ambition yoked to limited ability, of eternal hope invested in an ephemeral lifetime, of the driving need to try to create an inexorably predetermined future. It spoke of fear, and of hunger, and, most clearly, of the basic loneliness and alienation of the human animal. It described the universe through the eyes of man: a hostile embodiment of entropy into which we are all thrown alone, forbidden by our nature to touch another mind save secondhand, by proxy. It spoke of the blind perversity which forces man to strive hugely for a peace which, once attained, becomes boredom. And it spoke of folly, of the terrible paradox by which man is capable simultaneously of reason and unreason, forever unable to cooperate even with himself.

It spoke of Shara and her life.

Again and again cyclical statements of hope began, only to collapse into confusion and ruin. Again and again cascades of energy strove for resolution, and found only frustration. All at once she launched into a pattern that seemed familiar, and in moments I recognized it: the closing movement of *Mass Is A Verb* recapitulated—not repeated but reprised, echoed, the Three Questions given a more terrible urgency by this new context. And as before, it segued into that final relentless contraction, that ultimate drawing inward of all energies. Her body became derelict, abandoned, drifting in space, the essence of her being withdrawn to her center and invisible.

The quiescent aliens stirred for the first time.

And suddenly she exploded, blossoming from her contraction not as a spring uncoils, but as a flower bursts from a seed. The force of her release flung her through the void as though she were tossed, like a gull in a hurricane, by galactic winds. Her center appeared to hurl itself through space and time, yanking her body into a new dance.

And the new dance said, *This is what it is to be human: to see the essential existential futility of all action, all striving—and to act, to strive. This is what it is to be human: to reach forever beyond your grasp. This is what it is to be human: to live forever or die trying. This is what it is to be human: to perpetually ask the unanswerable questions, in the hope that the asking of them will somehow hasten the day when they will be answered. This is what it is to be human: to strive in the face of the certainty of failure.*

*This is what it is to be human: to persist.*

It said all this with a soaring series of cyclical movements that held all the rolling majesty of grand symphony, as uniquely different from each other as snowflakes, and as similar. And the new dance *laughed*, as much at tomorrow as at yesterday, and most of all at today.

*For this is what it means to be human: to laugh at what another would call tragedy.*

The aliens seemed to recoil from the ferocious energy, startled, awed, and perhaps a little frightened by Shara's indomitable spirit. They seemed to wait for her dance to wane, for her to exhaust herself, and her laughter sounded on my speaker as she redoubled her efforts, became a pinwheel, a catherine wheel. She changed the focus of her dance, began to dance *around* them, in pyrotechnic spatters of motion that came ever closer to the intangible spheroid which contained them. They cringed inward from her, huddling together in the center of the envelope, not so much physically threatened as cowed.

*This*, said her body, *is what it means to be human: to commit hara-kiri, with a smile, if it becomes needful.*

And before that terrible assurance, the aliens broke. Without warning fireflies and balloon vanished, gone, *elsewhere*.

I know that Cox and Tom were still alive, because I saw them afterwards, and that means they were probably saying and doing things in my hearing and presence, but I neither heard them nor saw them then; they were as dead to me as everything except Shara. I called out her name, and she approached the camera that was lit, until

I could make out her face behind the plastic hood of her p-suit.

"We may be puny, Charlie," she puffed, gasping for breath. "But by Jesus we're tough."

"Shara—come on in now."

"You know I can't."

"Carrington'll *have* to give you a free-fall place to live now."

"A life of exile? For what? To dance? Charlie, *I haven't got anything more to say*."

"Then I'll come out there."

"Don't be silly. Why? So you can hug a p-suit? Tenderly bump hoods one last time? Balls. It's a good exit so far—let's not blow it."

"*Shara!*" I broke completely, just caved in on myself and collapsed into great racking sobs.

"Charlie, listen now," she said softly, but with an urgency that reached me even in my despair. "Listen now, for I haven't much time. I have something to give you. I hoped you'd find it for yourself, but . . . will you listen?"

"Y—yes."

"Charlie, zero-gee dance is going to get awful popular all of a sudden. I've opened the door. But you know how fads are, they'll bitch it all up unless you move fast. I'm leaving it in your hands."

"What . . . what are you talking about?"

"About you, Charlie. You're going to dance again."

Oxygen starvation, I thought. But she can't be that low on air already. "Okay. Sure thing."

"For God's sake stop humoring me—I'm straight, I tell you. You'd have seen it yourself if you weren't so damned stupid. Don't you understand? *There's nothing wrong with your leg in free fall!*"

My jaw dropped.

"Do you hear me, Charlie? You can dance again!"

"No," I said, and searched for a reason why not. "I

. . . you can't . . . it's . . . dammit, the leg's not strong enough for inside work."

"Forget for the moment that inside work'll be less than half of what you do. Forget it and remember that smack in the nose you gave Carrington. Charlie, when you leaped over the desk: *you pushed off with your right leg.*"

I sputtered for awhile and shut up.

"There you go, Charlie. My farewell gift. You know I've never been in love with you . . . but you must know that I've always loved you. Still do."

"I love you, Shara."

"So long, Charlie. Do it right."

And all four thrusters went off at once. I watched her go down. Awhile after she was too far to see, there was a long golden flame that arced above the face of the globe, waned, and then flared again as the airtanks went up.

# 2

## The Stardancers

# Chapter 1

The flight from Washington was miserable. How can a man who's worked in free fall get airsick? Worse, I had awakened that morning with the same stinking cold I had had ever since returning Earthside, and so I spent the whole flight anticipating the knives that would be thrust through my ears when we landed. But I turned down the proffered drink as well as the meal.

I was not even depressed. Too much had happened to me in the last few weeks. I was wrung out, drained, just sort of . . . on standby, taking disinterested notes while my automatic pilot steered my body around. It helped to be in a familiar place—why, come to think, hadn't I once thought of Toronto, about a thousand years ago, as "home"?

There were reporters when I got through Customs, of course, but not nearly as many as there had been at first. Once, as a kid, I spent a summer working in a mental hospital, and I learned an extraordinary thing: I learned that anyone, no matter how determined, whom you *utterly* ignore will eventually stop pestering you and go away. I had been practicing the technique so consistently for the last three weeks that the word had gone out, and now only the most Skinnerian newstapers even troubled to stick

81

microphones in my face. Eventually there was a cab in front of me and I took it. Toronto cabbies can be relied upon not to recognize anybody, thank God.

I was "free" now.

Reentering the TDT studio was a strong déjà vu experience, strong enough almost to penetrate my armor. Once, geologic ages ago, I had worked here for three years, and briefly again thereafter. And once, in this building, I had seen Shara Drummond dance for the first time. I had come full circle.

I felt nothing.

Always excepting, of course, the god damned leg. After all the time in free fall it hurt much worse than I'd remembered, more than it had hurt since the original days of its ruining, unimaginably far in the past. I had to pause twice on the way upstairs, and I was soaking with sweat by the time I made the top. (Ever wonder why dance studios are *always* up at least one flight of stairs? Did you ever try to rent that much square footage at ground level?) I waited on the landing, regularizing my breathing, until I decided that my color had returned, and then a few seconds more. I knew I should feel agitated now, but I was still on standby.

I opened the door, and déjà vu smacked at me again. Norrey was across the old familiar room, and just as before she was putting a group of students through their paces. They might have been the same students. Only Shara was missing. Shara would always be missing. Shara was air pollution now, upper atmosphere pollution, much more widely distributed than most corpses get to be.

She had been cremated at the *top* of the atmosphere, and by it.

But her older sister was very much alive. She was in the midst of demonstrating a series of suspensions on half-toe as I entered, and I just had time to absorb an impression of glowing skin, healthy sweat, and superb muscle tone before she glanced up and saw me. She stif=

fened like a stop-frame shot, then literally fell out of an extension. Automatically her body tucked and rolled, and she came out of it at a dead run, crying and swearing as she came, arms outstretched. I barely had time to brace the good leg before she cannoned into me, and then we were rocking in each other's arms like tipsy giants, and she was swearing like a sailor and crying my name. We hugged for an endless time before I became aware that I was holding her clear of the floor and that my shoulders were shrieking nearly as loud as my leg. *Six months ago it would have buckled*, I thought vaguely, and set her down.

"All right, are you all right, are you all right?" her voice was saying in my ear.

I pulled back and tried to grin. "My leg is killing me. And I think I've got the flu."

"Damn you, Charlie, don't you dare misunderstand me. *Are you all right?*" Her fingers gripped my neck as if she intended to chin herself.

My hands dropped to her waist and I looked her in the eyes, abandoning the grin. All at once I realized I was no longer on standby. My cocoon was ruptured, blood sang in my ears, and I could feel the very air impinging on my skin. For the first time I thought about why I had come here, and partly I understood. "Norrey," I said simply, "I'm okay. Some ways I think I'm in better shape than I've been in twenty years."

The second sentence just slipped out, but I knew as I said it that it was true. Norrey read the truth in my eyes, and somehow managed to relax all over without loosing her embrace. "Oh, thank *God*," she sobbed, and pulled me closer. After a time her sobs lessened, and she said, almost petulantly, her voice tiny, "I'd have broken your *neck*," and we were both grinning like idiots and laughing aloud. We laughed ourselves right out of our embrace, and then Norrey said "Oh!" suddenly and turned bright red and spun round to her class.

It seemed that we were occupying the only portion of the room that was not intensely fascinating. They knew. They watched TV, they read the papers. Even as we watched, one of the students stepped out in front of the rest. "All right," she said to them, "let's take it from the top, I'll give you three for nothing and—*one*," and the whole group resumed their workout. The new leader would not meet Norrey's eyes, refused to accept or even acknowledge the gratitude there—but she seemed to be smiling gently, as she danced, at nothing in particular.

Norrey turned back to me. "I'll have to change."

"Not much, I hope."

She grinned again and was gone. My cheeks itched, and when I absently scratched them I discovered that they were soaking wet.

The afternoon outdoors struck us both with wonder. New colors seemed to boil up out of the spectrum and splash themselves everywhere in celebration of fall. It was one of those October days of which, in Toronto anyway, one can say either "Gee, it's chilly" or "Gee, it's warm" and be agreed with. We walked through it together arm in arm, speaking only occasionally and then only with our eyes. My stuffed head began to clear; my leg throbbed less.

Le Maintenant was still there then, but it looked shabbier than ever. Fat Humphrey caught sight of us through the kitchen window as we entered and came out to greet us. He is both the fattest happy man and the happiest fat man I've ever seen. I've seen him outdoors in February in his shirt sleeves, and they say that once a would-be burglar stabbed him three times without effect. He burst through the swinging doors and rushed toward us, a mountain with a smile on top. "Mist' Armstead, Miz Drummond! Welcome!"

"Hey there, Fat," I called out, removing my filters, "God bless your face. Got a good table?"

"Sure thing, in the cellar somewheres, I'll bring it up."

"I'm sorry *I* brought it up."

"There's certainly *some*thing wrong with your up-bringing," Norrey agreed dryly.

Fat Humphrey laughing aloud is like an earthquake in the Canadian Rockies. "Good to see you, good to see you both. You been away too long, Mist' Armstead."

"Tell you about it later, Fat, okay?"

"Sure thing. Lemme see: you look like about a pound of sirloin, some bake' potato, peas Italian hold the garlic and a bucket of milk. Miz Drummond, I figure you for tuna salad on whole wheat toast, side of slice' tomatoes and a glass of milk. Salad all around. Eh?"

We both burst out laughing. "Right again, as usual. Why do you bother to print menus?"

"Would you believe it? There's a law. How would you like that steak cooked?"

"Gee, that'd be terrific," I agreed, and took Norrey's coat and filtermask. Fat Humphrey howled and slapped his mighty thigh, and took my own gear while I was hanging Norrey's. "Been missin' you in this joint, Mist' Armstead. None of these other turkeys know a straight line when they hear it. This way." He led us to a small table in the back, and as I sat down I realized that it was the same table Norrey and Shara and I had shared so long ago. That didn't hurt a bit: it felt right. Fat Humphrey rolled us a joint by hand from his personal stash, and left the bag and a packet of Drums on the table. "Smoke hearty," he said and returned to the kitchen, his retreating buttocks like wrestling zeppelins.

I had not smoked in weeks; at the first taste I started to buzz. Norrey's fingers brushed mine as we passed the digit, and their touch was warm and electric. My nose, which had started to fill as we came indoors, flooded, and between toking and honking the joint was gone before a word had been spoken. I was acutely aware of how silly I must look, but too exhilarated to fret about it. I tried to review mentally all that must be said and all that must be asked, but I kept falling into Norrey's warm brown eyes and getting lost. The candle put highlights in them, and in her brown hair. I rummaged in my head for the right words.

"Well, here we are," is what I came up with.

Norrey half smiled. "That's a hell of a cold."

"My nose clamped down twenty hours after I hit dirt, and I've never properly thanked it. Do you have any *idea* how rotten this planet smells?"

"I'd have thought a closed system'd smell worse."

I shook my head. "There's a smell to space, to a space station I mean. And a p-suit can get pretty ripe. But Earth is a *stew* of smells, mostly bad."

She nodded judiciously. "No smokestacks in space."

"No garbage dumps."

"No sewage."

"No cow farts."

"How did she die, Charlie?"

*Oof.* "Magnificently."

"I read the papers. I *know* that's bullshit, and . . . and you were *there*."

"Yeah." I had told the story over a hundred times in the last three weeks—but I had never told a *friend*, and I discovered I needed to. And Norrey certainly deserved to know of her sister's dying.

And so I told her of the aliens' coming, of Shara's intuitive understanding that the beings communicated by dance, and her instant decision to reply to them. I told her of Shara's slow realization that the aliens were hostile, territorially aggressive, determined to have our planet for a spawning ground. And I told her, as best I could, of the *Stardance*.

"She danced them right out of the solar system, Norrey. She danced everything she had in her—and she had all of us in her. She danced what we are, what she was, and she scared them silly. They weren't afraid of military lasers, but she scared 'em right the hell back to deep space. Oh, they'll be back some day—I don't know why, but I feel it in my bones. But it might not be in our lifetime. She told them what it is to be human. She gave them the *Stardance*."

Norrey was silent a long time, and then she nodded. "Uh huh." Her face twisted suddenly. "But why did she have to die, Charlie?"

"She was done, honey," I said and took her hand. "She was acclimated all the way to free fall by then, and it's a one-way street. She could never have returned to Earth, not even to the one-sixth gee in Skyfac. Oh, she could have lived in free fall. But *Carrington* owns everything in free fall except military hardware—and she didn't have any more reason to take anything from him. She'd danced her *Stardance*, and I'd taped it, and she was done."

"Carrington," she said, and her fingers gripped my hand fiercely. "Where is he now?"

"I just found out myself this morning. He tried to grab all the tapes and all the money for Skyfac Incorporated, i.e., him. But he'd neglected to have Shara sign an actual contract, and Tom McGillicuddy found an airtight holograph will in her effects. It leaves everything fifty-fifty to you and me. So Carrington tried to buy a probate judge, and he picked the wrong judge. It would have hit the news this afternoon. The thought of even a short sentence in one gee was more than he could take. I think at the last he convinced himself that he had actually loved her, because he tried to copy her exit. He bungled it. He didn't know anything about leaving a rotating Ring, and he let go too late. It's the most common beginner's error."

Norrey looked puzzled.

"Instead of becoming a meteorite like her, he was last seen heading in the general direction of Betelgeuse. I imagine it's on the news by now." I glanced at my watch. "In fact, I would estimate that he's just running out of air about now—if he had the guts to wait."

Norrey smiled, and her fingers relaxed. "Let's hold that thought," she purred.

If captured—don't let them give you to the women.

The salad arrived then. Thousand Islands for Norrey and French for me, just as we would have ordered if we'd thought of it. The portions were unequal, and each was *precisely* as much as the recipient felt like eating. I don't know how Fat Humphrey does it. At what point does that kind of empathy become telepathy?

There was further sporadic conversation as we ate, but nothing significant. Fat Humphrey's cuisine demanded respectful attention. The meal itself arrived as we were finishing the salad, and when we had eaten our fill, both plates were empty and the coffee was cool enough to drink. Slices of Fat's fresh apricot pie were produced warm from the oven, and reverently dealt with. More coffee was poured. I took some pseudoephedrine for my nose. The conversation reawoke groggily, and there was only one question left for her to ask now so I asked her first.

"So what's happening with you, Norrey?"

She made a face. "Nothing much."

*Lovely answer. Push.*

"Norrey, on the day there is nothing much happening in your life, there'll be honest government in Ottawa. I hear you stood still, once, for over an hour—but the guy that said it was a famous liar. Come on, you know I've been out of touch."

She frowned, and that was it for me, that was the trigger. I had been thinking furiously ever since I came off standby in Norrey's arms back at the studio, and I had already figured out a lot of things. But the sight of that frown completed the process; all at once the jumble in my subconscious fell into shape with an almost audible click. They can come that way, you know. Flashes of insight. In the middle of a sentence, in a microsecond, you make a quantum jump in understanding. You look back on twenty years of blind stupidity without wincing, and perceive the immediate future in detail. Later you will marvel—at that instant you only accept and nod. The Sicilians have a thing like it, that they call *the thunderbolt*. It is said to bring deep calm and great gravity. It made me break up.

"What's so funny?"

"Don't know if I can explain it, hon. I guess I just figured out how Fat Humphrey does it."

"Huh?"

"Tell you later. You were saying . . . ."

The frown returned. "Mostly I wasn't saying. What's happening with me, in twenty-five words or less? I haven't asked myself in quite a while. Maybe too long." She sipped coffee. "Okay. You know that John Koerner album, the last commercial one he made? *Running Jumping Standing Still?* That's what I've been doing, I think. I've been putting out a lot of energy, doing satisfying things, and I'm not satisfied. I'm . . . I'm almost bored."

She floundered, so I decided to play devil's advocate. "But you're right where you've always wanted to be," I said, and began rolling a joint.

She grimaced. "Maybe that's the trouble. Maybe a life's ambition shouldn't be something that can be achieved —because what do you do then? You remember Koerner's movie?"

"Yeah. *The Sound of Sleep*. Nutball flick, nice cherries on top."

"Remember what he said the meaning of life was?"

"Sure. 'Do the next thing.'" I suited action to the word, licked it, sealed it and twisted the ends, then lit it. "Always thought it was terrific advice. It got me through some tough spots."

She toked, held it and exhaled before replying. "I'm

ready to do the next thing—but I'm not sure what that *is*. I've toured with the company, I've soloed in New York, I've choreographed, I've directed the whole damn school and now I'm an artistic director. I've got full autonomy now; I can even teach a class again if I feel like it. Every year from now until Hell freezes TDT's repertoire will include one of my pieces, and I'll always have superb bodies to work with. I've been working on childhood dreams all my life, Charlie, and *I hadn't thought ahead any farther than this when I was a kid*. I don't know what 'the next thing' is. I need a new dream."

She toked again, passed it to me. I stared at the glowing tip conspiratorially, and it winked at me. "Any clues? Directions at least?"

She exhaled carefully, spoke to her hands. "I thought I might like to try working with one of those commune-companies, where everybody choreographs every piece. I'd like to try working with a group-head. But there's really no one here I could start one with, and the only existing group-head that suits me is New Pilobolus—and for that I'd have to live in *America*."

"Forget that."

"Hell, yes. I . . . Charlie, I don't know, I've even thought of chucking it all and going out to PEI to farm. I always meant to, and never really did. Shara left the place in good shape, I could . . . oh, that's crazy. I don't really want to farm. I just want *something new*. Something different. Unmapped territory, something that— Charlie Armstead, what the hell are you grinning about?"

"Sometimes it's purely magical."

"What?"

"Listen. Can you hear them up there?"

"Hear who?"

"I oughta tell Humphrey. There's gonna be reindeer shit all over his roof."

"Charlie!"

"Go ahead, little girl, tug on the whiskers all you want

—they're real. Sit right here on my lap and place your order. Ho ho ho. Pick a number from one to two."

She was giggling now; she didn't know why but she was giggling. "Charlie . . . ."

"Pick a number from one to two."

"Two."

"That's a very good number. A very good number. You have just won one perfectly good factory-fresh dream, with all accessories and no warranty at all. This offer is not available through the stores. A very good number. How soon can you leave town?"

"Leave town! Charlie. . . ." She was beginning to get a glimmer. "You can't mean—"

"How would you like a half interest in a lot of vacuum, baby? I got *plenty* o' nuttin', or at least the use of it, and you're welcome to all you want. Talk about being on top of the world!"

The giggle was gone. "Charlie, you can't mean what I think you—"

"I'm offering you a simple partnership in a commune company—a *real* commune company. I mean, we'll all have to live together for the first season at least. *Lots* of real estate, but a bit of a housing shortage at first. We'll spring for expenses, and it's a free fall."

She leaned across the table, put one elbow in her coffee and the other in her apricot pie, grabbed my turtleneck and shook me. "Stop babbling and tell me straight, dammit."

"I am, honey, I am. I'm proposing a company of choreographers, a true commune. It'll have to be. Company members will live together, choreograph every piece together, perform together, share equally in the profits, and I'll put up all the expenses just for the hell of it. Oh yeah, we're rich, did I tell you? About to be, anyway."

"Charlie—"

"I'm straight, I tell you. I'm starting a company. And a school. I'm offering you a half interest and a full-time, year-round job, dead serious, and I'll need you to start right away. Norrey, I want you to come dance in free fall."

Her face went blank. "How?"

"I want to build a studio in orbit and form a company. We'll alternate performing with school like so: three months of classes dirtside—essentially auditions—and the graduates get to come study for three months in orbit. Any that are any good, we work into the next three months of performance taping. By then we've been in low or no gee for a long time, our bodies are starting to adapt, so we take three months vacation on Earth and then start the process over again. We can use the vacations to hunt out likely talent and recruit 'em—go concert-hopping, in other words. It'll be *fun*, Norrey. We'll make history and money both."

"*How*, Charlie? How are you going to get the backing for all this? Carrington's dead, and I won't work for his associates. Who else but Skyfac and the Space Command have space capacity?"

"Us."

"?"

"You and me. We *own* the *Stardance* tape, Norrey. I'll show it to you later, I have a dub in my pouch. At this point maybe a hundred people on Earth and a few dozen in space have seen that tape in its entirety. One of them was the president of Sony. He offered me a blank check."

"A blank—"

"Literally. Norrey, the *Stardance* may be the single most magnificent artistic utterance of man—irrespective of its historical importance and news value. I would estimate that within five years every sighted person in the solar system will know it. And we own the only tape. *And*, I own the only existing footage of Shara dancing on Earth, commercial value incalculable. Rich? Hell, we're *powerful!* Skyfac Incorporated is so anxious to come out of this looking good that if I phone up to Ring One and ask Tokugawa for the time, he'll take the next elevator down and give me his watch."

Her hands dropped from my sweater. I wiped apricot from one limp elbow, dried the other.

"I don't feel squeamish about profiting from Shara's death. We made the *Stardance*, together, she and I; I earned my half and she left you hers. The only thing wrong with that is that it leaves me filthy rich, and I don't want to be rich—not on *this* planet. The only way I can think of to piss away that kind of money in a way Shara would have approved is to start a company and a school. We'll specialize in misfits, the ones who for one reason or another don't fit into the mold here on Earth. Like Shara. The less than classically perfect dancer's bodies. That stuff is just irrelevant in space. More important is the ability to open yourself, to learn a whole new kind of dance, to . . . I don't know if this will make any sense . . . to encompass three hundred and sixty degrees. We'll be making the rules as we go along—and we'll employ a lot of dancers that aren't working now. I figure our investment capital is good for about five years. By that time the performing company should be making enough to cover the nut, underwrite the school, and still show a profit. All the company members share equally. Are you in?"

She blinked, sat back, and took a deep breath. "In what? What have you got?"

"Not a damn thing," I said cheerily. "But I know what I need. It'll take us a couple of years to get started at the very least. We'll need a business manager, a stage manager, three or four other dancers who can teach. A construction crew to get started, of course, and an elevator operator, but they're just employees. My cameras run themselves, by Christ, and I'll be my own gaffer. I can do it, Norrey —if you'll help me. Come on—join my company and see the world—from a decent perspective."

"Charlie, I . . . I don't even know if I can *imagine* free fall dance. I mean, I've seen both of Shara's shows several times of course, and I liked them a *lot*—but I still don't know where you could go from there. I can't picture it."

"Of course not! You're still hobbled with 'up' and 'down,' warped by a lifetime in a gravity well. But you'll catch on as soon as you get up there, believe me." (A year from now my blithe confidence would haunt me.) "You can learn to think spherically, I know you can, and the rest is just recoordination, like getting sea legs. Hell, if I can do it at my age, anybody can. You'll make a *good* dancing partner."

She had missed it the first time. Now her eyes enlarged. "A good *what?*"

Norrey and I go back a long time, and I'd have to tell you about most of it to explain how I felt just then. Remember when Alistair Sim, as Scrooge, has just awakened from his nightmare and vowed to make amends? And the more nice things he does, and the more people gape at him in bafflement, the more he giggles? And finally he slaps himself in the face and says, "I don't deserve to be this happy," and tries to get properly chaste? And then he giggles again and says, "But I just can't help myself" and breaks up all over again? *That's* how I felt. When a hangup of yours has been a burden to a friend for so many years, and all at once you not only realize that, but know that the burden is lifted, for both of you, there is an exquisite joy in sharing the news.

Remember how Scrooge sprung it on Bob Cratchit, by surprise? ". . . leaving me no alternative—but to raise your salary!" In the same childish way I had saved this, my *real* surprise Santa Claus announcement, for last. I intended to savor the moment.

But then I saw her eyes and I just said it flat out.

"The leg is functional in free fall, Norrey. I've been working out, hard, every day since I got back dirtside.

It's a little stiff, and I'll—we'll—always have to choreograph around it to some extent. But it does everything a weightless dancer needs it to. *I can dance again.*"

She closed her eyes, and the lids quivered. "Oh my God." Then she opened them and laughed and cried at once, "Oh my God, Charlie, oh my God, oh my God," and she reached across the table and grabbed my neck and pulled me close and I got apricot and coffee on my own elbows, and oh her tears were hot on my neck.

The place had gotten busy while we talked; no one seemed to notice us. I held her head in the hollow of my throat, and marveled. The only true measure of pain is relief—only in that moment, as layers of scar tissue sloughed off my heart, did I perceive their true weight for the first time.

Finally we were both cried out, and I pulled back and sought her eyes. "I can dance again, Norrey. It was Shara who showed me, I was too damn dumb to notice, too blocked to see it. It was about the last thing she ever did. I can't throw that away now, I've got to dance again, you see? I'm going to go back to space and dance, on my own property and on my own terms and fucking dance again.

"And I want to dance with *you*, Norrey. I want you to be my partner. I want you to come dance with me. Will you come?"

She sat up straight and looked me in the eye. "Do you know what you are asking me?"

*Hang on—here we go!* I took a deep breath. "Yes. I'm asking for a full partnership."

She sat back in her chair and got a faraway look. "How many years have we known each other, Charlie?"

I had to think. "I make it twenty-four years, off and on."

She smiled. "Yeah. Off and on." She retrieved the forgotten joint and relit it, took a long hit. "How much of that time do you estimate we've spent living together?"

More arithmetic; I toked while I computed. "Call it six or seven years." Exhale. "Maybe eight."

She nodded reflectively and took the joint back. "Some pretty crumby times."

"Norrey—"

"Shut up, Charlie. You waited twenty-four years to propose to me, you can shut up and wait while I give you my answer. How many times would you estimate I came down to the drunk tank and bailed you out?"

I didn't flinch. "Too many."

She shook her head. "One less than too many. I've taken you in when you needed it and thrown you out when you needed it and never once said the word 'love,' because I knew it would scare you away. You were so damned afraid that anyone might love you, because then they'd have to pity you for being a cripple. So I've sat by and watched you give your heart only to people who wouldn't take it—and then picked up the pieces every time."

"Norrey—"

"Shut up," she said. "Smoke this digit and shut up. I've loved you since before you knew me, Charlie, before your leg got chopped up, when you were still dancing. I knew you before you were a cripple. I loved you before I ever saw you offstage. I knew you before you were a lush, and I've loved you all the years since in the way that you wanted me to.

"Now you come before me on two legs. You still limp, but you're not a cripple any more. Fat Humphrey the telepath doesn't give you wine with your meal, and when I kiss you at the studio I notice you didn't have a drink on the plane. You buy me dinner and you babble about being rich and powerful and you try to sell me some crack-brained scheme for dancing in space, you have the goddam *audacity* to lay all this on me and *never once say the word 'love' with your mouth* and ask me to be your other half again." She snatched the roach out of my hand. "God dammit, Cratchit, you leave me no alternative . . . ."

And she actually paused and toked and held it and exhaled before she let the smile begin.

". . . but to raise your fucking salary."

And we were both holding hands in the apricots and grinning like gibbons. Blood roared in my ears; I literally shuddered with emotion too intense to bear. I groped for a cathartic wisecrack. "Who said I was buying dinner?"

A high, nasal voice from nearby said, "I'm buying, Mr. Armstead."

We looked up, startled to discover that the world still existed around us, and were further startled.

He was a short, slight young man. My first impression was of cascades of ringlets of exceedingly curly black hair, behind which lurked a face like a Brian Froud drawing of a puckish elf. His glasses were twin rectangles of wire and glass, thicker than the glass in airlock doors, and at the moment they were on the end of his nose. He squinted down past them at us, doing his best to look dignified. This was considerably difficult, as Fat Humphrey was holding him a clear foot off the floor, one big sausage-plate fist clutching his collar. His clothes were expensive and in excellent taste, but his boots were splendidly shabby. He was trying, unsuccessfully, not to kick his feet.

"Every time I pass your table I keep steppin' on his ears," Humphrey explained, bringing the little guy closer and lowering his voice. "So I figure him for a snoop or a newsie and I'm just givin' him the bum's rush. But if he's talkin' about buyin', it's your decision."

"How about it, friend? Snoop or newsie?"

Insofar as it was possible, he drew himself up. "I am an artist."

I queried Norrey with my eyes and was answered.

"Set that man down and get him a chair, Fat. We'll discuss the check later."

This was done, and the kid accepted the last of the roach, hitching his tunic into shape and pushing his glasses back up.

"Mr. Armstead, you don't know me, and I don't know this lady here, but I've got these terrific ears and no shame at all. Mr. Pappadopolous is right, I was eavesdropping just great. My name is Raoul Brindle, and—"

"I've heard of you," Norrey said. "I have a few of your albums."

"I do too," I agreed. "The next to last one was terrific."

"Charlie, that's a terrible thing to say."

Raoul blinked furiously. "No, he's right. The last one was trash. I owed a pound and paid."

"Well, I liked it. I'm Norrey Drummond."

"You're Norrey *Drummond*?"

Norrey got a familiar look. "Yes. Her sister."

"Norrey Drummond of TDT, that choreographed *Shifting Gears* and danced the *Question An Dancer* variations at the Vancouver conference, that—" He stopped, and his glasses slid down his nose. "Ohmigod. Shara Drummond is your *sister*? Ohmigod, of course. Drummond, Drummond, sisters, imbecile." He sat on his excitement and hitched up his glasses and tried to look dignified some more.

For my money he pulled it off. I knew something about Raoul Brindle, and I was impressed. He'd been a child-genius composer, and then in his college days he'd decided music was no way to make a living and became one of the best special effects men in Hollywood. Right after *Time* did a half-page sidebar on his work on *Children of the Lens*—which I mightily admired—he released a video-cassette album composed entirely of extraordinary visuals, laser optics and color effects, with synthesizer accompaniment of his own. It was sort of *Yellow Submarine* cubed, and it had sold like hell, and been followed by a half dozen more occasionally brilliant albums. He had designed and programmed the legendary million-dollar lightshow system for the Beatle's reunion as a favor for McCartney, and one of his audio-only tapes followed my deck everywhere it went. I resolved to buy *his* dinner.

"So how do you know me well enough to spot me in a restaurant, Raoul, and why have you been dropping eaves?"

"I didn't spot you here. I followed you here."

"Sonofabitch, I never saw you. Well, what did you follow me for?"

"To offer you my life."

"Eh?"

"I've seen the *Stardance*."

"You *have*?" I exclaimed, genuinely impressed. "How did you pull that off?"

He looked up at the ceiling. "Large weather we're having, isn't it? So I saw the *Stardance* and I made it my business to find you and follow you, and now you're going back to space to dance and I'm going with you. If I have to walk."

"And do what?"

"You said yourself, you're going to need a stage manager. But you haven't thought it through. I'm going to create a new art form for you. I'm going to beat my brains to peanut butter for you. I'm going to design free-fall sets and visuals and do the scores, and they'll both work integrally together and with the dances. I'll work for coffee and cakes, you don't even have to use my music if you don't want to, but I *gotta* design those sets."

Norrey cut him off with a gentle, compassionate hand over his mouth. "How do you mean, free-fall sets?" She took her hand away.

"It's free fall, don't you understand? I'll design you a sphere of trampolines, with cameras at the joints, and the framework'll be tubes of colored neon. For free-space work I'll give you rings of laser-lit metal flakes, loops of luminous gas, modified fireworks, giant blobs of colored liquid hanging in space to dance around and through— singing Jesus, as a special effects man I've been waiting all my *life* for zero gravity. It—it makes the Dykstraflex obsolete, don't you see?"

He was blinking hard enough to keep the insides of his glasses swept, glancing rapidly back and forth from Norrey to me. I was flabbergasted, and so was she.

"Look, I've got a microcassette deck here. I'll give it to you, Mister Armstead—"

"Charlie," I corrected absently.

"—and you take it home and listen. It's just a few tracks I cut after I saw the *Stardance*. It's just audio, just first impressions. I mean, it's not even the frame of a score, but I thought it . . . I mean, I thought maybe you'd . . . it's completely shitful, here, take it."

"You're hired," I said.

"Just promise me you'll hired?"

"Hired. Hey, Fat! You got a Betamax in the joint somewhere?"

So we went into the back room where Fat Humphrey Pappadopolous lives, and I fed the *Stardance* tape into his personal television, and the four of us watched it together while Maria ran the restaurant, and when it was over it was half an hour before any of us could speak.

# Chapter 2

So of course there was nothing to do then but go up to Skyfac.

Raoul insisted on paying for his own passage, which startled and pleased me. "How can I ask you to buy a pig in a poke?" he asked reasonably. "For all you know I may be one of those permanently spacesick people."

"I anticipate having at least some gravity in the living units, Raoul. And do you have any *idea* what an elevator costs a civilian?"

"I can afford it," he said simply. "You know that. And I'm no good to you if I have to stay in the house all day. I go on your payroll the day we know I can do the job."

"That's silly," I objected. "I plan to take carloads of student dancers up, with no more warranty than you've got, and they sure and hell won't be paying for their tickets. Why should I discriminate against you for not being poor?"

He shook his head doggedly, his eyeglasses tattooing the sides of his nose. "Because I want it that way. Charity is for those that need it. I've taken a lot of it, and I bless the people who gave it to me when I needed it, but I don't need it any more."

"All right," I agreed. "But after you've proved out, I'm going to rebate you, like it or not."

"Fair enough," he said, and we booked our passage.

Commercial transportation to orbit is handled by Space Industries Corp., a Skyfac subsidiary, and I have to congratulate them on one of the finest natural puns I've ever seen. When we located the proper gate at the spaceport, after hours of indignity at Customs and Medical, I was feeling salty. I still hadn't fully readapted after the time I'd spent in free fall with Shara, and the most I could pry out of the corporation medicos was three weeks—my "pull" with the top brass meant nothing to the Flight Surgeon in charge. I was busy fretting that it wasn't enough time and tightening my guts in anticipation of takeoff when I rounded the last corner and confronted the sign that told me I was in the right place.

It said:

## S.I.C. TRANSIT
### (gloria mundi)

I laughed so hard that Norrey and Raoul had to help me aboard and strap me in, and I was still chuckling when acceleration hit us.

Sure enough, Raoul got spacesick as soon as the drive cut off—but he'd been sensible enough to skip breakfast, and he responded rapidly to the injection. That banty little guy had plenty of sand: by the time we were docked at Ring One he was trying out riffs on his Soundmaster. White as a piece of paper and completely oblivious, eyes glued to the outboard video, fingers glued to the Soundmaster's keyboard, ears glued to its pickups. If elevator-belly ever troubled him again, he kept it to himself.

Norrey had no trouble at all. Neither did I. Our appointment with the brass had been set for an hour hence, just in case, so we stashed Raoul in the room assigned to him and spent the time in the Lounge, watching the stars wheel by on the big video wall. It was not crowded; the tourist trade had fallen off sharply when the aliens came, and never recovered. The New Frontier was less attractive with New Indians lurking in it somewhere.

My attempts to play seasoned old spacehound to Norrey's breathless tourist were laughably unsuccessful. No one *ever* gets jaded to space, and I took deep satisfaction in being the one who introduced Norrey to it. But if I couldn't pull off nonchalance, at least I could be pragmatic.

"Oh, Charlie! How soon can we go outside?"

"Probably not today, hon."

"Why *not*?"

"Too much to do first. We've got to insult Tokugawa, talk to Harry Stein, talk to Tom McGillicuddy, and when all that's done you're going to take your first class in EVA 101—indoors."

"Charlie, you've taught me all that stuff already."

"Sure. I'm an old spacehound, with all of six months experience. You dope, you've never even touched a real p-suit."

"Oh, welfare checks! I've memorized every word you've told me. I'm not scared."

"There in a nutshell is why I refuse to go EVA with you."

She made a face and ordered coffee from the arm of her chair.

"Norrey. Listen to me. You are not talking about putting on a raincoat and going to stand next to Niagara Falls. About six inches beyond that wall there is the most hostile environment presently available to a human. The technology which makes it possible for you to live there at all is not as old as you are. I'm not going to let you within ten meters of an airlock until I'm convinced that you're scared silly."

She refused to meet my eyes. "Dammit, Charlie, I'm not a child and I'm not an idiot."

"Then stop acting like both." She jumped at the volume and looked at me. "Or is there any other kind of person who believes you can acquire a new set of reflexes by being told about them?"

It might have escalated into a full-scale quarrel, but the waiter picked that moment to arrive with Norrey's coffee. The Lounge staff like to show off for the tourists; it increases the tip. Our waiter decided to come to our table the same way George Reeves used to leap tall buildings, and we were a good fifteen meters from the kitchen. Unfortunately, after he had left the deck, committing himself, a gaunt tourist decided to change seats without looking, and plotted herself an intersecting course. The waiter never flinched. He extended his left arm sideways, deploying the drogue (which looks just like the webbing that runs from Spiderman's elbow to his ribs); tacked around her; brought his hand to his chest to collapse the drogue; transferred the coffee to that hand; extended the other arm and came back on course; all in much less time than it has taken you to read about it. The tourist squawked and tumbled as he went by, landing on her rump and bouncing and skidding a goodly distance thereon; the waiter grounded expertly beside Norrey, gravely handed her a cup containing every drop of coffee he had started out with, and took off again to see to the tourist.

"The coffee's fresh," I said as Norrey goggled. "The waiter just grounded."

It's one of the oldest gags on Skyfac, and it always works. Norrey whooped and nearly spilled hot coffee on her hand—only the low gee gave her time to recover. That cut her laughter short; she stared at the coffee cup, and then at the waiter, who was courteously pointing out one of the half dozen LOOK BEFORE YOU LEAP signs to the outraged tourist.

"Charlie?"

"Yeah."

"How many classes will I need before I'm ready?"

I smiled and took her hand. "Not as many as I thought."

The meeting with Tokugawa, the new chairman of the board, was low comedy. He received us personally in what had been Carrington's office, and the overall effect was of a country bishop on the Pope's throne. Or perhaps "tuna impersonating a piranha" is closer to the image I want. In the vicious power struggle which followed Carrington's death, he had been the only candidate ineffectual enough to satisfy everyone. Tom McGillicuddy was with him, to my delight, the cast already gone from his ankle. He was growing a beard.

"Hi, Tom. How's the foot?"

His smile was warm and familiar. "Hello, Charlie. It's good to see you again. The foot's okay—bones knit faster in low gee."

I introduced Norrey to him, and to Tokugawa as an afterthought.

The most powerful man in space was short, gray, and scrutable. In deference to the custom of the day he wore traditional Japanese dress, but I was willing to bet that his English was better than his Japanese. He started when I lit up a joint, and Tom had to show him how to turn up the breeze and deploy the smoke filter. Norrey's body language said she didn't like him, and I trust her barometer even more than my own; she lacks my cynicism. I cut him off in the middle of a speech about Shara and the *Stardance* that must have used up four ghostwriters.

"The answer is 'no.'"

He looked as though he had never heard the expression before. "—I—"

"Listen, Toke old boy, I read the papers. You and Skyfac Inc. and Lunindustries Inc. want to become our patrons. You're inviting us to move right in and start dancing, offering to underwrite the whole bloody venture. And none of this has anything to do with the fact that antitrust legislation was filed against you this week, right?"

"Mister Armstead, I'm merely expressing my gratitude that you and Shara Drummond chose to bring your high art to Skyfac in the first place, and my fervent hope that you and her sister will continue to feel free to make use of—"

"Toke, where I come from we use that stuff for methane power." I took a lingering drag while he sputtered. "You know damn well how Shara came to Skyfac, and you sit in the chair of the man who killed her. He killed her by making her spend so many of her offstage hours in low or no gee, because that was the only way he could get it up. You ought to be bright enough to know that the day Norrey or I or any member of our company dances a step on Skyfac property, a red man with horns, a tail, and a pitchfork is going to come up to you and admit that it just froze over." The joint was beginning to hit me. "As far as I'm concerned, Christmas came this year on the day that Carrington went out for a walk and forgot to come back, and I will be go to hell before I'll live under his roof again, or make money for his heirs and assigns. Do we understand each other?" Norrey was holding my hand tightly, and when I glanced over she was grinning at me.

Tokugawa sighed and gave up. "McGillicuddy, give them the contract."

Pokerfaced, Tom produced a stiff folded parchment and passed it to us. I scanned it, and my eyebrows rose. "Tom," I said blandly, "is this honest?"

He never even glanced at his boss. "Yep."

"Not even a percentage of the gross? Oh my." I looked at Tokugawa. "A free lunch. It must be my good looks." I tore the contract in half.

"Mister Armstead," he began hotly, and I was glad that Norrey interrupted him this time. I was getting to like it too much.

"Mr. Tokugawa, if you'll stop trying to convince us that you're a patron of the arts, I think we can get along. We'll let you donate some technical advice and assistance, and we'll let you sell us materials and air and water at cost. We'll even give back some of the skilled labor we hire away from you when we're done with them. Not you, Tom—we want you to be our full-time business manager, if you're willing."

He didn't hesitate a second, and his grin was beautiful. "Ms. Drummond, I accept."

"Norrey. Furthermore," she went on to Tokugawa, "we'll make a point of telling everybody we know how nice you've been, any time the subject comes up. But we are going to own and operate our own studio, and it may suit us to put it on the far side of Terra, and we will be *independents*. Not Skyfac's in-house dance troupe: independents. Eventually we hope to see Skyfac itself settle into the role of the benevolent old rich uncle who lives up the road. But we don't expect to need you for longer than you need us, so there will be no contract. Have we a meeting of the minds?"

I nearly applauded out loud. I'm pretty sure he'd never had a personal executive secretary hired right out from under his nose before. His grandfather might have committed seppuku; he in his phony kimono must have been seething. But Norrey had played things just right, grudgingly offering him equals-status if he cared to claim it—and he *needed* us.

Perhaps you don't understand just how badly he needed us. Skyfac was the first new multinational in years, and it had immediately begun hurting the others where they lived. Not only could it undersell any industry requiring vacuum, strain-free environment, controlled radiation, or wide-range temperature or energy density gradients—and quite a few profitable industries do—but it could also sell things that simply could not be made on Earth, even expensively. Things like *perfect* bearings, *perfect* lenses, strange new crystals—none of which will form in a gravity well. All the raw materials came from space, unlimited free solar energy powered the factories, and delivery was cheap (a delivery module doesn't have to be a spaceship; all it has to do is fall correctly).

It wasn't long before the various nationals and multinationals who had not been invited into the original Skyfac consortium began to feel the pinch. The week before, antitrust actions had been filed in the US, USSR, China, France, and Canada, and protests had been lodged in the United Nations, the first steps in what would turn out to be the legal battle of the century. Skyfac's single most precious asset was its monopoly of space—Tokugawa was running scared enough to need any good press he could get.

And the week before *that*, the tape of the *Stardance* had been released. The first shock wave was still running around the world; we were the best press Tokugawa was ever likely to get.

"You'll cooperate with our PR people?" was all he asked.

"As long as you don't try to quote me as 'heartbroken' by Carrington's death," I said agreeably. I really had to hand it to him: he almost smiled then.

"How about 'saddened'?" he suggested delicately.

We settled on "shocked."


We left Tom in our cabin with four full briefcases of paperwork to sort out, and went to see Harry Stein.

We found him where I expected to, in a secluded corner of the metals shop, behind a desk with stacks of pamphlets, journals and papers that would have been improbable in a full gee. He and a Tensor lamp were hunched over an incredibly ancient typewriter. One massive roll fed clean paper into it, another took up the copy. I noted with approval that the manuscript's radius was two or three centimeters thicker than when last I'd seen it. "Say hey, Harry. Finishing up chapter one?"

He looked up, blinked. "Hey, Charlie. Good to see you." For him it was an emotional greeting. "You must be her sister."

Norrey nodded gravely. "Hi, Harry. I'm glad to meet you. I hear those candles in *Liberation* were your idea."

Harry shrugged. "She was okay."

"Yes," Norrey agreed. Unconsciously, instinctively, she was taking on his economical word usage—as Shara had before her.

"I," I said, "will drink to that proposition."

Harry eyed the thermos on my belt, and raised an eyebrow in query.

"Not booze," I assured him, unclipping it. "On the wagon. Jamaican Blue Mountain coffee, fresh from Japan. Real cream. Brought it for you." Damn it, I was doing it too.

Harry actually smiled. He produced three mugs from a nearby coffeemaker unit (personally adapted for low gee), and held them while I poured. The aroma diffused easily in low gee; it was exquisite. "To Shara Drummond," Harry said, and we drank together. Then we shared a minute of warm silence.

Harry was a fifty-year-old ex-fullback who had kept himself in shape. He was so massive and formidably packed that you could have known him a long time without ever suspecting his intelligence, let alone his genius —unless you had happened to watch him work. He spoke mostly with his hands. He hated writing, but put in two methodical hours a day on The Book. By the time I asked him why, he trusted me enough to answer. "Somebody's gotta write a book on space construction," he said. Certainly no one could have been better qualified. Harry literally made the first weld on Skyfac, and had bossed virtually all construction since. There was another guy who had as much experience, once, but he died (his "suit sold out," as the spacemen say: lost its integrity). Harry's writing was astonishingly lucid for such a phlegmatic man (perhaps because he did it with his fingers), and I knew even then that The Book was going to make him rich. It didn't worry me; Harry will never get rich enough to retire.

"Got a job for you, Harry, if you want it."

He shook his head. "I'm happy here."

"It's a space job."

He damn near smiled again. "I'm unhappy here."

"All right, I'll tell you about it. My guess is a year of design work, three or four years of heavy construction, and then a kind of permanent maintenance job keeping the whole thing running for us."

"What?" he asked economically.

"I want an orbiting dance studio."

He held up a hand the size of a baseball glove, cutting me off. He took a minicorder out of his shirt, set the mike for "ambient" and put it on the desk between us. "What do you want it to *do*?"

Five and a half hours later all three of us were hoarse, and an hour after that Harry handed us a set of sketches. I looked them over with Norrey, we approved his budget, and he told us a year. We all shook hands.

Ten months later I took title.

We spent the next three weeks in and around Skyfac property, while I introduced Norrey and Raoul to life without up and down. Space overawed them both at first. Norrey, like her sister before her, was profoundly moved by the personal confrontation with infinity, spiritually traumatized by the awesome perspective that the Big Deep brings to human values. And unlike her sister before her, she lacked that mysteriously total self-confidence, that secure ego-strength that had helped Shara to adjust so quickly. Few humans have ever been as sure of themselves as Shara was. Raoul, too, was only slightly less affected.

We all get it at first, we who venture out into space. From the earliest days, the most unimaginative and stolid jocks NASA could assemble for astronauts frequently came back down spiritually and emotionally staggered, and some adapted and some didn't. The ten percent of Skyfac personnel who spend much time EVA, who have any way of knowing they're not in Waukegan besides the low gee, often have to be replaced, and no worker is depended on until his or her second tour. Norrey and Raoul both came through it—they were able to expand their personal interior universe to encompass that much external universe, and came out of the experience (as Shara and I had) with a new and lasting inner calm.

The spiritual confrontation, however, was only the first step. The major victory was much subtler. It was more than just spiritual malaise that washed out seven out of ten exterior construction workers in their first tour: It was also physiological—or was it psychological?—distress.

Free fall itself they both took to nearly at once. Norrey was much quicker than Raoul to adapt—as a dancer, she knew more about her reflexes, and he was more prone to forget himself and blunder into impossible situations, which he endured with dogged good humor. But both were proficient at "jaunting," propelling oneself through an enclosed space, by the time we were ready to return to Earth. (I myself was pleasantly astonished at how fast unused dance skills came back to me.)

The real miracle was their equally rapid acclimation to sustained EVA, to extended periods outdoors in free space. Given enough time, nearly anyone can acquire new reflexes. But startlingly few can learn to live without a local vertical.

I was so ignorant at that time that I hadn't the slightest *idea* what an incredible stroke of good fortune it was that both Norrey and Raoul could. No wonder the gods smile so seldom—we so often fail to notice. Not until the next year did I realize how narrowly my whole venture—my whole life—had escaped disaster. When it finally dawned on me, I had the shakes for days.

That kind of luck held for the next year.

That first year was spent in getting the ball rolling. Endless millions of aggravations and petty details—have you ever tried to order dancing shoes for *hands*? With velcro palms? So few of the things we needed could be ordered from the Johnny Brown catalog, or put together out of stock space-hardware. Incredible amounts of imaginary dollars flowed through my and Norrey's right hands, and but for Tom McGillicuddy the thing simply would not have been possible. He took care of incorporating both the Shara Drummond School of New Modern Dance and the performing company, Stardancers, Inc., and became business manager of the former and agent for the latter. A highly intelligent and thoroughly honorable man, he had entered Carrington's service with his eyes—and his ears—wide open. When we waved him like a wand, magic resulted. How many honest men understand high finance?

The second indispensable wizard was, of course, Harry. And bear in mind that during five of those ten months, Harry was on mandatory dirtside leave, readapting his body and bossing the job by extreme long distance phone (God, I hated having phones installed—but the phone company's rates were fractionally cheaper than buying our own orbit-to-Earth video equipment, and of course it tied the Studio into the global net). Unlike the majority of Skyfac personnel, who rotate dirtside every fourteen months, construction men (those who make it) spend so much time in total weightlessness that six months is the recommended maximum. I figured us Stardancers for the same shift, and Doc Panzella agreed. But the first month and the last four were under Harry's direct supervision, and he actually turned it in under budget—doubly impressive considering that much of what he was doing had never been done before. He would have beat his original deadline; it wasn't his fault that we had to move it up on him.

Best of all, Harry turned out (as I'd hoped) to be one of those rare bosses who would rather be working with his hands than bossing. When the job was done he took a month off to collate the first ten inches of copy on his takeup reel into The First Book, sold it for a record-breaking advance and Santa Claus royalties, and then hired back on with us as set-builder, prop man, stage manager, all-around maintenance man, and resident mechanic. Tokugawa's boys had made astonishingly little fuss when we hired Harry away from them. They simply did not know what they were missing—until it was *months* too late to do anything about it.

We were able to raid Skyfac so effectively only because it was what it was: a giant, heartless multinational that saw people as interchangeable components. Carrington probably knew better—but the backers he had gotten together and convinced to underwrite his dream knew even less about space than I had as a video man in Toronto. I'm certain they thought of it, most of them, as merely an extremely foreign investment.

I needed all the help I could get. I needed that entire year—and more!—to overhaul and retune an instrument that had not been used in a quarter of a century: my dancer's body. With Norrey's support, I managed, but it wasn't easy.

In retrospect, all of the above strokes of luck were utterly necessary for the Shara Drummond School of New Modern Dance to have become a reality in the first place. After so many interlocking miracles, I guess I should have been expecting a run of bad cards. But it sure didn't *look* like one when it came.

For we truly did have dancers coming out of our ears when we finally opened up shop. I had expected to need good PR to stimulate a demand for the expensive commodity, for although we absorbed the bulk of student expenses (we *had* to—how many could afford the hundred-dollar-a-kilo elevator fee alone?) we kept it expensive enough to weed out the casually curious—with a secret scholarship program for deserving needy.

Even at those prices, I had to step lively to avoid being trampled in the stampede.

The cumulative effect of Shara's three tapes on the dance consciousness of the world had been profound and revolutionary. They came at a time when Modern dance as a whole was in the midst of an almost decade-long stasis, a period in which everyone seemed to be doing variations of the already-done, in which dozens of choreographers had beat their brains out trying to create the next New Wave breakthrough, and produced mostly gibberish. Shara's three tapes, spaced as she had intuitively sensed they must be, had succeeded in capturing the imagination of an immense number of dancers and dance lovers the world over—as well as millions of people who had never given dance a thought before.

Dancers began to understand that free fall meant free dance, free from a lifetime in thrall to gravity. Norrey and I, in our naiveté, had failed to be secretive enough about our plans. The day after we signed the lease on our dirtside studio in Toronto, students began literally arriving at our door in carloads and refusing to leave—much before we were ready for them. We hadn't even figured out how to audition a zero-gee dancer on Earth yet. (Ultimately it proved quite simple: Dancers who survived an elimination process based on conventional dance skills were put on a plane, taken up to angels thirty, dumped out, and filmed on the way down. It's not the *same* as free fall—but it's close enough to weed out gross unsuitables.)

We were sleeping 'em like torpedomen at the dirtside school, feeding them in shifts, and I began having pan-

icky second thoughts about calling up to Harry and putting off our deadline so he could triple the Studio's living
quarters. But Norrey convinced me to be ruthlessly se-
lective and take ONLY the most promising ten—out of
hundreds—into orbit.

Thank God—we damned near lost three of those
pigeons in two separate incidents, and we conclusively
washed out nine. That run of bad cards I mentioned
earlier.

Most often it came down to a failure to adapt, an inability to evolve the consciousness beyond dependence on
up and down (the one factor skydiving *can't* simulate: a
skydiver *knows* which way is down). It doesn't help to
tell yourself that north of your head is "up" and south
of your feet is "down"—from that perspective the whole
universe is in endless motion (you're hardly ever motionless in free fall), a perception most brains simply reject.
Such a dancer would persistently "lose his point," his
imaginary horizon, and become hopelessly disoriented.
Side effects included mild to extreme terror, dizziness,
nausea, erratic pulse and blood pressure, the grand-daddy
of all headaches and involuntary bowel movement.

(Which last is uncomfortable and embarrassing. P-suit
plumbing makes country outhouses look good. Men have
the classic "relief tube," of course, but for women and for
defecation in either sex we rely on a strategic deployment
of specially treated . . . oh, hell, we wear a diaper and
try to hold it until we get indoors. End of first inevitable
digression.)

Even in inside work, in the Goldfish Bowl or Raoul's
collapsible trampoline sphere, such dancers could not learn
to overcome their perceptual distress. Having spent their
whole professional lives battling gravity with every move
they made, they found that they were lost without their
old antagonist—or at least without the linear, right-angled
perceptual set that it provided: we found that some of

them could actually learn to acclimate to weightlessness inside a cube or rectangle, as long as they were allowed to think of one wall as the "ceiling" and its opposite as the "floor."

And in the one or two cases where their vision was adequate to the new environment, their bodies, their instruments, were not. The new reflexes just failed to jell.

They simply were not meant, any of them, to live in space. In most cases they left friends—but they all left.

All but one.

Linda Parsons was the tenth student, the one that didn't wash out, and finding her was good fortune enough to make up for the run of bad cards.

She was smaller than Norrey, almost as taciturn as Harry (but for different reasons), much calmer than Raoul, and more open-hearted and giving than I will be if I live to be a thousand. In the villainous overcrowding of that first free-fall semester, amid flaring tempers and sullen rages, she was the *only* universally loved person—I honestly doubt whether we could have survived without her (I remember with some dismay that I seriously contemplated spacing a pimply young student whose only crime was a habit of saying, "There you go" at every single pause in the conversation. *There he goes*, I kept thinking to myself, *there he goes . . .* ).

Some women can turn a room into an emotional maelstrom, simply by entering it, and this quality is called "provocative." So far as I know, our language has no word for the opposite of provocative, but that is what Linda was. She had a talent for getting people high together, without drugs, a knack for resolving irreconcilable differences, a way of brightening the room she was in.

She had been raised on a farm by a spiritual community in Nova Scotia, and that probably accounted for her empathy, responsibility, and intuitive understanding of group-energy dynamics. But I think the single overriding quality that made her magic work was inborn: she genuinely loved people. It could not have been learned behavior; it was just too clearly intrinsic in her.

I don't mean that she was a Pollyanna, nauseatingly cheerful and syrupy. She could be blistering if she caught you trying to call irresponsibility something else. She insisted that a high truth level be maintained in her presence, and she would not allow you the luxury of a hidden grudge, what she called "holding a stash on someone." If she caught you with such psychic dirty laundry, she would haul it right out in public and force you to clean it up. "Tact?" she said to me once. "I always understood that to mean a mutual agreement to be full of shit."

These attributes are typical of a commune child, and usually get them heartily disliked in so-called polite society—founded, as it is, on irresponsibility, untruth, and selfishness. But again, something innate in Linda made them work for her. She could call you a jerk to your face without triggering reflex anger; she could tell you publicly that you were lying without calling you a liar. She plainly knew how to hate the sin and forgive the sinner; and I admire that, for it is a knack I never had. There was never any mistaking or denying the genuine caring in her voice, even when it was puncturing one of your favorite bubbles of rationalization.

At least, that's what Norrey or I would have said. Tom, when he met her, had a different opinion.

"Look, Charlie, there's Tom."

I should have been fuming mad when I got out of Customs. I felt a little uneasy *not* being fuming mad. But after six months of extraterrestrial cabin fever, I was finding it curiously difficult to dislike *any* stranger—even a Customs man.

Besides, I was too *heavy* to be angry.

"So it is. Tom! Hey, Tom!"

"Oh my," Norrey said, "something's wrong."

*Tom* was fuming mad.

"Hell. What put the sand in his shorts? Hey, where're Linda and Raoul? Maybe there's a hassle?"

"No, they got through before we did. They must have taken a cab to the hotel already—"

Tom was upon us, eyes flashing. "So that's your paragon? Jesus Christ! Fucking bleeding heart, I'll wring her scrawny neck. Of all the—"

"Whoa! Who? Linda? What?"

"Oh Christ, later—here they come." What looked like a vigilante committee was converging on us, bearing torches. "Now look," Tom said hurriedly through his teeth, smiling as though he'd just been guaranteed an apartment in Paradise, "give these bloodsuckers your best I mean your best shot, and *maybe* I can scavenge something from this stinking mess." And he was striding toward them, opening his arms and smiling. As he went I heard him mutter something under his breath that began with "Ms. Parsons," contained enough additional sibilants to foil the shotgun-mikes, and moved his lips not at all.

Norrey and I exchanged a glance. "Pohl's Law," she said, and I nodded (Pohl's Law, Raoul once told us, says that nothing is so good that somebody somewhere won't hate it, and vice versa). And then the pack was upon us.

"This way Mister when does your next tape come over here please tell our viewers what it's really believe that this this new artform is a valid passport or did you look this way Mr. Drummond is it true that you haven't been able to smile for the cameraman for the *Stardance*, weren't you going to look this way to please continue or are readers would simply love to no but didn't you miss Drummond pardon me Miz Drummond do you think you're as good as your sister Sharon in the profits in their own country are without honor to welcome you back to Earth *this* way please," said the mob, over the sound of clicking, whirring, snapping, and whining machinery and through the blinding glare of what looked like an explosion at the galactic core seen from close up. And I smiled and nodded and said urbanely witty things and answered the rudest questions with good humor and by the time we could get a cab I *was* fuming mad. Raoul and Linda had indeed gone ahead, and Tom had found our luggage; we left at high speed.

"Bleeding Christ, Tom," I said as the cab pulled away, "next time schedule a press conference for the next day, will you?"

"*God damn it*," he blazed, "you can have this job back any time you want it!"

His volume startled even the cabbie. Norrey grabbed his hands and forced him to look at her.

"Tom," she said gently, "we're your friends. We don't want to yell at you; we don't want you to yell at us. Okay?"

He took an extra deep breath, held it, let it out in one great sigh and nodded. "Okay."

"Now I know that reporters can be hard to deal with. I understand that, Tom. But I'm tired and hungry and my feet hurt like hell and my body's convinced it weighs three hundred and thirteen kilos and next time could we maybe just lie to them a little?"

He paused before replying, and his voice came out calm. "Norrey, I am really not an idiot. All that madness to the contrary, I *did* schedule a press conference for tomorrow, and I *did* tell everybody to have a heart and leave you alone today. Those jerks back there were the ones who ignored me, the sons of—"

"Wait a minute," I interrupted. "Then why the hell did we give *them* a command performance?"

"Do you think I wanted to?" Tom growled. "What the hell am I going to say tomorrow to the honorable ones who got scooped? But I had no *choice*, Charlie. That dizzy bitch left me no choice. I had to give those crumbs *some*-thing, or they'd have run what they had already."

"Tom, what on earth are you talking about?"

"Linda Parsons, that's what I'm talking about, your new wonder discovery. Christ, Norrey, the way you went on about her over the phone, I was expecting . . . I don't know, anyway a professional."

"You two, uh, didn't hit it off?" I suggested.

Tom snorted. "First she calls me a tight-ass. Practically the first words out of her mouth. Then she says I'm ignorant, and I'm not treating her right. Treating her right, for Christ's sake. Then she chews me out for having reporters there—and Charlie, I'll take that from you and Norrey, I *should*'ve had those jerks thrown out, but I don't have to take that crap from a rookie. So I start to explain about the reporters, and *then* she says I'm being defensive. Christ on the pogie, if there's anything I hate it's somebody that comes on aggressive and then says you're being defensive, smiling and looking you right in the eye and trying to rub my fucking *neck*!"

I figured he'd let off enough steam by now, and I was losing count of the grains of salt. "So Norrey and I made nice for the newsies because they taped you two squabbling in public?"

"*No!*"

We got the story out of him eventually. It was the old Linda magic at work again, and I can offer you no more typical example. Somehow a seventeen-year-old girl had threaded her way through the hundreds of people in the spaceport terminal straight to Linda and collapsed in her arms, sobbing that she was tripping and losing control and would Linda please make it all *stop*? It was at that point that the mob of reporters had spotted Linda as a Stardancer and closed in. Even considering that she weighed six times normal, had just been poked full of holes by Medical and insulted by Immigration, and was striking large sparks off of Tom, I'm inclined to doubt that Linda lost her temper; I think she abandoned it. Whatever, she apparently scorched a large hole through that pack of ghouls, bundled the poor girl into it and got her a cab.

While they were getting in, some clown stuck a camera in the girl's face and Linda decked him.

"Hell, Tom, I might have done the same thing myself," I said when I got it straight.

"*God's teeth, Charlie!*" he began; then with a super-human effort he got control of his voice (at least). "Look. Listen. This is not some four-bit kids' game we are playing here. Megabucks pass through my fingers, Charlie, mega-bucks! You are not a bum any more, you don't have the privileges of a bum. Do you—"

"Tom," Norrey said, shocked.

"—have any *idea* how fickle the public has become in the last twenty years? Maybe I've got to tell you how much public opinion has to do with the *existence* of that orbiting junkheap you just left? Or maybe you're going to tell me that those tapes in your suitcase are as good as the *Stardance*, that you've got something so hot you can beat up reporters and get away with it. Oh *Jesus*, what a mess!"

He had me there. All the choreography plans we had brought into orbit with us had been based on the assumption that we would have between eight and twelve dancers. We had thought we were being pessimistic. We had to junk everything and start from scratch. The resulting tapes relied heavily on solos—our weakest area at that point—and while I was confident that I could do a lot with editing, well . . . .

"It's okay, Tom. Those bums got something their editors'll like better than a five-foot lady making gorillas look like gorillas—they worry a little about public opin-ion, too."

"And what do I tell Westbrook tomorrow? And Mortie and Barbara Frum and UPI and AP and—"

"Tom," Norrey interrupted gently, "it'll be all right."

"All right? How it is all right? Tell me how it's all right."

I saw where she was going. "Hell, yeah. I never thought

of that, hon, of *course*. That pack o' jackals drove it clean out of my mind. Serves 'em right." I began to chuckle. "Serves 'em bloody right."

"If you don't mind, darling."

"Huh? Oh. No . . . no, I don't mind." I grinned. "It's been long enough coming. Let's do it up."

"Will somebody *please* tell me what the hell is—"

"Tom," I said expansively, "don't worry about a thing. I'll tell your scooped friends the same thing I told my father at the age of thirteen, when he caught me in the cellar with the mailman's daughter."

"What the hell is that?" he snapped, beginning to grin in spite of himself and unsure why.

I put an arm around Norrey. " 'It's okay, Pa. We're gettin' married tomorrow.' "

He stared at us blankly for several seconds, the grin fading, and then it returned full force.

"Well I'll be dipped in shit," he cried. "Congratulations! That's terrific, Charlie, Norrey, oh congratulations you two—it's about time." He tried to hug us both, but at that moment the cabbie had to dodge a psychopath and Tom was flung backwards, arms outstreched. "That's tremendous, that's . . . you know, I think that'll do it—I think it'll work." He had the grace to blush. "I mean, the hell with the reporters, I just—I mean—"

"You may always," Norrey said gravely, "leave these little things to us. "

The desk phoned me when Linda checked in, as I had asked them to. I grunted, hung the phone up on thin air, stepped out of bed and into a hotel wastebasket, cannoned into the bedside table destroying table and accompanying lamp, and ended up prone on the floor with my chin sunk deep into the pile rug and my nose a couple of centimeters from a glowing clockface that said it was 4:42. In the morning. At the moment that I came completely awake, the clock expired and its glow went out.

Now it was *pitch* dark.

Incredibly, Norrey still had not awakened. I got up, dressed in the dark, and left, leaving the wreckage for the morning. Fortunately the good leg had sustained most of the damage; I could walk, albeit with a kind of double limp.

"Linda? It's me, Charlie."

She opened up at once. "Charlie, I'm sorry—"

"Skip it. You done good. How's the girl?" I stepped in.

She closed the door behind me and made a face. "Not terrific. But her people are with her now. I think she's going to be okay."

"That's good. I remember the first time a trip went sour on me."

She nodded. "You know it's going to stop in eight hours, but that doesn't help; your time rate's gone eternal."

"Yeah. Look, about Tom—"

She made another face. "Boy, Charlie, what a jerk."

"You two, uh, didn't hit it off?"

"I just tried to tell him that he was being too uptight, and he came on like he couldn't imagine what I was talking about. So I told him he wasn't as ignorant as he gave himself credit for, and asked him to treat me like a friend instead of a stranger—from all you told me about him, that seemed right. 'Okay,' he says, so I ask him as a friend to try and keep those reporters off of us for a day or so and he blows right up at me. He was so defensive, Charlie."

"Look, Linda," I began, "there was this screwup that—"

"Honestly, Charlie, I tried to calm him down, I tried to show him I wasn't *blaming* him. I—I was rubbing his neck and shoulders, trying to loosen him up, and he, he pushed me away. I mean, really, Charlie, you and Norrey said he was so nice and what a creep."

"Linda, I'm sorry you didn't get along. Tom *is* a nice guy, it's just—"

"I think he wanted me to just tell Sandra to get lost, just let Security take her away and—"

I gave up. "I'll see you in the mor . . . in the afternoon, Linda. Get some sleep; there's a press conference in the Something-or-other Room at two."

"Sure. I'm sorry, it must be late, huh?"

I met Raoul in the corridor—the desk had called him right after me, but he woke up slower. I told him that Linda and patient were doing as well as could be expected, and he was relieved. "Cripes, Charlie, her and Tom, you shoulda seen 'em. Cats and dogs, I never would have believed it."

"Yeah, well, sometimes your best friends just can't stand each other."

"Yeah, life's funny that way."

On that profundity I went back to bed. Norrey was still out cold when I entered, but as I climbed under the covers and snuggled up against her back she snorted like a horse and said, "Awright?"

"All right," I whispered, "but I think we're going to have to keep those two separated for awhile."

She rolled over, opened one eye and found me with it. "Darl'n," she mumbled, smiling with that side of her mouth, "there's hope for you yet."

And then she rolled over and went back to sleep, leaving me smug and fatuous and wondering what the hell she was talking about.

# *Chapter 3*

Those first-semester tapes sold like hell anyway, and the critics were more than kind, for the most part. Also, we rereleased *Mass Is A Verb* with Raoul's soundtrack at that time, and finished our first fiscal year well in the black.

By the second year our Studio was taking shape.

We settled on a highly elongated orbit. At perigee the Studio came as close as 3200 kilometers to Earth (not very close—Skylab was up less than 450 klicks), and at apogee it swung way out to about 80,000 klicks. The point of this was to keep Earth from hogging half the sky in every tape; at apogee Terra was about fist-sized (subtending a little more than 9° of arc), and we spent most of our time far away from it (Kepler's Second Law: the closer a satellite to its primary, the faster it swings around). Since we made a complete orbit almost twice a day, that gave two possible taping periods of almost eight hours apiece in every twenty-four hours. We simply adjusted our "inner clocks," our biological cycle, so that one of these two periods came between "nine" and "five" subjective. (If we fudged a shot, we had to come back and reshoot some multiple of eleven hours later to get a background Earth of the proper apparent size.)

As to the Studio complex itself:

The largest single structure, of course, is the Fishbowl, an enormous sphere for inside work, without p-suits. It is effectively transparent when correctly lit, but can be fitted with opaque foil surfaces in case you don't *want* the whole universe for a backdrop. Six very small and very good camera mounts are built into it at various places, and it is fitted to accept plastic panels which convert it into a cube within a sphere, although we only used them a few times and probably won't again.

Next largest is the informal structure we came to call Fibber McGee's Closet. The Closet itself is only a long "stationary" pole studded with stanchions and line-dispensing reels, but it is always covered with junk, tethered to it for safekeeping. Props, pieces of sets, camera units and spare parts, lighting paraphernalia, control consoles and auxiliary systems, canisters and cans and boxes and slabs and bundles and clusters and loops and coils and assorted disorderly packages of whatever anyone thought it might be handy to have for free fall dance and the taping thereof, all cling to Fibber McGee's Closet like interplanetary barnacles. The size and shape of the ungainly mass change with use, and the individual components shift lazily back and forth like schizophrenic seaweed at all times.

We had to do it that way, for it is not at all convenient to reenter and exit the living quarters frequently.

Imagine a sledgehammer. A big old roustabout's stake pounder, with a large, barrel-shaped head. Imagine a much smaller head, coke-can size, at the butt end of the handle. That's my house. That's where I live with my wife when I'm at home in space, in a three-and-a-half-room walkdown with bath. Try to balance that sledgehammer horizontally across one finger. You'll want to lay that finger right up near the *other* end, just short of the much massier hammerhead. That's the point around which my house pivots, and the countermass pivots, in chasing concentric circles, to provide a net effect of one-sixth gee at home.

The countermass includes life-support equipment and supplies, power supply, medical telemetry, home computer and phone hardware, and some damn big gyros. The "hammer handle" is quite long: it takes a shaft of about 135 meters to give one-sixth gee at a rotation rate of one minute. That slow a rate makes the Coriolis differential minimal, as imperceptible as it is on a torus the size of Skyfac's Ring One but without a torus's vast cubic and inherently inefficient layout (Skyfac axiom: anywhere you want to go will turn out to be all the way round the bend; as, in short order, will you).

Since only a Tokugawa can afford the energies required to start and stop spinning masses in space on a whim, there are only two ways to leave the house. The axis of spin aims toward Fibber McGee's Closet and Town Hall (about which more later); one can merely go out the "down" airlock ("the back door") and let go at the proper time. If you're not an experienced enough spacehand, or if you're going somewhere on a tangent to the axis of rotation, you go out the "up" lock or front door, climb up the runged hammer handle to the no-weight point and step off, then jet to where you want to go. You *always* come home by the front door; that's why it's a walkdown. The plumbing is simplicity itself, and habitual attention must be paid to keep the Closet and Hall from being peppered with freeze-dried dung.

(No, we don't save it to grow food on, or any such ecological wizardry. A closed system the size of ours would be too small to be efficient. Oh, we reclaim most of the moisture, but we give the rest to space, and buy our food and air and water from Luna like everybody else. In a pinch we could haul 'em up from Terra.)

We went through all these hoops, obviously, to provide a sixth-gee home environment. After you've been in space for long enough, you find zero gee much more comfortable and convenient. Any gravity at all seems like an arbitrary bias, a censorship of motion—like a pulp writer being required to write only happy endings, or a musician being restricted to a single meter.

But we spent as much time at home as we could manage. Any gravity at all will slow your body's mindless attempt to adapt irrevocably to zero gee, and a sixth-gee is a reasonable compromise. Since it is local normal for both Lunar surface and Skyfac, the physiological parameters are standard knowledge. The more time spent at home, the longer we could stay up—and our schedule was fixed. None of us wanted to be marooned in space. That's how we thought of it in those days.

If we slipped, if physicals showed one of us adapting too rapidly, we could compensate to some degree. You go out the back door, climb into the exercise yoke dangling from the power winch, and strap yourself in. It looks a little like one of those Jolly Jumpers for infants, or a modified bosun's chair. You ease off the brake, and the yoke begins to "descend," on a line with the hammer handle since there's no atmospheric friction to drag you to one side. You lower away, effectively increasing the length of your hammer handle and thus your gee force. When you're "down" far enough, say at a half gee (about 400 meters of line), you set the brake and exercise on the yoke, which is designed to provide a whole-body workout. You can even, if you want, use the built-in bicycle pedals to pedal yourself back up the line, with a built-in "parking brake" effect so that if it gets too much for you and you lose a stroke, you don't break your legs and go sliding down to the end of your tether. From low-enough gee zones you can even hand-over-hand your way up, with safety line firmly snubbed—but below half-gee level you do not unstrap from the yoke for *any* reason. Imagine hanging by your hands at, say, one gravity over all infinity, wearing a snug plastic bag with three hours' air.

We all got pretty conscientious about . . . er . . . watching our weight.

The big temptation was Town Hall, a sphere slightly smaller than the Goldfish Bowl. It was essentially our communal living room, the place where we could all hang out together and chew the fat in person. Play cards, teach each other songs, argue choreography, quarrel choreography (two different things), play 3-D handball, or just appreciate the luxury of free fall without a p-suit or a job to do. If a couple happened to find themselves alone in Town Hall, and were so inclined, they could switch off half the external navigation lights—signifying "Do Not Disturb"—and make love.

(One-sixth gee sex is nice, too—but zero gee is *different*. Nobody's on top. It's a wholehearted cooperative effort or it just doesn't happen [I can't imagine a free-fall rape]. You get to use *both* hands, instead of just the one you're not lying one. And while a good half of the Kama Sutra goes right out the airlock, there are compensations. I have never cared for simultaneous oral sex, the classic "69," because of the discomfort and distraction. Free fall makes it not only convenient, but logical, inevitable. End of second inevitable digression.)

For one reason and another, then, it was tempting to hang out overlong at Town Hall—and so many standard daily chores *must* be done there that the temptation had to be sharply curbed. Extensive physiological readouts on all of us were sent twice daily to Doc Panzella's medical computer aboard Skyfac: as with air, food, and water, I was prepared to deal elsewhere if Skyfac ever lost its smile, but while I could have them I wanted Panzella's brains. He was to space medicine what Harry was to space construction, and he kept us firmly in line, blistering us by radio when we goofed, handing out exercise sessions on the Jolly Jumper like a tough priest assigning novenas for penance.

We originally intended to build five sledge hammers, for a maximum comfortable population of fifteen. But we had rushed Harry, that first year; when the first group of students got off the elevator, it was a miracle that as many as three units were operational. We had to dismiss Harry's crew early with thanks and a bonus: we needed the cubic they were using. Ten students, Norrey, Raoul, Harry, and me totals fourteen bodies. Three units totals nine rooms. It was a hell of a courtship . . . but Norrey and I came out of it *married*; the ceremony was only a formality.

By the second season we had completed one more three-room home, and we took up only seven new students, and everybody had a door they could close and crouch behind when they needed to, and all seven of them washed out. The fifth hammer never got built.

It was that run of bad cards I mentioned earlier, extending itself through our second season.

Look, I was just beginning to become a Name in dance, and rather young for it, when the burglar's bullet smashed my hip joint. It's been a long time, but I remember myself as having been pretty damn good. I'll never be that good again, even with the use of my leg back. A few of the people we washed out were better dancers than I *used* to be—in dirtside terms. I had believed that a really good dancer almost automatically had the necessary ingredients to learn to think spherically.

The first season's dismal results had shown me my error, and so for the second semester we used different criteria. We tried to select for free-thinking minds, unconventional minds, minds unchained by preconception and consistency. Raoul described them as "science-fiction-reader types." The results were ghastly. In the first place, it turns out that people who can question even their most basic assumptions intellectually can not necessarily do so physically—they could imagine what needed doing, but couldn't do it. Worse, the free-thinkers could not cooperate with other free-thinkers, could not work with *anyone*'s preconception consistently. What we wanted was a choreographer's commune, and what we got was the classic commune where no one wanted to do the dishes. One chap would have made a terrific solo artist—when I let him go, I recommended to the Betamax people that they finance him to a Studio of his own—but we couldn't work with him.

And two of the damned idiots killed themselves through thoughtlessness.

They were all *well* coached in free-fall survival, endlessly drilled in the basic rules of space life. We used a double-buddy system with every student who went EVA until they had demonstrated competence, and we took every precaution I could or can think of. But Inge Sjoberg could not be bothered to spend a whole hour a day inspecting and maintaining her p-suit. She managed to miss all six classic signs of incipient coolant failure, and one sunrise she boiled. And nothing could induce Alexi Nikolski to cut off his huge mane of brown hair. Against all advice he insisted on tying it back in a kind of doubled-up pony tail, "as he had always done." The arrangement depended on a *single hairband*. Sure as hell it failed in the middle of a class, and quite naturally he gasped. We were minutes away from pressure; he would surely have drowned in his own hair. But as Harry and I were towing him to Town Hall he unzipped his p-suit to deal with the problem.

Both times we were forced to store the bodies in the Closet for a gruesomely long time, while next-of-kin debated whether to have the remains shipped to the nearest spaceport or go through the legal complication of arranging for burial in space. Macabre humor saved our sanity (Raoul took to calling it Travis McGee's Closet), but it soured the season.

And it wasn't much more fun to say good-bye to the last of the live ones. On the day that Yeng and DuBois left, I nearly bottomed out. I saw them off personally, and the "coitus with a condom" imagery of shaking hands with p-suits on was just too ironically appropriate. The whole semester, like the first, had been coitus with a condom—hard work, no product—and I returned to Town Hall in the blackest depression I had known since . . . since Shara died. By association, my leg hurt; I wanted to bark at someone. But as I came in through the airlock Norrey, Harry and Linda were watching Raoul make magic.

He was not aware of them, of anything external, and Norrey held up a warning hand without meeting my eyes. I put my temper on hold and my back against the wall beside the airlock; the velcro pad between my shoulder-blades held me securely. (The whole sphere is carpeted in "female" velcro; pads of "male" are sewn into our slippers—which also have "thumbs"—our seats, thighs, backs, and the backs of our gloves. Velcro is the cheapest furniture there is.)

Raoul was making magic with common household ingredients. His most esoteric tool was what he referred to as his "hyperdermic needle." It looked like a doctor's hypo with elephantiasis: the chamber and plunger were oversized, but the spike itself was standard size. In his hands it was a magic wand.

Tethered to his skinny waist were all the rest of the ingredients: five drinking bulbs, each holding a different colored liquid. At once I identified a source of subconscious unease, and relaxed: I had been missing the vibration of the air conditioner, missing the draft. Twin radial tethers held Raoul at the center of the sphere, in the slight crouch typical of free fall, and he *wanted* still air —even though it severely limited his working time. (Shortly, exhaled carbon dioxide would form a sphere around his head; he would spin gently around his tethers and the sphere would become a donut; by then he must be finished. Or move. I would have to be careful myself to keep moving, spiderlike, as would the others.)

He speared one of the bulbs with his syringe, drew off a measured amount. Apple juice, by the color of it, admixed with water. He emptied the syringe gently, thin knuckly fingers working with great delicacy, forming a translucent golden ball that hung motionless before him, perfectly spherical. He pulled the syringe free, and the ball . . . shimmered . . . in spherically symmetrical waves that took a long time to ebb.

He filled his syringe with air, jabbed it into the heart of the ball and squeezed. The bulb filled with a measured amount of air, expanding into a nearly transparent golden bubble, around which iridescent patterns chased each other in lazy swirls. It was about a meter in diameter. Again Raoul disengaged the syringe.

Filling it in turn from bulbs of grape juice, tomato juice and unset lime jello, he filled the interior of the golden bubble with spherical beads of purple, red, and green, pumping them into bubbles as he formed them. They shone, glistened, jostling but declining to absorb each other. Presently the golden bubble was filled with Christmas-tree balls in various sizes from grape to grape-fruit, shimmering, borrowing colors from each other. Marangoni Flow—gradients in surface tension—made them spin and tumble around each other like struggling kittens. Occasional bubbles were pure water, and these were rainbow scintillations that the eye ached to fragment and follow individually.

Raoul was drifting for air now, holding the macro-bubble in tow with the palm of his hand, to which the whole thing adhered happily. If he were to strike it sharply now, I knew, the whole cluster would *snap* at once into a single, large bubble around the surface of which streaks of colors would run like tears (again, by Marangoni Flow). I thought that was his intention.

The master lighting panel was velcro'd to his chest. He dialed for six tight spots, focusing them on the bubble-jewel with sure fingers. Other lights dimmed, winked out. The room was spangled with colors and with color, as the facets of the manmade jewel flung light in all directions. With a seemingly careless wave of his hand, Raoul set the scintillating globe spinning, and Town Hall swam in its eerie rainbow fire.

Drifting before the thing, Raoul set his Musicmaster for external speaker mode, velcro'd it to his thighs, and began to play.

Long, sustained warm tones first. The globe thrilled to them, responding to their vibrations, expressing the music visually. Then liquid trills in a higher register, with pseudowoodwind chords sustained by memory-loop beneath. The globe seemed to ripple, to pulse with energy. A simple melody emerged, mutated, returned, mutated again. The globe spangled in perfect counterpoint. The tone of the melody changed as it played, from brass to violin to organ to frankly electronic and back again, and the globe reflected each change with exquisite subtlety. A bass line appeared. Horns. I kicked myself free of the wall, both to escape my own exhalations and to get a different perspective on the jewel. The others were doing likewise, drifting gently, trying to become organic with Raoul's art. Spontaneously we danced, tossed by the music like the glistening jewel, by the riot of color it flung around the spherical room. An orchestra was strapped to Raoul's thighs now, and it made us free-fall puppets.

Improv only; not up to concert standard. Simple group exercises, luxuriating in the sheer physical *comfort* of free fall and sharing that awareness. Singing around the campfire, if you will, trying out unfamiliar harmonies on each other's favorite songs. Only Harry abstained, drifting somehow "to one side" with the odd, incongruous grace of a polar bear in the water. He became thereby a kind of second focus of the dance, became the camera eye toward which Raoul aimed his creation, and we ours. (Raoul and Harry had become the fastest of friends, the chatterbox and the sphinx. They admired each other's hands.) Harry floated placidly, absorbing our joy and radiating it back.

Raoul tugged gently on a line, and a large expandable wire loop came to him. He adjusted it to just slightly larger than the bubblejewel, captured that in the loop and expanded the loop rapidly at once. Those who have only seen it masked by gravity have no idea how powerful a force surface tension is. The bubblejewel became a concave lens about three meters in diameter, within which multicolored convex lenses bubbled, each literally perfect. He oriented it toward Harry, added three low-power lasers from the sides, and set the lens spinning like the Wheel of Kali. And we danced.

After awhile the knock-knock light went on beside the airlock. That should have startled me—we don't get much company—but I paid no mind, lost in zero-gee dance and in Raoul's genius, and a little in my own in hiring him. The lock cycled and opened to admit Tom McGillicuddy —which should have startled hell out of me. I'd had no idea he was thinking of coming up to visit, and since he hadn't been on the scheduled elevator I'd just put Yeng and DuBois on, he must have taken a *very* expensive special charter to get here. Which implied disaster.

But I was in a warm fog, lost in the dance, perhaps a little hypnotized by the sparkling of Raoul's grape-juice, tomato-juice and lime-jello kaleidoscope. I may not even have nodded hello to Tom, and I know I was not even remotely surprised by what he did, then.

He joined us.

With no hesitation, casting away the velcro slippers he'd brought from the airlock's dressing chamber, he stepped off into thick air and joined us within the sphere, using Raoul's guy wires to position himself so that our triangle pattern became a square. And then he danced with us, picking up our patterns and the rhythm of the music.

He did a creditable job. He was in damned good shape for someone who'd been doing all our paperwork—but infinitely more important (for terrestrial physical fitness is so *useless* in space), he was clearly functioning without a local vertical, and enjoying it.

Now I *was* startled, to my bones, but I kept poker-faced and continued dancing, trying not to let Tom catch me watching. Across the sphere Norrey did likewise—and Linda, above, seemed genuinely oblivious.

Startled? I was flabbergasted. The single factor that had washed out sixteen students out of seventen was the same thing that washed out Skyfac construction men, the same thing that had troubled eight of the nine Skylab crewmen back when the first experiments with zero-gee life had been made: inability to live without a local vertical.

If you bring a goldfish into orbit (the Skylab crew did), it will flounder helplessly in its globe of water. Show the fish an *apparent* point of reference, place a flat surface against its water-sphere (which will then form a perfect hemisphere thereon quite naturally), and the fish will decide that the plane surface is a stream bed, aligning its body perpendicularly. Remove the plate, or add a second plate (no local vertical or too many), and the gold-fish will soon die, mortally confused. Skylab was purposely built to have three *different* local verticals in its three major modules, and eight out of nine crewmen faithfully and chronically adjusted to a module's local vertical as they entered it, without conscious thought. Traveling all the way through all three in one jaunt gave them head-aches; they hated the docking adapter which was designed to have no local vertical at all. It is physically impossible to get dizzy in zero gee, but they said they *felt* dizzy, any time they were prevented from coming into focus with a defined "floor" and "walls."

All of them except one—described as "one of the most intelligent of the astronauts, as well as one of the most perverse." He took to the docking adapter—to life with-out up and down—like a duck to water. He was the only one of nine who made the psychological breakthrough. *Now* I knew how lucky I had been that Norrey and

Raoul had both turned out to be Stardancer material. And how few others ever could be.

But Tom was unquestionably one of them. One of us. His technique was raw as hell, he thought his hands were shovels and his spine was all wrong, but he was trainable. And he had that rare, indefinable *something* that it takes to maintain equilibrium in an environment that forbids equilibration. He was at home in space.

I should have remembered. He had been ever since I'd known him. It seemed to me in that moment that I perceived all at once the totality of my bloody blind stupidity—but I was wrong.

The impromptu jam session wound down eventually; Raoul's music frivolously segued into the closing bars of *Thus Spake Zarathustra*, and as that last chord sustained, he stabbed a rigid hand through his lens, shattering it into a million rainbow drops that dispersed with the eerie grace of an expanding universe.

"Hoover that up," I said automatically, breaking the spell, and Harry hastened to kick on the air scavenger before Town Hall became sticky with fruit juice and jello. Everyone sighed with it, and Raoul the magician was once again a rabbity little guy with a comic-opera hypo and a hula hoop. And a big wide smile. The tribute of sighs was followed by a tribute of silence; the warm glow was a while in fading. *I'll be damned*, I thought, *I haven't made memories this good in twenty years*. Then I put my mind back in gear.

"Conference," I said briefly, and jaunted to Raoul. Harry, Norrey, Linda and Tom met me there, and we grabbed hands and feet at random to form a human snowflake in the center of the sphere. This left our faces every-which-way to each other, of course, but we ignored it, the way a veteran DJ ignores the spinning of a record label he's reading. Even Tom paid no visible mind to it. We got right down to business.

"Well, Tom," Norrey said first, "what's the emergency?"

"Is Skyfac bailing out?" Raoul asked.

"Why didn't you call first?" I added. Only Linda and Harry were silent.

"Whoa," Tom said. "No emergency. None at all, everybody relax. Businesswise everything continues to work like a ridiculously overdesigned watch."

"Then why spring for the chartered elevator? Or were you stowing away in the regular that just left?"

"No, I had a charter, all right—but it was a taxi. I've been in free fall almost as long as you have. Over at Skyfac."

"Over at—" I thought things through, with difficulty. "And you went to the trouble of having your calls and mail relayed so we wouldn't catch on."

"That's right. I've spent the last three months working out of our branch office aboard Skyfac." That branch office was a postal address somewhere in the lower left quadrant of Tokugawa's new executive secretary's desk.

"Uh huh," I said. "*Why?*"

He looked at Linda, whose left ankle he happened to be holding, and chose his words. "Remember that first week after we met, Linda?" She nodded. "I don't think I've been so exasperated before in my whole life. I thought you were the jackass of the world. That night I blew up at you in Le Maintenant, that last time that we argued religion—remember? I walked out of there that night and took a copter straight to Nova Scotia to that damned commune you grew up in. Landed in the middle of the garden at three in the morning, woke half of 'em up. I raved and swore at them for over an hour, *demanding* to know how in the hell they could have raised you to be such a misguided idiot. When I was done they blinked and scratched and yawned and then the big one with the really improbable beard said, 'Well, if there's that much juice between you, we would recommend that you probably ought to start courting,' and gave me a sleeping bag."

The snowflake broke up as Linda kicked free, and we

all grabbed whatever was handiest or drifted. Tom reversed his attitude with practiced ease so that he tracked Linda, continued to speak directly to her.

"I stayed there for a week or so," he went on steadily, "and then I went to New York and signed up for dance classes. I studied dance when I was a kid, as part of karate discipline; it came back, and I worked hard. But I wasn't sure it had anything to do with zero-gee dance—so I sneaked up to Skyfac without telling any of you, and I've been working like hell over there ever since, in a factory sphere I rented with my own money."

"Who's minding the store?" I asked mildly.

"The best trained seals money can buy," he said shortly. "Our affairs haven't suffered. But I have. I hadn't intended to tell you *any* of this for another year or so. But I was in Panzella's office when the Termination of Monitoring notices came in on Yeng and DuBois. I knew you were hurting for bodies. I'm self-taught and clumsy as a pig on ice and on Earth it'd take me another five years to become a fourth-rate dancer, but I think I can do the kind of stuff you're doing here."

He wriggled to face me and Norrey. "I'd like to study under you. I'll pay my own tuition. I'd like to work with you people, besides just on paper, and be part of your company. I think I can make a Stardancer." He turned back to Linda. "And I'd like to start courting you, by your customs."

*Then* it was that the totality of my stupidity truly did become apparent to me. I was speechless. It was Norrey who said, "We accept," on behalf of the company, at the same instant that Linda said the same thing for herself. And the snowflake reformed, much smaller in diameter.

Our company was formed.

As to the nature of our dance itself, there is not much to be said that the tapes themselves don't already say. We borrowed a lot of vocabulary from New Pilobolus and the Contact Improv movement (which had been among the last spasms of inventiveness before that decade-long stasis in dance I mentioned earlier), but we had to radically adapt almost everything we borrowed. Although the Contact Improv people say they're into "free fall," this is a semantic confusion: *they* mean "falling freely"; *we* mean "free of falling." But a lot of their discoveries *do* work, at least in some fashion, in zero gee—and we used what worked.

Linda's own dance background included four years with the New Pilobolus company: if you don't know them, or the legendary Pilobolus company they sprang from, they're sort of Contact Improv without the improv —carefully choreographed stuff. But they too are into "using each other as the set"—dancing on, over, and around one another, cooperating in changing *each other's* vectors. Dancing acrobats, if you will. We ourselves tried to achieve a balanced blend of both choreographed and spontaneous dance in the stuff we taped.

Linda was able to teach us a lot about mutually inter-reacting masses, hyperfulcrums, and the like—and a lot more about the *attitude* they require. To truly interact with another dancer, to spontaneously create shapes together, you must attempt to attune yourself to them empathically. You must know them—how they dance and how they're feeling at the moment—to be able to sense what their next move will be, or how they will likely react to yours. When it works, it's the most exhilarating feeling I've ever known.

It's *much* harder with more than one partner, but the exhilaration increases exponentially.

Because free fall requires mutual cooperation, mutual awareness on a spherical level, our dance became an essentially spiritual exercise.

And so, with a company of adequate size and an increasing grasp of what zero-gee dance was really about, we began our second and last season of taping.

# Chapter 4

I fell through starry space, balanced like an inbound comet on a tail of fluorescent gas, concentrating on keeping my spine straight and my knees and ankles locked. It helped me forget how nervous I was.

"Five," Raoul chanted steadily, "four, three, two, NOW," and a ring of his bright orange "flame" flared soundlessly all around me. I threaded it like a needle.

"Beautiful," Norrey whispered in my ear, from her vantage point a kilometer away. At once I lifted my arms straight over my head and bit down hard on a contact. As I passed through the ring of orange "flame," my "tail" turned a rich, deep purple, expanding lazily and symmetrically behind me. Within the purple wake, tiny novae sparkled and died at irregular intervals: Raoul magic. Just before the dye canisters on my calves emptied, I fired my belly thruster and let it warp me "upward" in an ever-increasing curve while I counted seconds.

"Light it up, Harry," I said sharply. "I can't see you." The red lights winked into being *above* my imaginary horizon and I relaxed, cutting the ventral thrust in plenty of time. I was not heading precisely for the camera, but the necessary corrections were minor and would not visibly spoil the curve. Orienting myself by a method I can only call informed writhing, I cut main drive and selected my point.

On Earth you can turn forever without getting dizzy if you select a point and keep your eyes locked on it, whipping your head around at the last possible second for each rotation. In space the technique is unnecessary: once out of a gravity well, your semicirculars fill up and your whole balance system shuts down; you *can't* get dizzy. But old habit dies hard. Once I had my point star I tumbled, and when I had counted ten rotations the camera was close enough to see and coming up fast. At once I came out of my spin, oriented, and braked *sharply*— maybe three gees—with all thrusters. I had cut it fine: I came to rest relative to the camera barely fifty meters away. I cut all power instantly, went from the natural contraction of high acceleration to full release, giving it everything I had left, held it for a five-count and whispered, "Cut!"

The red lights winked out, and Norrey, Raoul, Tom, and Linda cheered softly (nobody does anything loudly in a p-suit).

"Okay, Harry, let's see the playback."

"Coming up, boss."

There was a pause while he rewound, and then a large square section of distant space lit up around the edges. The stars within it rearranged themselves and took on motion. My image came into frame, went through the maneuver I had just finished. I was pleased. I had hit the ring of orange "flame" dead center and triggered the purple smoke at just the right instant. The peelout curve was a little ragged, but it would do. The sudden growth of my oncoming image was so startling that I actually flinched—which is pretty silly. The deceleration was nearly as breathtaking to watch as it had been to do, the pullout was fine, and the final triumphant extension was frankly terrific.

"That's a take," I said contentedly. "Which way's the bar?"

"Just up the street," Raoul answered. "I'm buying."

"Always a pleasure to meet a patron of the arts. How much did you say your name was?"

Harry's massive construction-man's spacesuit, festooned with tools, appeared from behind and "beneath" the camera. "Hey," he said, "not yet. Gotta at least run through the second scene."

"Oh hell," I protested. "My air's low, my belly's empty, and I'm swimming around in this overgrown galosh."

"Deadline's coming," was all Harry said.

I wanted a shower so bad I could taste it. Dancers are all different; the only thing we *all* have in common is that we all sweat—and in a p-suit there's nowhere for it to go. "My thrusters're shot," I said weakly.

"You don't need 'em much for Scene Two," Norrey reminded me. "Monkey Bars, remember? Brute muscle stuff." She paused. "And we are pushing deadline, Charlie."

Dammit, voice on stereo earphones seems to come from the same place that the voice of your conscience does.

"They're right, Charlie," Raoul said. "I spoke too soon. Come on, the night is young."

I stared around me at an immense sphere of starry emptiness, Earth a beachball to my left and the Sun a brilliant softball beyond it. "Night don't *come* any older than this," I grumbled, and gave in. "Okay, I guess you're right. Harry, you and Raoul strike that set and get the next one in place, okay? The rest of you warm up in place. Get sweaty."

Raoul and Harry, as practiced and efficient as a pair of old beat cops, took the Family Car out to vacuum up the vacuum. I sat on nothing and brooded about the damned deadline. It *was* getting time to go dirtside again, which meant it was time to get this segment rehearsed and shot, but I didn't have to like it. No artist likes time pressure, even those who can't produce without it. So I brooded.

The show must go on. The show must always go on, and if you are one of those millions who have always wondered exactly why, I will tell you. The tickets have already been sold.

But it's uniquely hard (as well as foolish) to brood in space. You hang suspended within the Big Deep, infinity in all directions, an emptiness so immense that although you know that you're falling through it at high speed, you make no slightest visible progress. Space is God's Throne Room, and so vasty a hall is it that no human problem has significance within it for long.

Have you ever lived by the sea? If so, you know how difficult it is to retain a griping mood while contemplating the ocean. Space is like that, only more so.

Much more so.

By the time the Monkey Bars were assembled, I was nearly in a dancing mood again. The Bars were a kind of three-dimensional gymnast's jungle, a huge partial icosahedron composed of transparent tubes inside which neon fluoresced green and red. It enclosed an area of about 14,000 cubic meters, within which were scattered a great many tiny liquid droplets that hung like motionless dust motes, gleaming in laserlight. Apple juice.

When Raoul and Harry had first shown me the model for the Monkey Bars, I had been struck by the aesthetic beauty of the structure. By now, after endless simulations and individual rehearsals, I saw it only as a complex collection of fulcrums and pivots for Tom, Linda, Norrey and me to dance on, an array of vector-changers designed for maximal movement with minimal thruster use. Scene Two relied almost entirely on muscle power, a paradox considering the technology implicit in its creation. We would pivot with all four limbs on the Bars and on each other, borrowing some moves from the vocabulary of trapeze acrobatics and some from our own growing experience with free-fall lovemaking, constantly forming and dissolving strange geometries that were new even to dance. (We were using choreography rather than improv techniques: the Bars and their concept were too big for the Goldfish Bowl, and you can't afford mistakes in free space.)

Though I had taught individual dancers their parts and rehearsed some of the trickier clinches with the group, this would be our first full run-through together. I found I was anxious to assure myself that it would actually work. All the computer simulation in the world is no substitute for actually doing it; things that look lovely in compsim can dislocate shoulders in practice.

I was about to call places when Norrey left her position and jetted my way. Of course there's only one possible reason for that, so I turned off my radio too and waited. She decelerated neatly, came to rest beside me, and touched her hood to mine.

"Charlie, I didn't mean to crowd you. We can come back in eleven hours and—"

"No, that's okay, hon," I assured her. "You're right: 'Deadline don't care.' I just hope the choreography's right."

"It's just the first run-through. And the simulations were great."

"That's not what I mean. Hell, I know it's *correct*. By this point I can think spherically just fine. I just don't know if it's *any good*."

"How do you mean?"

"It's exactly the kind of choreography Shara would have loathed. Rigid, precisely timed, like a set of tracks."

She locked a leg around my waist to arrest a slight drift and looked thoughtful. "She'd have loathed it for herself," she said finally, "but I think she'd really have enjoyed watching us do it. It's a *good* piece, Charlie—and you know how the critics love anything abstract."

"Yeah, you're right—again," I said, and put on my best Cheerful Charlie grin. It's not fair to have a bummer at curtain time; it brings the other dancers down. "In fact, you may have just given me a better title for this whole mess: *Synapstract*."

There was relief in her answering grin. "If it's got to be a pun, I like *ImMerced* better."

"Yeah, it does have a kind of Cunningham flavor to it. Bet the old boy takes the next elevator up after he sees it." I squeezed her arm through the p-suit, added "Thanks, hon," and cut in my radio again. "All right, boys and girls, *'let's shoot this turkey.'* Watch out for leg-breakers and widowmakers. Harry, those cameras locked in?"

"Program running," he announced. "Blow a gasket." It's the Stardancer's equivalent of "Break a leg."

Norrey scooted back into position, I corrected my own, the lights came up hellbright on cameras 2 and 4, and we took our stage, while on all sides of us an enormous universe went about its business.

You can't fake cheerfulness well enough to fool a wife like Norrey without there being something real to it; and, like I said, it's hard to brood in space. It really was exhilarating to hurl my body around within the red and green Bars, interacting with the energy of three other dancers I happened to love, concentrating on split-second timing and perfect body placement. But an artist is capable of self-criticism even in the midst of the most involving performance. It's the same perpetual self-scrutiny that makes so many of us so hard to get along with for any length of time—and that makes us artists in the first place. The last words Shara Drummond ever said to me were, "Do it right."

And even in the whirling midst of a piece that demanded all my attention, there was still room for a little whispering voice that said that this was only the best I had been able to do and still meet my deadline.

I tried to comfort myself with the notion that every artist who ever worked feels exactly the same way, about nearly every piece they ever do—and it didn't help me any more than it ever does any of us. And so I made the one small error of placement, and tried to correct with thrusters in too much of a hurry and triggered the wrong one and smacked backward hard into Tom. His back was to me as well, and our air tanks *clanged* and one of mine blew. A horse kicked me between the shoulder blades and the Bars came up fast and caught me across the thighs, tumbling me end over end. I was more than twenty meters from the set, heading for forever, before I had time to black out.

Happening to smack into the Bars off center was a break. It put me into an acrobat's tumble, which centrifuged air into my hood and boots, and blood to my head and feet, bringing me out of blackout quicker. Even so, precious seconds ticked by while I groggily deduced my problem, picked my point and began to spin correctly. With the perspective that gave me I oriented myself, still groggy, figured out intuitively which thrusters would kill the spin, and used them.

That done, it was easy to locate the Bars, a bright cubist's Christmas tree growing perceptibly smaller as I watched. It was between me and the blue beachball I'd been born on. At least life would not be corny enough to award me Shara's death. But Bryce Carrington's didn't appeal to me much more.

My thighs ached like hell, the right one especially, but my spine hadn't begun to hurt yet—I hadn't yet worked out that it ought to. There were voices in my headphones, urgent ones, but I was still too fuzzy to make any sense out of what they were saying. Later I could spare time to retune my ears; right now figures were clicking away in my mind and the answers kept getting worse. There's much more pressure in an air tank than in a thruster. On the other hand, I had ten aimable thrusters with which to cancel the velocity imparted by that one diffused burst. On the third hand, I had started this with badly depleted thrusters . . . .

Even as I concluded that I was dead I was doing what I could to save my life: one by one I lined up my thrusters on the far side of my center of mass and fired them to exhaustion. Left foot, fore and aft. Right foot, likewise. Belly thruster. My back began to moan, then cry, then shriek with agony; not the localized knifing I'd expected but a general ache. I couldn't decide if that was a good sign or bad. Back thruster, clamping my teeth against a whimper. Left hand, fore and aft—

—*Save a little*. I reserved my right hand pair for last minute maneuvers, and looked to see if I'd done any good.

The Monkey Bars were still shrinking, fairly rapidly.

I was almost fully conscious now, feeling that my brains were just catching up with me. The voices in my headphones began to make sense at last. The first one that I identified, of course, was Norrey's—but she wasn't saying anything, only crying and swearing.

"Hey, honey," I said as calmly as I could, and she cut off instantly. So did the others. Then—

"Hang on, darling. *I'm coming!*"

"That's right, boss," Harry agreed. "I've been tracking you with the radar gun since you left, and the computer's doing the piloting."

"She'll get you," Raoul cried. "The machine says 'yes.' With available fuel, it can get her to you and then back here, Charlie, it says 'yes.'"

Sure enough, just to the side of the Bars I could see the Family Car, nose-on to me. It was not shrinking as fast as the Bars were—but it did appear to be shrinking. That had been a hell of a clout that can of air fetched me.

"Boss," Harry said urgently, "*is your suit honest?*"

"Yeah, sure, the force of the blast was outwards, didn't even damage the other can." My back throbbed just thinking about it, and yes, damn it, the Car's visible disk was definitely shrinking, not a whole lot but certainly *not* growing, and at that moment of moments I recalled that the warranty on that computer's software had expired three days ago.

*Say something heroic before you moan.*

"Well, that's settled," I said cheerfully. "Remind me to sue the bas—hey! *How's Tom?*"

"We got it patched," Harry said briefly. "He's out, but telemetry says he's alive and okay."

No wonder Linda was silent. She was praying.

"Is there a doctor in the house?" I asked rhetorically.

"I called Skyfac. Panzella's on his way. We're proceeding home on thrusters to get Tom indoors now."

"Go, all three of you. Nothing you can do out here. Raoul, take care of Linda."

"Yah."

Silence fell, except of course for the by-now unheard constants of breathing and rustling cloth. Norrey began to cry again, briefly, but controlled it. The disc that was her and the Car was growing now, I had to stare and measure with my thumb but yes, it was growing.

"Attaway, Norrey, you're gaining on me," I said, trying to keep it light.

"That I am," she agreed, and when the *rate* of the Car's growth had just reached a visibly perceptible crawl, the corona of her drive flame winked out. "What the—?"

Visualize the geometry. I leave the Monkey Bars at a hell of a clip. Maybe a full thirty seconds elapse before Norrey is in the saddle and blasting. Ideally the computer has her blast to a velocity higher than mine, hold it, then turnover and begin decelerating so that she will begin to return toward the Bars *just as our courses intersect*. A bit tricky to work out in your head, but no problem for a ballistic computer half as good as ours.

The kicker was fuel.

Norrey *had to* cut thrust precisely halfway through projected total fuel consumption. She had used up half the content of her fuel tanks; the computer saw that at these rates of travel rendezvous could be accomplished eventually; it cut thrust with a computer's equivalent of a smile of triumph. I did primitive mental arithmetic, based on guesswork and with enormous margins for error, and went pale and cold inside my plastic bag.

The second kicker was air.

"Harry," I rapped, "run that projection through again for me, but include the following air supply data—"

"Oh Jesus God," he said, stunned, and then repeated back the figures I gave him. "Hold on."

"Charlie," Norrey began worriedly, "Oh my God, Charlie!"

"Wait, baby. Wait. Maybe it's okay."

Harry's voice was final. "No good, boss. You'll be out of air when she gets there. She'll be damn low when she gets back."

"Then turn around and start back now, hon," I said as gently as I could.

"Hell no," she cried.

"Why risk your neck, darling? *I'm already buried—* buried in space. Come on now—"

"No."

I tried brutality. "You want my corpse that bad?"

"*Yes.*"

"Why, to have it hanging around the Closet?"

"No. To ride with."

"Huh?"

"Harry, plot me a course that'll get me to him before his air runs out. Forget the round trip: Give me a minimum-time rendezvous."

"No!" I thundered.

"Norrey," Harry said earnestly, "there's *nothing else to come get you with.* There's not a ship in the sky. You blast any more and you'll never even get started back here, you'll never even stop leaving. You've got more air than him, but both your air combined wouldn't last one of you 'til help could arrive, even if we could keep tracking you that long." It was the longest speech I'd ever heard Harry make.

"I'm damned if I want to be a widow," she blazed, and cut in acceleration on manual overrride.

She was as dead as me, now.

"Goddammit," Harry and I roared together, and then "Help her, Harry!" I screamed and "I am!" he screamed back and an endless time later he said sadly, "Okay, Norrey, let go. The new course is locked in." She was still dead, had been from the moment she overrode the computer. But at least now we'd go together.

"All right, then," she said, still angry but mollified. "Twenty-five *years* I waited to be your wife, Armstead. I will be *damned* if I'll be your widow."

"Harry," I said, knowing it was hopeless but refusing to accept, "refigure, assuming that we leave the Car when it runs out of juice and use all of Norrey's suit thrusters together. Hers aren't as low as mine were."

It must have been damned awkward for Harry, using two fingers to keep himself headed for home at max thrust, holding the big computer terminal and pushing keys with the rest. It must have been even more awkward for Raoul and Linda, towing the unconscious Tom between them, watching their patch job leak.

"Forget it, boss," Harry said almost at once. "There's two of you."

"Well then," I said desperately, "can we trade off breathing air for thrust?"

He must have been just as desperate; he actually worked the problem. "Sure. You could start returning, get back here in less than a day. But it'd take *all* your air to do it. You're dead, boss."

I nodded, a silly habit I'd thought I'd outgrown. "That's what I thought. Thanks, Harry. Good luck with Tom."

Norrey said not a word. Presently the computer shut down her drive again, having done its level best to get her to me quickly with the fuel available. The glow around the Car (now plainly growing) winked out, and still she was silent. We were all silent. There was either nothing to say or too much, no in-between. Presently Harry reported docking at home. He gave Norrey her turnover data, gave her back manual control, and then he and the others went off the air.

Two people breathing makes hardly any noise at all.

She was a long long time coming, long enough for the pain in my back to diminish to the merely incredible. When she was near enough to see, it took all my discipline to keep from using the last of my jump-juice to try and match up with her. Not that I had anything to save it for. But matching in free space is like high-speed highway merging—one of you had better maintain a constant velocity, two variables are too many. Norrey did a textbook job, coming to a dead stop relative to me at the extreme edge of lifeline range.

The precision was wasted. But you don't stop trying to live just because a computer says you can't.

At the same split second that she stopped decelerating she fired the lifeline. The weight at the end tapped me gently on the chest: *very* impressive shooting, even with the magnet to help. I embraced it fiercely, and it took me several seconds of concentrated effort to let go and clip it to my belt. I hadn't realized how lonely and scared I was.

As soon as she was sure I was secure, she cut the drag and let the Car reel me in.

"Who says you can never get a cab when you need one?" I said, but my teeth were chattering and it spoiled the effect.

She grinned anyhow, and helped me into the rear saddle. "Where to, Mac?"

All of a sudden I couldn't think of anything funny to say. If the Car's fuselage hadn't been reinforced, I'd have crushed it between my knees. "Wherever you're going,"

I said simply, and she spun around in her saddle and gave it the gun.

It takes a really sensitive hand to pilot a tractor like the Family Car accurately, especially with a load on. It's quite difficult to keep the target bubble centered, and the controls are mushy—you have to sort of outguess her or you'll end up oscillating and throw your gyro. A dancer is, of course, better at seat-of-the-pants mass balancing than any but the most experienced of Space Command pilots, and Norrey was the best of the six of us. At that she outdid herself.

She even outdid the computer. Which is not too astonishing—there's always more gas than it says on the gauge —and of course it wasn't nearly enough to matter. We were still dead. But after a time the distant red and green spheroid that was the Bars stopped shrinking; instruments confirmed it. After a longer time I was able to convince myself that it was actually growing some. It was, naturally, at that moment that the vibration between my thighs ceased.

All the time we'd been accelerating I'd been boiling over with the need to talk, and had kept my mouth shut for fear of distracting Norrey's attention. Now we had done all we could do. Now we had nothing left to do in our lives but talk, and I was wordless again. It was Norrey who broke the silence, her tone just precisely right.

"Uh, you're not going to believe this . . . but we're out of gas."

"The hell you say. Let me out of this car; I'm not that kind of boy." *Thank you, hon.*

"Aw, take it easy. It's downhill from here. I'll just put her in neutral and we'll coast home."

"Hey listen," I said, "when you navigate by the seat of your pants like that, is that what they call a bum steer?"

"Oh Charlie, I don't want to die."

"Well then, don't."

"I wasn't *finished* yet."

"Norrey!" I grabbed her shoulder from behind. Fortunately I used my left hand, triggering only empty thrusters.

There was a silence.

"I'm sorry," she said at last, still facing away from me. "I made my choice. These last minutes with you are worth what I paid for them. That just slipped out." She snorted at herself. "Wasting air."

"I can't think of anything I'd rather spend air on than talking with you. That you can do in p-suits, I mean. I don't want to die either—but if I've got to go, I'm glad I've got your company. Isn't that selfish?"

"Nope. I'm glad you're here too, Charlie."

"Hell, I *called* this meeting. If I wasn't here, nobody would be." I broke off then, and scowled. "That's the part that bothers me the most, I think. I used to try and guess, sometimes, what it would be that would finally kill me. Sure enough, I was right: my own damn stupidity. Spacing out. Taking my finger off the number. Oh dammit, Norrey—"

"Charlie, it was an accident."

"I spaced out. I wasn't paying attention. I was thinking about the god damned deadline, and I blew it." (I was very close to something, then; something bigger than my death.)

"Charlie, that's cheating. At least half of that guilt you're hogging belongs to the crook that inspected that air tank at the factory. Not to mention the flaming idiot who forgot to gas the Car this morning."

It's a rotating duty. "Who was that idiot?" I asked, before I could think better of it.

"Same idiot who took off without grabbing extra air. Me."

That produced an uncomfortable silence. Which started me trying to think of something meaningful or useful to say. Or do. Let's see, I had less than an eighth of a can of air. Norrey maybe a can and a quarter: she hadn't used up as much in exercise. (Space Command armor, like the NASA Standard suits before them, hold about six hours' air. A Stardancer's p-suit is good for only half as much—but they're prettier. And we *always* have plenty of air bottles—strapped to every camera we use.) I reached forward and unshipped her full tank, passed it silently over her shoulder. She took it, as silently, and got the first-aid kit out of the glove compartment. She took a Y-joint from it, made sure both male ends were sealed, and snapped it onto the air bottle. She got extension hoses from the kit and mated them to the ends of the Y. She clipped the whole assembly to the flank of the Car until we needed it, an air soda with two straws. Then she reversed herself in the saddle, awkwardly, until she was facing me.

"I love you, Charlie."

"I love you, Norrey."

Don't ever let anybody tell you that hugging in p-suits is a waste of time. Hugging is *never* a waste of time. It hurt my back a lot, but I paid no attention.

The headphones crackled with another carrier wave: Raoul calling from Tom and Linda's place. "Norrey? Charlie? Tom's okay," he said agitatedly. "I mean, he's a mess, but he's okay. The doctor's on his way, Charlie, but he's not going to get here in time to do you any good. I called the Space Command, there's no scheduled traffic *near* here, there's just nothing in the neighborhood, Charlie, just nothing at all what the hell are we going to *do?*" Harry must have been very busy with Tom, or he'd have grabbed the mike by now.

"Here's what you're going to do, buddy," I said calmly, spacing my words to slow him down. "Push the 'record' button. Okay? Now put the speakers on so Harry and Linda can witness. Ready? Okay. 'I, Charles Armstead, being of sound mind and body—' "

"Charlie!"

"Don't spoil the tape, buddy. I haven't got time for too many retakes, and I've got better things to do. 'I, Charles Armstead—' "

It didn't take very long. I left everything to the Company—and I made Fat Humphrey a full partner. Le Maintenant had closed the month before, strangled by bureaucracy. Then it was Norrey's turn, and she echoed me almost verbatim.

What was there to do then? We said our good-byes to Raoul, to Linda, and to Harry, making it as short as possible. Raoul cried. Linda was grave, solemn. Harry was brief. Then we switched off our radios. Sitting backwards in the saddle was uncomfortable for Norrey; she turned around again and I hugged her from behind like a motorcycle passenger. Our hoods touched. What we said then is really none of your damned business.

An hour went by, the fullest hour I had ever known. All infinity stretched around us. Both of us being ignorant of astronomy, we had given names of our own to the constellations on our honeymoon. The Banjo. The Leering Gerbil. Orion's Truss. The Big Pot Pipe and the Little Hash Pipe. One triplet near the Milky Way quite naturally became the Three Musketeers. Like that. We renamed them all, now, re-evoking that honeymoon. We talked of our lost plans and hopes. In turns, we freaked out and comforted each other, and then we both freaked out together and both comforted each other. We told each other those last few secrets even happily-marrieds hold out. Twice, we agreed to take off our p-suits and get it over with. Twice, we changed our minds. We talked about the children we didn't have, and how lucky it was for them that we didn't have them. We sucked sugar water from our hood nipples. We talked about God, about death, about how uncomfortable we were and how absurd it was to die uncomfortable—about how absurd it was to die at all.

"It was deadline pressure killed us," I said finally,

"stupid damned deadline pressure. In a big hurry. Why? So we wouldn't get marooned in space by our metabolisms. What was so wrong with that?" (I was very close, now.) "What were we so scared of? What has Earth got, that we were risking our necks to keep?"

"People," Norrey answered seriously. "Places. There aren't many of either up here."

"Yeah, places. New York. Toronto. Cesspools."

"Not fair. Prince Edward Island."

"Yeah, and how much time did we get to spend there? And how long before *it's* a bloody city?"

"*People*, Charlie. Good people."

"Seven billion of 'em, squatting on the same disintegrating anthill."

"Charlie, look out there." She pointed to the Earth. "Do you see an 'oasis hanging in space'? Does that look crowded to you?"

She had me there. From space, one's overwhelming impression of our home planet is of one vast, godforsaken wilderness. Desert is by far the most common sight, and only occasionally does a twinkle or a miniature mosaic give evidence of human works. Man may have polluted hell out of his atmosphere—seen edge-on at sunset it looks no thicker than the skin of an apple—but he has as yet made next to no visible mark on the face of his planet.

"No. But it is, and you know it. My leg hurts all the time. There's never a moment of real silence. It stinks. It's filthy and germ-ridden and riddled with evil and steeped in contagious insanity and hip-deep in despair. I don't know what the hell I ever wanted to go back there for."

"Charlie!" I only realized how high my volume had become when I discovered how loud she had to be to outshout me. I broke off, furious with myself. *Again you want to freak out? The last time wasn't bad enough?*

*I'm sorry,* I answered myself, *I've never died before. I*

*understand it's been done worse.* "I'm sorry, hon," I said aloud. "I guess I just haven't cared much for Earth since Le Maintenant closed." It started out to be a wisecrack, but it didn't come out funny.

"Charlie," she said, her voice strange.

*You see? There she goes now, and we're off and running again.* "Yeah?"

"Why are the Monkey Bars blinking on and off?"

At once I checked the air bottle, then the Y-joint, hoses, and joins. No, she was getting air. I looked then, and sure as hell the Monkey Bars were blinking on and off in the far distance, a Christmas-tree bulb on a flasher circuit. I checked the air again, carefully, to make sure we weren't both hallucinating, and returned to our spoon embrace.

"Funny," I said, "I can't think of a circuit malf that'd behave that way."

"Something must have struck the sunpower screen and set it spinning."

"I guess. But what?"

"The hell with it, Charlie. Maybe it's Raoul trying to signal us."

"If it is, to hell with him indeed. There's nothing more I want to say, and I'm damned if there's anything I want to hear. Leave the damn phone off the hook. Where were we?"

"Deciding Earth sucks."

"It certainly does—hard. Why does *anybody* live there, Norrey? Oh, the hell with that too."

"Yeah. It can't be such a bad place. We met there."

"That's true." I hugged her a little tighter. "I guess we're lucky people. We each found our Other Half. And before we died, too. How many are that lucky?"

"Tom and Linda, I think. Diane and Howard in Toronto. I can't think of anybody else I know of, for sure."

"Me either. There used to be more happy marriages around when I was a kid." The Bars began blinking twice as fast. A second improbable meteor? Or a chunk of the panel breaking loose, putting the rest in a tighter spin? It was an annoying distraction; I moved until I couldn't see it. "I guess I never realized just how incredibly lucky we are. A life with you in it is a square deal."

"Oh, Charlie," she cried, moving in my arms. Despite the awkwardness she worked around in her saddle to hug me again. My p-suit dug into my neck, the earphone on that side notched my ear, and her strong dancer's arms raised hell with my throbbing back, but I made no complaint. Until her grip suddenly convulsed even tighter.

"*Charlie!*"

"Nnngh."

She relaxed her clutch some, but held on. "What the hell is that?"

I caught my breath. "What the hell is what?" I twisted in my seat to look. "*What the hell is that?*" We both lost our seats on the Car and drifted to the ends of our hoses, stunned limp.

It was practically on top of us, within a hundred meters, so impossibly enormous and foreshortened that it took us seconds to recognize, identify it as a ship. My first thought was that a whale had come to visit.

*Champion*, said the bold red letters across the prow. And beneath, *United Nations Space Command*.

I glanced back at Norrey, then checked the air line one more time. " 'No scheduled traffic,' " I said hollowly, and switched on my radio.

The voice was incredibly loud, but the static was so much louder that I knew it was off-mike, talking to someone in the same room. I remember every syllable.

"pid fucking idiots are too God damned dumb to turn on their radios, sir. Somebody's gonna have to tap 'em on the shoulder."

Further off-mike, a familiar voice began to laugh like hell, and after a moment the radioman joined in. Norrey and I listened to the laughter, speechless. A part of me considered laughing too, but decided I might never stop.

"Jesus Christ," I said finally. "How far does a man have to go to have a little privacy with his wife?"

Startled silence, and then the mike was seized and the familiar voice roared, "You son of a bitch!"

"But seeing you've come all this way, Major Cox," Norrey said magnificently, "we'll come in for a beer."

"You dumb son of a bitch," Harry's voice came from afar. "You dumb son of a bitch." The Monkey Bars had stopped winking. We had the message.

"After you, my love," I said, unshipping the air tank, and as I reached the airlock my last thruster died. Bill Cox met us at the airlock with three beers, and mine was *delicious*.

The two sips I got before the fun started.

Like Phillip Nolan, I had renounced something out loud—and had been heard.

# Chapter 5

I took those two sips right away, and made them last. Officers and crew were frankly gaping at Norrey and me. At first I naturally assumed they were awed by anyone dumb enough to turn off their radios in an emergency. Well, I hadn't thought of being dead as an emergency. But on the second sip I noticed a certain subtle classification of gaping. With one or two exceptions, all the female crew were gaping at me and all the male crew were gaping at Norrey. I had not exactly forgotten what we were wearing under our p-suits; there was almost nothing to forget. We were "decently" covered by sanitary arrangements, but just barely, and what is commonplace on a home video screen on Earth is not so in the ready room of a warship.

Bill, of course, was too much of a gentleman to notice. Or maybe he realized there was not one practical thing to do about the situation except ignore it. "So reports of your demise were exaggerated, eh?"

"On the contrary," I said, wiping my chin with my glove. "They omitted our resurrection. Which by me is the most important part. Thanks, Bill."

He grinned, and said a strange thing very quickly. "Don't ask any of the obvious questions." As he said it, his eyes flickered slightly. On Earth or under acceleration they would have flicked from side to side. In free fall, a new reflex controls, and he happened to be oriented out of phase to my local vertical: his pupils described twin circles, perhaps a centimeter in diameter, and returned to us. The message was plain. The answers to my obvious next questions were classified information. Wait.

Hmmm.

I squeezed Norrey's hand hard—unnecessarily, of course—and groped for a harmless response.

"We're at your disposal," is what I came up with.

He flinched. Then in a split second he decided that I didn't mean whatever he'd thought I meant, and his grin returned. "You'll want a shower and some food. Follow me to my quarters."

"For a shower," Norrey said, "I will follow you through hell." We kicked off.

There was my second chance to gawk like a tourist at the innards of a genuine warship—and again I was too busy to pay any attention. Did Bill really expect his crew to believe that he had just happened to pick us up hitchhiking? Whenever no one was visibly within earshot, I tried to pump him—but in Space Command warships the air pressure is so low that sounds travel poorly. He outflew my questions—and how much expression does a man wear on the soles of his feet?

At last we reached his quarters and swung inside. He backed up to a wall and hung facing us in the totally relaxed "spaceman's crouch," and tossed us a couple of odd widgets. I examined mine: it looked like a wristwatch with a miniature hair dryer attached. Then he tossed us a pair of cigarettes and I got it. Mass priorities in military craft differ from those of essentially luxury operations like ours or Skyfac's: the *Champion*'s air system was primitive, not only low-pressure but inefficient. The widgets were combination air-cleaner/ashtrays. I slipped mine over my wrist and lit up.

"Major William Cox," I said formally, "Norrey Armstead. Vice versa."

It is of course impossible to bow when your shoulders are velcro'd to the wall, but Bill managed to signify. Norrey gave him what we call the free-fall curtsy, a movement we worked out idly one day on the theory that we might someday give curtain calls to a live audience. It's indescribable but spectacular, as frankly sexual as a curtsy and as graceful.

Bill blinked, but recovered. "I am honored, Ms. Armstead. I've seen all the tapes you've released, and—well, this will be easy to misunderstand, but you're her sister."

Norrey smiled. "Thank you, Major—"

"Bill."

"—Bill. That's high praise. Charlie's told me a lot about you."

"Likewise, one drunken night when we met dirtside. Afterwards."

I remembered the night—weeks before I had consciously realized that I was in love with Norrey—but not the conversation. My subconscious tells me only what it thinks I ought to know.

"Now you must both forgive me," he went on, and I noticed for the first time that he was in a hurry. "I'd like nothing better than to chat, but I can't. Please get out of your p-suits, quickly."

"Even more than a shower, I'd like some answers, Bill," I said. "What the hell brings you out our way, just in the nicotine? Like that. I don't believe in miracles, not that kind anyway. And why the hush?"

"Yes," Norrey chimed in, "and why didn't your own Ground Control know you were in the area?"

Cox held up both hands. "Whoa. The answer to your questions runs about twenty minutes minimum. In—" he glanced at his watch, "less than three we accelerate at two gravities. That's why I want you out of those suits—my bed *will* accommodate air tank fittings, but you'd be uncomfortable as hell."

"What? Bill, what the hell are you talking about? Accelerate where? Home is a couple o' dozen klicks that-away."

"Your friends will be picked up by the same shuttle that is fetching Dr. Panzella," Cox said. "They'll join us at Skyfac in a matter of hours. But you two can't wait."

"For *what?*" I hollered.

Bill arm-wrestled me with his eyes, and lost. "Damn it," he said, then paused. "I have specific orders not to tell you a thing." He glanced at his chronometer. "And I really do have to get back to the Worry Hole. Look, if you'll trust me and pay attention, I can give you the whole twenty minutes in two sentences, all right?"

"I—yeah. Okay."

"The aliens have been sighted again, in the close vicinity of Saturn. They're just sitting there. Think it through."

He left at once, but before he cleared the doorway I was halfway out of my p-suit, and Norrey was reaching for the straps on the right half of the Captain's couch.

And we were both beginning to be terrified. Again.


Think it through, Bill had said.

The aliens had come boldly knocking on our door once, and been met by a shotgun blast named Shara. They were learning country manners; this time they had stopped at the fence gate, shouted "hello the house," and waited prudently. (Saturn was just about our fence gate, too— as I recalled, a manned expedition to Saturn was being planned at that time, for the usual obscure scientific reasons.) Clearly, they wanted to parley.

Okay, then: if you were the Secretary General, who would *you* send to parley? The Space Commando? Prominent politicians? Noted scientists? A convention of used copter salesmen? You'd most likely send your most seasoned and flexible career diplomats, of course, as many as could go.

But would you omit the only artists in human space who have demonstrated a working knowledge of pidgin Alien?

I was drafted—at my age.

But that was only the first step in the logic chain. The reason that Saturn probe story had made enough of a media splash to attract even my attention was that it was a kind of kamikaze mission for the crew. Whose place we were assuming.

Think it through. Whatever they planned to send us to Saturn on, it was sure to take a *long* time. Six years was the figure I vaguely recalled hearing mentioned. And any transit over that kind of distance would have to be spent almost entirely in free fall. You could rotate the craft to provide gravity at either end—but one gee's worth of rotation of a space that small would create so much Coriolis differential that anyone who didn't want to puke or pass out would have to stay lying down for six years. Or hang like bolas from exercise lines on either end—not much more practical.

If we didn't dodge the draft, we would never walk Earth again. We would be free-fall exiles, marooned in space. Our reward for serving as mouthpieces between a bunch of idiot diplomats and the things that had killed Shara.

Assuming that we survived the experience at all.

At any other time, the implications would have been too staggering for my brain to let itself comprehend; my mind would have run round in frightened circles. Unless I could talk my way out of this with whoever was waiting for us at Skyfac (why Skyfac?), Norrey and I had taken our last walk, seen our last beach, gone to our last concert. We would never again breathe uncanned air, eat with a fork, get rained on, or eat fresh food. We were dead to the world (*S.I.C. TRANSIT: gloria mundi*, whispered a phantom memory that had been funny enough the first time). And yet I faced it squarely, calmly.

Not more than an hour ago I had renounced all those things.

*And* resigned myself to the loss of a lot of more important things, that it looked like I was now going to be able to keep. Breathing. Eating. Sleeping. Thinking. Making love. Hurting. Scratching. Bowel movements. Bitching. Why, the list was endless—and I had all those things back, at least six years' worth! Hell, I told myself, there were damned few city dwellers any better off—few of *them* ever got walks, beaches, concerts, uncanned air or fresh food. What with airlocks and nostril filters, city folk might as well be in orbit for all the outdoors they could enjoy— and how many of them could feel confident of six more years? I couldn't begin to envision the trip to Saturn, let alone what lay at the end of it—but I knew that space held no muckers, no muggers, no mad stranglers or crazed drivers, no tenement fires or fuel shortages or race riots or blackouts or gang wars or reactor meltdowns—

*How does Norrey feel about it?*

It had taken me a couple of minutes to get this far; as I turned my head to see Norrey's face the acceleration warning sounded. She turned hers, too; our noses were scant centimeters apart, and I could see that she too had thought it through. But I couldn't read her reaction.

"I guess I don't mind much going," I said.

"I *want* to go," she said fervently.

I blinked. "Phillip Nolan was the Man Without A Country," I said, "and he didn't care for it. *We'll* be the Couple Without A Planet."

"I don't care, Charlie." Second warning sounded.

"You seemed to care back there on the Car, when I was bum-rapping Earth."

"You don't understand. Those fuckers killed my sister. I want to learn their language so I can cuss them out."

It didn't sound like a bad idea.

But thinking about it was. Two gees caught us both without heads sideways, smacking our cheeks into the couch and wrenching our necks. An eternity later, turnover gave us just enough time to pop them back into place, and then deceleration came for another eternity.

There were "minor" maneuvering accelerations, and then "acceleration over" sounded. We unstrapped, both borrowed robes from Bill's locker, and began trading neckrubs. By and by Bill returned. He glanced at the bruises we were raising on opposite sides of our faces and snorted. "Lovebirds. All right, all ashore. Powwow time." He produced off-duty fatigues in both our sizes, and a brush and comb.

"With who?" I asked, dressing hastily.

"The Secretary-General of the United Nations," he said simply.

"Jesus Christ."

"If he was available," Bill agreed.

"How about Tom?" Norrey asked. "Is he all right?"

"I spoke with Panzella," Bill answered. "McGillicuddy is all right. He'll look like strawberry yoghurt for a while, but no significant damage—"

"Thank God."

"—Panzella's bringing him here with the others, ETA—" he checked his chronometer pointedly—"five hours away."

"*All* of us?" I exclaimed. "How big is the bloody ship?" I slipped on the shoes.

"All I know is my orders," Bill said, turning to go. "I'm to see that the six of you are delivered to Skyfac, soonest. And, I trust you'll remember, to keep my damn mouth shut." *Why Skyfac?* I wondered again.

"Suppose the others don't volunteer?" Norrey asked.

Bill turned back, honestly dumbfounded. "Eh?"

"Well, they don't have the personal motivations Charlie and I have."

"They have their duty."

"But they're *civilians*."

He was still confused. "Aren't they humans?"

She gave up. "Lead us to the Secretary-General."

None of us realized at the time that Bill had asked a good question.


Tokugawa was in Tokyo. It was just as well; there was no room for him in his office. Seven civilians, six military officers. Three of the latter were Space Command, the other three national military; all thirteen were of high rank. It would have been obvious had they been naked. All of them were quiet, reserved; none of them spoke an unnecessary word. But there was enough authority in that room to sober a drunken lumberjack.

And it was agitated authority, nervous authority, faced not with an issue but a genuine crisis, all too aware that it was making history. Those who didn't look truculent looked extremely grave. A jester facing an audience of lords in this mood would have taken poison.

And then I saw that all of the military men and one of the civilians were trying heroically to watch everyone in the room at once without being conspicuous, and I put my fists on my hips and laughed.

The man in Carrington's—excuse me, in Tokugawa's chair looked genuinely startled. Not offended, not even annoyed—just surprised.

There's no point in describing the appearance or recounting the accomplishments of Siegbert Wertheimer. As of this writing he is still the Secretary-General of the United Nations, and his media photos, like his record, speak for themselves. I will add only that he was (inevitably) shorter than I had expected, and heavier. And one other, entirely subjective and apolitical impression: in those first seconds of appraisal I decided that his famous massive dignity, so beloved by political cartoonists, was intrinsic rather than acquired. It was the cause of his impressive track record, I was certain, and not the result of it. He did not *seem* like a humorless man—he was simply astounded that someone had *found* some humor in this mess. He looked unutterably weary.

"Why is it that you laugh, sir?" he asked mildly, with that faintest trace of accent.

I shook my head, still grinning uncontrollably. "I'm not sure I can make you see it, Mr. Secretary-General." Something about the set of his mouth made me decide to try. "From my point of view, I've just walked into a Hitchcock movie."

He considered it, momentarily imagining what it must be like to be an ordinary human thrust into the company of agitated lions, and grinned himself. "Then at least we shall try to make the dialogue fresh," he said. A good deal of his weariness seemed to be low-gee malaise, the discomfort of fluids rising to the upper body, the feeling of fullness in the head and the vertigo. But only his body noticed it. "Let us proceed. I am impressed by your record, Mr.—" He glanced down, and the paper he needed was not there. The American civilian had it, and the Russian general was looking over his shoulder. Before I could prompt him, he closed his eyes, jogged his memory, and continued, "—Armstead. I own three copies of the *Stardance*, and the first two are worn out. I have recently viewed your own recordings, and interviewed several of your former students. I have a job that needs doing, and I think you and your troupe are precisely the people for that job."

I didn't want to get Bill in trouble, so I hung a dumb look on my face and waited.

"The alien creatures you encountered with Shara Drummond have been seen again. They appear to be in a parking orbit around the planet Saturn. They have been there for approximately three weeks. They show no sign of any intention to move, nearer to or farther from us. Radio signals have been sent, but they have elicited no response. Will you kindly tell me when I come to information that is new to you?"

I knew I was caught, but I kept trying. In low gee, you *chase* spilled milk—and often catch it. "*New* to me? Christ, all of it's—"

He smiled again. "Mr. Armstead, there is a saying in the UN. We say, 'There are no secrets in space.'"

It is true that between all humans who choose to live in space, there is a unique and stronger bond than between any of them and anyone who spends all his life on Earth. For all its immensity, space has always had a better grapevine than a small town. But I hadn't expected the Secretary-General to know that.

Norrey spoke while I was still reevaluating. "We know that we're going to Saturn, Mr. Secretary-General. We don't know how, or what will happen when we get there."

"Or for that matter," I added, "why this conference is taking place in Skyfac cubic."

"But we understand the personal implications of a space trip that long, as you must have known we would, and we know that we have to go."

"As I hoped you would," he finished, respectfully. "I will not sully your bravery with words. Shall I answer your questions, then?"

"One moment," I interjected. "I understand that you want our entire troupe. Won't Norrey and I do? We're the best dancers—why multiply your payload?"

"Payload mass is not a major consideration," Wertheimer said. "Your colleagues will be given their free choice—but if I can have them, I want them."

"Why?"

"There will be four diplomats. I want four interpreters. Mr. Stein's experience and proven expertise are invaluable —he is, from his record, unique. Mr. Brindle can help us learn the aliens' response to visual cues designed by computers which have seen the *Stardance* tapes—the same sort of augmentation he provides for you now. A sort of expanded vocabulary. He will also provide a peaceful excuse for us to judge the aliens' reaction to laser beams."

His answer raised several strong objections in my mind, but I decided to reserve them for later. "Go on."

"As to your other questions. We are guests of Skyfac Incorporated because of a series of coincidences that almost impels me to mysticism. A certain unusual transfer is required in order to get a mission to Saturn at all expediently. This transfer, called Friesen's Transfer, must be begun from a 2:1 resonance orbit. Skyfac has such an orbit. It is a convenient outfitting base unequalled in space. And by chance *Siegfried*, the Saturn probe which was just nearing completion, is in a precessing ellipse orbit which brought it within the close vicinity of Skyfac at the right time. An incredible coincidence. On a par with the coincidence that the launch window for Saturn opened concurrent with the aliens' appearance there.

"I do not believe in good fortune of that magnitude. I suspect personally that this is some kind of intelligence and aptitude test—but I have no evidence beyond what I have told you. My speculations are as worthless as anyone's—we must have more information."

"How long does that launch window remain open?" I asked.

Wertheimer's watch was as Swiss as he, exquisite and expensive but so old fashioned that he had to look at it. "Perhaps twenty hours."

Oof. Now for the painful one. "How long is the round trip?"

"Assuming zero time in negotiation, three years. Approximately one year out and two back."

I was pleasurably startled at first: three years instead of twelve to be cooped up in a canful of diplomats. But then I began to grasp the accelerations implied—in an untested ship built by a government on low-bid contracts. And it was still more than enough time for us all to adapt permanently to zero gee. Still, they obviously had something special and extraordinary up their sleeves.

I grinned again. "Are you going?"

A lesser man would have said, "I regret that I cannot," or something equally self-absolutory—and might have been completely honest at that. Secretary-Generals don't go chasing off to Saturn, even if they want to.

But all he said was, "No," and I was ashamed that I had asked the question.

"As to the question of compensation," he went on quietly, "there is of course none adequate to the sacrifice you are making. Nevertheless, should you, upon your return, elect to continue performing, all your operating costs will be covered in perpetuity by the United Nations. Should you be disinclined to continue your careers, you will be guaranteed unlimited lifetime transport to and from, and luxury accommodations at, any place within United Nations jurisdiction."

We were being given a paid-up lifetime plane ticket to anywhere in human space. If we survived to collect it.

"This is in no sense to be considered payment; any attempt at payment would be laughable and grotesque. But you have chosen to serve; your species is grateful. Is this satisfactory to you?"

I thought about it, turned to Norrey. We exchanged a few paragraphs by facial telegraph. "We accept the blank check," she said. "We don't promise to cash it."

He nodded. "Perhaps the only sensible answer. All right, let us—"

"Sir," I said urgently, "I have something I have to say first."

"Yes?" He did me the honor of displaying patience.

"Norrey and I are willing to go, for our own reasons. I can't speak for the others. But I *must* tell you that I have no great confidence that *any* of us can do this job for you. I will try my best—but frankly I expect to fail."

The Chinese general's eyes locked onto me. "Why?" he snapped.

I continued to look at Wertheimer. "You assume that because we are Stardancers, we can interpret for you. I cannot guarantee that. I venture to say that I know the *Stardance* tapes, even the classified ones, better than any person here. I shot them. I've monkeyed with speed and image-field until I know every frame by name and I will be damned if I understand their language. Oh, I get flashes, insights, but . . .

"Shara understood them—crudely, tentatively, and with great effort. I'm not half the choreographer she was, nor half the dancer. None of us is. No one I've ever seen is. She told me herself that what communication took place was more telepathy than choreography. I have no idea whether any of us can establish such a telepathic rapport through dance. I wasn't *there*; I was in this oversized donut, four bulkheads away from here, filming the show." I was getting agitated, all the pressure finding release. "I'm sorry, General," I said to the Chinese, "but this is not something you can order done."

Wertheimer was not fazed. "Have you used computers?"

"No," I admitted. "I always meant to when I got time."

"You did not think we would fail to do so? No more than you, do we have an alien/human dictionary—but we know much. You can choreograph by computer?"

"Sure."

"Your ship's computer memories should offer you a year's worth of study on the trip out. They will provide you with at least enough 'vocabulary' to begin the process of acquiring more, and they will provide extensive if hypothetical suggestions for doing so. The research has been done. You and your troupe may be the only humans alive capable of assessing the data and putting them to use. I have seen your performance tapes, and I believe you can do it if anyone can. You are all unique people, at least in your work. You think as well as a human . . . but not *like* a human."

It was the most extraordinary thing anyone had ever said to me; it stunned me more than anything else that was said that day.

"All of you, apparently," he went on. "Perhaps you will meet with failure. In that case you are the best imaginable teachers and guides for the diplomat team, of whom only one has even minimal experience with free-fall conditions. They will need people who are at home in space to help them, whatever happens."

He took out a cigarette, and the American civilian turned up the air for him unobtrusively. He lit it with a match, himself. It smoked an odd color: it was tobacco.

"I am confident that all of you will do your best. All of your company who choose to go. I hope that will be all of you. But we cannot wait until the arrival of your friends, Mr. Armstead; there are enormous constraints on us all. If you are to be introduced to the diplomatic mission before take-off, it must be now."

*Wuh oh. Red alert. You're inspecting your housemates for the next two years—just before signing the lease. Pay attention: Harry and the others'll be interested.*

I took Norrey's hand; she squeezed mine hard.

*And to think I could have been an alcoholic, anonymous video man in New Brunswick.*

"Go ahead, sir," I said firmly.

"You're shitting me," Raoul exclaimed.

"Honest to God," I assured him.

"It sounds like a Milton Berle joke," he insisted.

"You're too young to remember Milton Berle," Norrey said. She was lying down on the near bunk, nodding off in spite of herself.

"So don't I have a tape library?"

"I agree with you," I said, "but the fact remains. Our

diplomatic team consists of a Spaniard, a Russian, a Chinaman, and a Jew."

"My God," Tom said from his reclining position on the other bed, where he had been since he arrived. He did indeed look like strawberry yoghurt, lightly stirred, and he complained of intermittent eye and ear pain. But he was shot full of don't-hurt and keep-going, and his hands were full of Linda's; his voice was strong and clear. "It even makes sense."

"Sure," I agreed. "If he's not going to send one delegate from each member nation, Wertheimer's only option is to keep it down to The Big Three. It's the only restriction most everybody can live with. It's *got* to be a multinational team; that business about mankind uniting in the face of the alien menace is the bunk."

"Headed by the proverbial Man Above Reproach," Linda pointed out.

"Wertheimer himself would have been perfect," Raoul put in.

"Sure," I agreed drily, "but he had some pressing obligations elsewhere."

"Ezequiel DeLaTorre will do just fine," Tom said thoughtfully.

I nodded. "Even I've heard of him. Okay, I've told you all we know. Comments? Questions?"

"I want to know about this one-year trip-time business," Tom spoke up. "As far as I know, that's impossible."

"Me too," I agreed. "We've been in space a long time. I don't know if they can understand how *little* prolonged acceleration we can take at this point. What about it, Harry? Raoul? Can the deed be done?"

"I don't think so," Harry said.

"Why not? Can you explain?"

Guest privileges aboard Skyfac include computer access. Harry jaunted to the terminal, punched up a reference display.

The screen said:

$$t_2 - t_1 = \sqrt{2p^3/u} \left[ \tan \frac{f_2}{2} + \frac{1}{3} \tan^3 \frac{f_2}{2} - \tan \frac{f_1}{2} - \frac{1}{3} \tan^3 \frac{3f_1}{2} \right]$$

"That's the simplest expression for a transfer time from planet to planet," he said.

"Jesus."

"And it's too simple for your problem."

"Uh—they said something about a freezing transfer."

"Got it," Raoul said. "Friesen's Transfer, on the tip of my mind. Sure, it'd work."

"How?" everyone said at once.

"I used to study all the papers on Space Colonization when I was a kid," Raoul bubbled. "Even when it was obvious that L-5 wasn't going to get off the ground, I never gave up hope—it seemed like the only way I might ever get to space. Lawrence Friesen presented a paper at Princeton once . . . sure, I remember, '80 or a little earlier. Wait a minute." He hopped rabbitlike to the terminal, used its calculator function.

Harry was working his own belt-buckle calculator. "How're you gonna get a characteristic velocity of 28 klicks a second?" he asked skeptically.

"Nuclear pulse job?" Tom suggested.

That was what I had been afraid of. I've read that there are people who seriously propose propelling themselves into deep space by goosing themselves with hydrogen bombs—but you'll never get me up in one of them things.

"Hell no," Raoul said—thank goodness. "You don't need that kind of thrust with a Friesen. Watch." He set the terminal for engineering display and began sketching the idea. "You gotta start from an orbit like this:"

"A 2:1 resonance orbit?" I asked.

"That's right," he affirmed.

"Like Skyfac?" I asked.

"Yeah, sure, that'd—hey! Hey, yeah—we're just where we want to be. Gee, what a funny coincidence, huh?"

Harry, I could see, was beginning to smell the same rat Wertheimer had. Maybe Tom was, too; all that yoghurt got in the way. "So then?" I prompted.

Raoul cleared the screen and calculated some more. "Well, you'd want to make your ship lose, let's see, a little less than a kilometer per second. That's—well, nearly two minutes acceleration at one gravity. Hmmm. Or a tenth-gee, say, about a seventeen-minute burn. Nothing.

"That starts us falling toward Earth. What we want to do then is slingshot around it. So we apply an extra . . . 5.44 klicksecs at just the right time. About nine minutes at one gravity, but they won't use one gravity because you need it *fast*. Might be, lemme see, 4.6 minutes at two gees, or it might be 2.3 at four."

"Oh, fine," I said cheerfully. "Only a couple of minutes at four gees. Our faces'll migrate around the back of our heads, and we'll be the only animals in the system with frontbones. Go on."

"So you get this," Raoul said, keying the drafting display again:

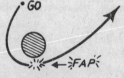

"And that gives us a year of free fall, in which to practice our choreography, throw up, listen to our bones rot, kill the diplomats and eat them, discuss Heinlein's effect on Proust, and bone up on Conversational Alien. Then we're at Saturn. Gee, that's another lucky break, the launch window for a one-year Friesen being open—"

"Yeah," Harry interrupted, looking up from his calculator, "that gets you to Saturn in a year—at twelve klick-secs relative. That's more'n escape velocity for Earth."

"We let the ship get captured by Titan," Raoul said triumphantly.

"Oh," Harry said. "Oh. Dump eight or nine klicksecs—"

"Sure," Raoul went on, punching keys. "Easy. A tenth gee for two-and-a-half hours. Or make it easy on our-selves, a hundredth of a gee for a little more than a day. Uh, twenty-five and a half hours. A hundredth gee isn't enough to make pee trickle down your leg, even if you're free-fall adapted."

I had actually managed to follow most of the salient points—computer display is a wondrous aid for the ig-norant. "Okay then," I said sharply, in my "pay attention, here comes your blocking" voice, focusing everyone's attention by long habit. "Okay. This thing can be done. We've been talking it over ever since two hours before your shuttle docked here. I've told you what they want of us, and why they want all of us. My inclination is to tell you to have your answers ready along about next fall. But the bus is leaving soon. That launch window business you mentioned, Raoul." Harry's eyes flashed suspiciously, and yes, Tom too had picked up on the improbability of such luck. "So," I went on doggedly, "I have to ask for your final answers within the hour. I know that's pre-posterous, but there's no choice." I sighed. "I advise you to use the hour."

"Damn it, Charlie," Tom said in real anger, "is this a family or isn't it?"

"I—"

"What kind of shit is that?" Raoul agreed. "A man shouldn't insult his friends."

Linda and Harry also looked offended.

"Listen, you idiots," I said, giving it my very best shot, "*this is forever*. You'll never ski again, never swim, never walk around under even Lunar gravity. You'll never take a shit without technological assistance again."

"Where on Earth can you take a shit without technological assistance today?" Linda asked.

"Come on," I barked, "don't give me satire, *think about it*. Do I have to get personal? Harry—Raoul—how many women you figure you're going to date in space? How many would leave behind a whole world to stay with you? Seriously, now. Linda—Tom—do you know of any evidence at all to suggest that childbirth is *possible* in free fall? Do you want to bet two lives someday? Or had you planned to opt for sterilization? Now the four of you stop talking like comic book heroes and *listen to me*, God dammit." I discovered to my transient surprise that I genuinely was blazing mad; my tension was perfectly happy to find release as anger. I realized, for the first time, that a little histrionics can be a dangerous thing. "We have no way of knowing whether we can communicate with the goddam fireflies. On a gamble with odds that long, stakes this high, two lives is enough to risk. *We don't need you guys anyway*," I shouted, and then I caught myself.

"No," I went on finally, "that's a lie.. I won't try to claim that. But we can *do* it without you if it can be done at all. Norrey and I have personal reasons for going—but what do *you* people want to throw away a planet for?"

There was a glutinous silence. I had done my best; Norrey had nothing to add. I watched four blank, expressionless faces and waited.

At last Linda stirred. "We'll solve zero-gee childbirth," she said with serene confidence, and added, "when we have to," a second later.

Tom had forgotten his discomfort. He looked long at Linda, smiling with puffy lips amid his burst capillaries, and said to her, "I was raised in New York. I've known cities all my life. I never realized how much tension was involved in city life until I stayed at your family's home for a week. And I never realized how much I hated that tension until I noticed how much I was getting to dread having to go dirtside again. You only realize how stiff your neck and shoulders were when someone rubs them out for you." He touched her cheek with blood-purple fingernails. "It will be a long time before we have to put a lock on our airlock. Sure, we'll have a child someday—and we won't have to teach it how to adapt to a jungle."

She smiled, and took his purple fingers in her own. "We won't have to teach it how to walk."

"In zero gee," Raoul said meditatively, "I'm taller." I thought he meant the few centimeters that every spine stretches in free fall, but then he said, "In zero gee *nobody* is short."

By golly, he was right. "Eye-level" is a meaningless term in space; consequently so is height.

But his voice was speculative; he had not committed himself yet.

Harry sucked beer from a bulb, belched, and studied the ceiling. "On my mind. For a long time. This adapting stuff. I could work all year insteada half. See a job through for once. Was thinking of doing it anyway." He looked at Raoul. "Don't figure I'll miss the ladies any."

Raoul met his eyes squarely. "Me either," he said, and this time his voice held commitment.

Light dawned in the cerebral caverns, and my jaw hung down. "Jesus Christ in a p-suit!"

"It's just a blind spot, Charlie," Linda said compassionately.

She was right. It has nothing to do with wisdom or maturity or how observant I am. It's just a personal quirk, a blind spot: I never will learn to notice love when it's under my nose.

"Norrey," I said accusingly. "You know I'm an idiot, why didn't you *tell* me? Norrey?"

She was sound asleep.

And all four of them were laughing like hell at me, and after a second I had to laugh too. Any man who does not know himself a fool is a damned fool; any man who tries to hide it is a double-damned fool, for he is alone. Together, we laughed, diminishing my foolishness to a shared thing, and Norrey stirred and half-smiled in her sleep.

"All right," I said when I could get my breath, "someone for all and all for someone. I won't try to fight the weather. I love you all, and will be glad of your company. Tom, you stretch out and get some sleep yourself; Raoul, get the light; the four of us'll go get briefed and come back for you and Norrey, Tom; we'll pack your comic books and your other tunic. You still mass around seventy-two, right?" I bent and kissed Norrey's forehead. "Let's *roll* it."

# 3

## Starseed

# *Chapter 1*

It was a week after that day that we next found an opportunity to all talk together—and we spent the first hour and a half of our opportunity in relative silence. A week locked in a steel can with many strangers had turned out to be even less fun than a comparable period with as many students. Most of these strangers were our employers, the other two were our Space Command keepers, none of them were our subordinates and nearly all of them were temperamentally unsuited to live with artists. All things considered, we handled the close quarters and tension much better than we had in the early days of the Studio—which surprised me.

But as soon as we could, we all went out for a stroll together. And discovered that we had *much* more important things to do than compare notes, first.

Distance shrank the mighty *Siegfried*, but refused to turn it into a Space Commando model; it retained its massive dignity even when viewed from truly Olympian perspective. I felt an uncharacteristic rush of pride at belonging to the species that had built it and hurled it at the sky. It lightened my mood like a shot of oxygen. I tugged at the three kilometers of line that connected me to the great ship, enjoyed the vast snakelike ripples I caused, let their influence put me in a slow roll like an infinite swan dive.

Space turned around me.

Tom and Linda came into view. I didn't call out to them—their breathing told me that they were in deep meditative trance, and my eyes told me how they had got there. You take that oldest and most enduring of children's toys, the Slinky. You weld thin flat plates on either end, and bring the accordionlike result out into free space. You place the plates together, so that the Slinky describes a circle. Then you let go. Watch the result for long enough, and you will go into deep trance. The Worm Ourobouros endlessly copulating with himself. They would hear me if I called them by name; they would hear nothing else.

Raoul came into frame next, seen side-on to me. With deadly, matter-of-fact accuracy, he and Harry were hurling that other most durable of toys—a Frisbee (neon-rimmed for visibility)—back and forth across a couple of kilometers of emptiness. This too was more a meditational exercise than anything else; there is next to no skill involved. A flying saucer, it turns out, really *is* the most dynamically stable shape for a spacecraft. (Take a missile shaped like the old science fiction spaceships, fins and all, and throw it any way you want, with "Kentucky rifle" spin or without: sooner or later it will tumble. A sphere is okay—but unless it was formed in free fall, it's imperfect: it'll wobble, worse and worse as it goes.) They were practiced partners; their thruster was minimal.

Norrey was skipping rope with a bight of her lifeline. Naturally she was rotating in the opposite direction. It was incredibly beautiful to watch, and I canceled my rotation to enjoy it. Perhaps, I thought lazily, we could work that into a dance someday. Dynamic balance, yin and yang, as simple and as complex as a hydrogen atom.

*"Don't atoms dance, Charlie?"*

I stiffened, then grinned at myself and relaxed. *You can't haunt me, Shara*, I told the hallucinatory voice. *You and I are at peace. Without me you could never have done the thing you did; without you I might never have been whole again. Rest in peace.*

I watched Norrey some more, in a curiously detached state of mind. Considered objectively, my wife was nowhere near as stunningly beautiful as her dead sister had been. Just strikingly beautiful. And never once in the decades of our bizarre relationship had I ever felt for Norrey the kind of helpless consuming passion I had felt for Shara every minute of the few years I knew her. Thank God. I remembered that passion, that mindless worship that sees a scuff on an apartment floor and says *There she placed her foot*, that sees a battered camera and says *With that I taped her*. The sleepless nights and the rivers of scotch and the insulted hookers and the terrible awakenings; through it all the continuous yearning that nothing will abate and only the presence of the loved one will assuage. My passion for Shara had died, vanished forever, almost at the same moment that she did. Norrey had been right, two years ago in Le Maintenant: you only conceive a passion like that for someone you think you can't have. And the very worst thing that can happen to you is to be wrong.

Shara had been very kind to me.

The love I now shared with Norrey was much quieter, much gentler on the nervous system. Why, I'd managed to overlook it for years. But it was a richer kind of love in the end.

Look, I used this metaphor before I ever *dreamed* of coming to space, and it's still good. Picture us all as being in free fall, all of us that are alive. Literally falling freely, at one gee, down a tube so unimaginably long that its ultimate bottom cannot be seen. The vast tube is studded with occasional obstacles—and the law of averages says that at some finite future time you will smash into one:

you will die. There are literally billions of us in this tube, all falling, all sure to hit some day; we carom off each other all the time, whirling more or less at random in and out of lives and groups of lives. Most of us construct belief-structures which deny either the falling or the obstacles, and place them underneath our feet like skateboards. A good rider can stay on for a lifetime.

Occasionally you reach out and take a stranger's hand, and fall together for a while. It's not so bad, then. Some-times if you're really desperate with fear, you clutch some-one like a drowning man clinging to an anchor, or you strive hopelessly to reach someone in a different trajectory, someone you can't possibly reach, just to be doing some-thing to make you forget that your death is rushing up toward you.

That was the kind of need I had had for Shara. I had learned better, from her and from space, and finally from my Last Ride with Norrey a week ago. I had reconciled myself to falling. Norrey and I now fell through life together with great serenity, enjoying the view with a truly binocular vision.

"Has it occurred to any of you," I asked lazily, "that living in space has just about matured us to the point of early childhood?"

Norrey giggled and stopped skipping. "What do you mean, love?"

Raoul laughed. "It's obvious. Look at us. A Slinky, a Frisbee, and a jump rope. The thrusting apex of modern culture, kids in the biggest playground God ever made."

"On tethers," Norrey said, "like country kids, to keep us out of the garden."

"Feels good to me," Harry put in.

Linda was coming out of meditation; her voice was slow, soft. "Charlie is right. We have matured enough to become childlike."

"That's closer to what I meant," I said approvingly. "Play is play, whether it's a tennis racquet or a rattle. I'm not talking about the kinds of toys we choose, so much. It's more like. . . ." I paused to think, and they waited. "Listen, it seems to me that I have felt like an old old man since I was about, what, nine years old. This past few years has been the adolescence I never had, and now I'm happy as a child again."

Linda began to sing:

> " 'Can't remember when I've ever been so happy
> Happier than I can say
> I used to feel older than my own grandpappy
> But I'm getting younger every day'

"It's an old Nova Scotia song," she finished quietly.

"Teach it to me," Raoul said.

"Later. I want to pursue this thought."

So did I—but just then my alarm watch went off. I fumbled the stud home through the p-suit, and it subsided. "Sorry, gang. Halfway through our air. Let's get together for the group exercises. Form up on Linda and we'll try the Pulsing Snowflake."

"Shit—work again?" "Phooey—we've got a year to get into shape," "Wait'll I catch this sonumbitch, boss," and "Let's get it over with," were the entirely natural-sounding responses to the code phrase. We closed ranks and diddled with our radios.

"There we go," I said as I closed. "Right, and Harry, you cross over and take Tom's . . . that's right. Wait, *look out!* Oh Christ!" I screamed.

"No!" Harry shouted.

"Ohmigod," Raoul bubbled, "Ohmigod his suit's ripped *his suit's ripped.* Somebody *do* something, ohmigod—"

"May Day," I roared. "*Siegfried* from Stardancers, May Day, God damn it. We've got a blown suit, I don't think I can fix it, *answer me,* will you?"

Silence, except for Harry's horrible gurgling.

"*Siegfried,* for the love of God, come *in.* One of your precious interpreters is dying out here!"

Silence.

Raoul swore and raged, Linda said calming things to him, Norrey prayed softly.

Silence.

"I guess that damper circuit works, Harry," I said approvingly at last. "We've got privacy. By the way, that gurgling was horrible."

"When did I have a chance to rehearse?"

"You got that heavy-breathing tape going?"

"In circuit," Harry agreed. "Heavy breathing and cadence counts, no repeats. Hour and a half's worth."

"So if anyone's listening, they're just, uh, getting into our pants," Raoul said almost inevitably.

"*O*-kay," I said, "let's talk family talk. We've each spent some time with our assigned partners. What's the consensus?"

Some more silence.

"Well, has anybody got presentiments of doom? Choice gossip? Tom? You follow politics, you knew most of these people by reputation anyway. Tell us all about that first, and then we can compare personal impressions."

"All right, let's see—is there anything to be said about DeLaTorre? If he is not a man of honor and compassion, no one is. Even his critics admire him, and a good half of them are willing to admit it. I'll be honest: I'm not as certain of *Wertheimer*'s integrity as I am of DeLaTorre's. Except of course that he *picked* DeLaTorre to head this posse, which raises him a notch. Anybody feel different? Charlie, he's your puppetmaster, what do you say?"

"A heartfelt ditto. I'd turn my back on him in the airlock. Go on."

"Ludmilla Dmirov has a similar reputation for moral toughness, unpusharoundable. She was the first diplomatic official ever to turn down a state-owned *dacha* in Sovmin. Those of you who don't know *nomenklatura*, the patronage system in Moscow, a *dacha* is sort of a country cabin for high-ranking officials, and turning one down is like a freshman senator refusing to vacation or junket, or a rookie cop turning down the usuals. Unthinkable . . . and dangerous." He paused. "But I can't be as certain that it's integrity with her. It may just be orneriness. And compassionate she is *not*."

Norrey was assigned to Dmirov; she spoke up. "I'm not sure I agree, Tom. Oh, she plays chess like a machine, and she sure knows how to be impenetrable—and maybe she *doesn't* know enough about when and how to turn it off. But she showed me all her son's baby pictures, and she told me that the *Stardance* made her cry. 'Weep from the chest,' she said. I think the compassion's in there."

"Okay," Tom said. "I'll take your word. And she *was* one of the ones who pushed hard for a UN Space Command. Without her there just might not *be* a UN anymore, and space might have become the next Alsace-Lorraine. I'm willing to believe her heart's in the right place." He paused again. "Uh, with all due respect, I don't think I'd be prepared to turn my back on her in the airlock yet. But my mind's open.

"Now, Li," he went on, "was also a prime mover in the formation of the Space Command—but I'll lay odds that it was a chess-player's move for him. I think he took a cold extrapolative look at the future and decided that if the world *did* blow itself up over the issue of space, it would seriously restrict his political career. He is reputed to be one sharp horse trader and one cold son of a bitch, and they say the road to Hell is paved with the skins of his enemies. He owns a piece of Skyfac Inc. I wouldn't turn my back on him on live network TV, and Linda, I hope you won't either."

"That is certainly the image he has cultivated," she agreed. "But I must add a few things. He is impeccably polite. He is a philosopher of incredible perception and subtlety. And he is rock steady. Hunger, lack of sleep, danger—none of these will affect his performance or his judgment in any measurable way. Yet I find his mind to be open, to change and to changes. I believe he might well be a real *statesman*." She broke off, took a deep breath, and finished, "But I don't think I trust him either. Yet."

"Yeah," Tom said. "Is he a statesman for mankind or for the People's Republic? Okay, that leaves my own man. Whatever else you can say about the others, they're probably all statespersons. Sheldon Silverman is a politician. He's held just about every elective office except President and Vice President. He could have been the latter any time he was silly enough to want to; only some incredibly subtle errors cost him the former. I think he bought or bribed his way onto this trip somehow, as his last chance to earn a whole page in the history books. I think he sees *himself* as the leader of the team, by virtue of being an American. I despise him. He costs Wertheimer the notch that DeLaTorre earned him, as far as I'm concerned." He shut up suddenly.

"I think you may be holding his past against him," Linda said.

"Damn right," he agreed.

"Well—he's old. Some old people change, quite radically. Zero gee has been working on him; wait and see. We should bring him out here some time."

"My love, your fairness is showing."

"Damn right," she said, forcing a grin from him. "It sort of has to."

"Huh?"

"He gives me the *creeps*."

"Oh. I see. I think."

"Harry, Raoul," I said, "you've been hanging out with the Space Commandos."

Raoul took it, of course. "Cox we all know or know about. I'd let him hold the last air bottle while I took a leak. His second-in-command is an old-time NASA science officer type."

"Jock," Harry put in.

Raoul chuckled. "You know, she is. Susan Pha Song

was a Viet Nam War baby, raised in Nam by her aunt after her father split and her mother got napalmed. Hasn't got much use for America. Physicist. Military through and through; if they told her to she'd nuke Viet Nam and drop rose petals on Washington. She disapproves of music and dance. And me and Harry."

"She'll follow orders," Harry asserted.

"Yeah. For sure. She's a chicken colonel as of last week, and in the event Commander Cox drops dead, the chain of command goes to her, then Dmirov, presumably. She's got pilot training, she's a space freak."

"If it comes to that extreme," I said, "I for one am going free lance."

"Chen Ten Li has a gun," Linda said suddenly.

"*What?*" Five voices at once.

"What kind?" from Harry.

"Oh, I don't know. A small handgun, squarish looking. Not much barrel."

"How did you get a look at it?" I asked.

"Jack-in-the-box effect. Took him by surprise, and he recovered late."

The jack-in-the-box effect is one of the classic surprises of free fall, predictable but unexpected, and it gets virtually every new fish. Any container, cabinet or drawer you open will spew its contents at you—unless you have thought to velcro them all in place. The practical joke possibilities are nearly inexhaustible. But I smelled a rat. "How about that, Tom?"

"Eh?"

"If Chen Ten Li has been one of the major forces behind intelligent use of space, wouldn't he know about jack-in-the-box?"

Tom's voice was thoughtful. "*Huh.* Not necessarily. Li is one of those paradoxes, like Isaac Asimov refusing to fly. For all his understanding of the issues of space, this is the first time he's been further off-planet than a jetliner goes. He's a groundlubber at heart."

"Still," I objected, "jack-in-the-box is standard tourist anecdote. He'd only need have spoken with one returned spacegoer, for any length of time."

"I don't know about the rest of you," Raoul said, "but there was a lot about zero gee that I knew about intellectually, that I still tripped over when I got there. Besides, what motive could Li have for letting Linda see a gun?"

"That's what bothers me," I admitted. "I can think of two or three reasons offhand—and they all imply either great clumsiness or great cunning. I don't know which I'd prefer. Well . . . anyone else see any heat?"

"I haven't seen a thing," Norrey said judiciously, "but I wouldn't be surprised if Ludmilla has a weapon of some kind."

"Anybody else?"

Nobody responded. But each of the diplomats had fetched a sizable mass of uninspected luggage.

"Okay. So the upshot is, we're stuck in a subway with three rival gangleaders, two cops and a nice old man. This is one of the few times I've ever been grateful that the eyes of the world are upon us."

"Much more than the eyes of the world," Linda corrected soberly.

"It'll be okay," Raoul said. "Remember: a diplomat's whole function is to maintain hostilities short of armed conflict. They'll all pull together at the showdown. Most of 'em may be chauvinists—but underneath I think they're all *human* chauvinists, too."

"That's what I mean," Linda said. "Their interests and ours may not coincide."

Startled silence, then, "What do you mean, darling? We're not human?" from Tom.

"Are we?"

I began to understand what she was driving at, and I felt my mind accelerate to meet her thought.

What does it mean to be human? Considering that the

overwhelming mass of the evidence has been taken from observation of humans under one gravity, pinned against a planet? By others in the same predicament?

"Certainly," Tom said. "Humans are humans whether they float or fall."

"Are you sure?" Linda asked softly. "We are different from our fellows, different in basic ways. I don't mean just that we can never go back and live with them. I mean spiritually, psychologically. Our thought patterns change, the longer we stay in space—our brains are adapting just like our bodies."

I told them what Wertheimer had said to me the week before—that we choreographed as well as humans but not like humans.

"That's John Campbell's classic definition of 'alien,'" Raoul said excitedly.

"Our souls are adapting, too," Linda went on. "Each of us spends every working day gazing on the naked face of God, a sight that groundhogs can only simulate with vaulting cathedrals and massive mosques. We have more perspective on reality than a holy man on the peak of the highest mountain on Earth. There are no atheists in space —and *our* gods make the hairy thunderers and bearded paranoids of Earth look silly. Hell, you can't even make out Olympus from the Studio—much less from here." The distant Earth and Moon were already smaller than we were used to.

"There's no denying that space is a profoundly moving place," Tom maintained, "but I don't see that it makes us other than human. I *feel* human."

"How did Cro-Magnon know he was different from Neanderthal?" Raoul asked. "Until he could assess discrepancies, how would he know?"

"The swan thought he was an ugly duckling," Norrey said.

"But his *genes* were swan," Tom insisted.

"Cro-Magnon's genes started out Neanderthal," I said. "Have you ever examined yours? Would you know a really subtle mutation if you saw one?"

"Don't tell me you're buying into this silliness, Charlie?" Tom asked irritably. "Do you feel inhuman?"

I felt detached, listening with interest to the words that came out of my mouth: "I feel other than human. I feel like more than a new man. I'm a new thing. Before I followed Shara into space, my life was a twisted joke, with too many punchlines. Now I am alive. I love and can be loved. I didn't leave Earth behind. I put space ahead."

"Aw, phooey," Tom said. "Half of that's your leg—and I know what the other half is because it happened to me, at Linda's family's place. It's the city-mouse-in-the-country effect. You find a new, less stressful environment, get some insights, and start making better, more satisfying decisions. Your life straightens out. So something must be magic about the place. Nuts."

"The Mountain *is* magic," Linda said gently. "Why is magic a dirty word for you?" At that stage of their relationship, it suited Tom and Linda to maintain a running pseudodisagreement on matters spiritual. Occasionally they realized what was obvious to the rest of us: that they almost never actually disagreed with each other on anything but semantics.

"Tom," I said insistently, "this is *different*. I've *been* to the country. I'm telling you that I'm not an improved version of the man I was—I'm something altogether different now. I'm the man I could never have been on Earth, had lost all hope of being. I—I believe in things that I haven't believed in since I was a kid. Sure I've had some good breaks, and sure, opening up to Norrey has made my life more than I ever thought it could be. But my whole makeup has changed, and no amount of lucky breaks will do that. Hell, I used to be a drunk."

"Drunks smarten up every day," Tom said.

"Sure—if they can find the strength to maintain cold turkey for the rest of their lives. I take a drink when I feel like it. I just hardly ever feel like it. I stopped *needing* booze, just like that. How common is that? I smoke less these days, and treat it less frivolously when I do."

"So space grew you up in spite of yourself?"

"At first. Later I had to pitch in and work like hell—but it started without my knowledge or consent."

"When did it begin?" Norrey and Linda asked together.

I had to think. "When I began to learn how to see spherically. When I finally learned to cut loose of up and down."

Linda spoke. "A reasonably wise man once said that anything that disorients you is good. Is instructive."

"I know that wise man," Tom sneered. "Leary. Brain-damage case if I ever heard of one."

"Does that make him incapable of having ever been wise?"

"Look," I said, "we are all unique. We've all come through a highly difficult selection process, and I don't suppose the first Cro-Magnon *felt* any different. But the overwhelming evidence suggests that our talent is not a normal human attribute."

"Normal people can live in space," Norrey objected. "Space Command crews. Construction gangs."

"If they've got an artificial local vertical," Harry said. "Take 'em outdoors, you gotta give 'em straight lines and right angles or they start going buggy. Most of 'em. S'why we get rich."

"That's true," Tom admitted. "At Skyfac a good outside man was worth his mass in copper, even if he was a mediocre worker. Never understood it."

"Because you are one," Linda said.

"One *what*?" he said, exasperated.

"A Space Man," I said, spacing it so the capitals were apparent. "Whatever comes after *Homo habilis* and *Homo sapiens*. You're space-going Man. I don't think the Romans had the concept, so *Homo novis* is probably the best you can do in Latin. New Man. The next thing."

Tom snorted. "*Homo excastra* is more like it."

"No, Tom," I said forcefully, "you're wrong. We're *not* outcasts. We may be literally 'outside the camp,' 'outside the fortress'—but the connotation of 'exile' is all wrong. Or are you regretting the choice you made?"

He was a long time answering. "No. No, space is where I want to live, all right. I don't feel exiled—I think of the whole solar system as 'human territory.' But I feel like I've let my citizenship in its largest nation lapse."

"Tom," I said solemnly, "I assure you that that is the diametric opposite of a loss."

"Well, the world does look pretty rotten these days, I'll grant you that. There isn't a *lot* of it I'll miss."

"You miss my point."

"So explain."

"I talked about this with Doc Panzella some, before we left. What is the normal lifespan for a Space Man?"

He started to speak twice, stopped trying.

"Right. There's no way to frame a guess—it's a completely new ball game. We're the first. I asked Panzella, and he told me to come back when two or three of us had died. We may all die within a month, because fatigue products refuse to collect in our feet or our corns migrate to our brains or something. But Panzella's guess is that free fall is going to add at *least* forty years to our lifespans. I asked him how sure he was and he offered to bet cash."

Everyone started talking at once, which doesn't work on radio. The consensus was, "Say *what*?" The last to shut up and drop out was Tom. "—possibly *know* a thing like that, yet?" he finished, embarrassed.

"Exactly," I said. "We won't *know* 'til it's too late. But it's *reasonable*. Your heart has less work to do, arterial deposits seem to diminish—"

"So it won't be heart trouble that gets us," Tom stipulated, "assuming that lowering the work load drastically turns out to be good for a heart. But that's one organ out of many."

"Think it through, Tom. Space is a sterile environment. With reasonable care it always will be. Your immune system becomes almost as superfluous as your semicircular canals—and do you have any idea how much energy fighting off thousands of wandering infections drains from your life system? That might have been used for maintenance and repair? Or don't you notice your energy level drop when you go dirtside?"

"Well sure," he said, "but that's just. . . ."

"—the gravity, you were gonna say? See what I mean? We're healthier, physically and mentally, than we *ever* were on Earth. When did you ever have a cold in space? For that matter, when was the last time you got deeply depressed, morose? How come we hardly ever, any of us, have dog days, black depressions and sulks and the like? Hell, the *word* depression is tied to gravity. You *can't* depress something in space, you can only move it. And the very word gravity has come to be a synonym for humorlessness. If there's two things that'll kill you early it's depression and lack of a sense of humor."

In a vivid rush came the memory of what it had felt like to live with a defective leg under one gravity. Depression, and an atrophying sense of humor. It seemed so long ago, so very far away. Had I ever really been that despairing?

"Anyway," I went on, "Panzella says that people who spend a lot of time in free fall—and even the people in Luna who stay in one-sixth gee, those exile/miners—show a lower incidence of heart and lung trouble, naturally. But he also says they show a much lower incidence of cancers of all kinds than the statistical norm."

"Even with the higher radiation levels?" Tom asked skeptically. Whenever there's a solar flare, we all see green polliwogs for awhile, as the extra radiation impacts our eyeballs—and it doesn't make any difference whether we're indoors or out.

"Yep," I assured him. "Coming out from under the atmosphere blanket was the main health hazard we all gambled on in living in space—but it seems to've paid off. It *seemed* there should have been a *higher* risk of cancer, but it just doesn't seem to be turning out that way. Go ask why. And the lower lung trouble is obvious—we breath real air, better filtered than the Prime Minister's, dust free and zero pollen count. Hell, if you had all the money on Earth, you couldn't have a healthier environment tailor-made. How about old Mrs. Murphy on Skyfac? What is she, sixty-five?"

"Sixty-six," Raoul said. "And free-fall handball champ. She whipped my ass, three games running."

"It's almost as though we were *designed* to live in space," Linda said wonderingly.

"All right," Tom cried in exasperation. "All right, I give up. I'm sold. We're all going to live to be a hundred and twenty. Assuming that the aliens don't decide we're delicious. But I still say that this 'new species' nonsense is muddy thinking, delusions of grandeur. For one thing, there's no guarantee we'll breed true—or, as Charlie pointed out, at all. But more important, *Homo novis* is a 'species' without a natural habitat! *We're not self-sustaining*, friends! We're utterly dependent on *Homo sapiens*, unless and until we learn how to make our own air, water, food, metals, plastics, tools, cameras—"

"What are you so pissed off about?" Harry asked.

"I'm not pissed off!" Tom yelled.

We all broke up, then, and Tom was honest enough to join us after a while.

"All right," he said. "I am angry. I'm honestly not sure why. Linda, do you have any handles on it?"

"Well," she said thoughtfully, " 'anger' and 'fear' are damned close to synonyms. . . ."

Tom started.

Raoul spoke up, his voice strained. "If it will help any, I will be glad to confess that our pending appointment with these super-fireflies has me, for one, scared shitless. And *I* haven't met 'em personally like you and Charlie have. I mean, this little caper could cost us a lot more than just Earth."

That was such an odd sentence that we just let it sit there a while.

"I know what you mean," Norrey said slowly. "Our job is to establish telepathic rapport with what seems to be a group-mind. I'm almost . . . almost afraid I might succeed."

"Afraid you might get lost, darling?" I said. "Forget it— I wouldn't let go of you long enough. I didn't wait twenty years to be a widower." She squeezed my hand.

"That's the point," Linda said. "The worst we're facing is death, in one form or another. And we always *have* been under sentence of death, all of us, for being human. That's the ticket price for this show. Norrey, you and Charlie looked death right in the eye a week ago. Sure as hell you will again some day. It might turn out to be a year from now, at Saturn: so what?"

"That's the trouble," Tom said, shaking his head. "Fear doesn't go away just because it's illogical."

"No," Linda agreed, "but there *are* methods for dealing with it—and repressing it until it comes out as anger is *not* one of them. Now that we're down to the root, though, I can teach you techniques of self-discipline that'll at least help a lot."

"Teach me too," Raoul said, almost inaudibly.

Harry reached out and took his hand. "We'll learn together," he said.

"We'll all learn together," I said. "Maybe we are other than human, but we're not *that* different. But I would like to say that you are about the bravest folks I know, all of you. If anybody—wups! There goes the alarm again. Let's get some real dancing done, so we come home sweaty. We'll do this again in a couple of days. Harry, take that heavy-breathing tape out of circuit and we'll boost our signal strength together at three, two, one, *mark*."

I repeat the above conversation in its entirety partly because it is one of the few events in this chronicle of which I possess a complete audio recording. But also partly because it contains most of the significant information you need to know about that one-year trip to Saturn. There is no point in describing the interior of *Siegfried*, or the day-to-day schedules or the month-by-month objectives or the interpersonal frictions that filled up one of the most busy, boring years of my life.

As is common and perhaps inevitable on expeditions of this kind, crew, diplomats, and dancers formed three reasonably tight cliques outside working hours, and maintained an uneasy peace during them. Each group had its own interests and amusements—the diplomats, for instance, spent much of their free time (and a substantial percentage of their working time) fencing, politely and otherwise. DeLaTorre's patience soon earned the respect of every person aboard. Read any decent book on life in a submarine, then throw in free fall, and you've got that year. Raoul's music helped keep as all sane, though; he became the only other universally respected passenger.

The six of us somehow never discussed the "new species" line of thought again together, although I know Norrey and I kicked it around hood-to-hood a few times, and Linda and I spoke of it occasionally. And of course we never mentioned it *at all* anywhere aboard *Siegfried*—spaceships are *supposed* to be thoroughly bugged. The notion that we six dancers were somehow other-than-human was not one that even DeLaTorre would have cared for—and he was about the only one who treated us as anything but hired hands, "mere interpreters" (Silverman's expression). Dmirov and Li knew better, I believe, but they couldn't help it; as experienced diplomats they were not conditioned to accept interpreters as social equals. Silverman thought dance was that stuff they did on variety shows, and why *couldn't* we translate the concept of Manifest Destiny into a dance?

I will say one thing about that year. The man I had been when I first came to space could not have survived it. He'd have blown out his brains, or drunk himself to death.

Instead I went out for lots of walks. And made lots of love with Norrey. With music on, for privacy.

Other than that the only event of note was when Linda announced that she was pregnant, about two months out of Saturn. We were committed to solving zero-gee childbirth without an obstetrician. Or, for that matter, a GP.

Things got livelier as we neared Saturn.

# *Chapter* 2

We had not succeeded in persuading any of the diplomats to join us in EVA of any kind. Three refused for the predictable reason. EVA is measurably more dangerous than staying safely indoors (as I had been forcibly reminded on the day I had gotten into this), and duty forbade them from taking *any* avoidable risk on their way to what was literally the biggest and most important conference in history. We dancers were considered more expendable, but pressure was put on us to avoid having all four dancers outboard at the same time. I stuck to my guns, maintaining that a group dance must be planned, choreographed, and rehearsed *ensemble*—that what Stardancers, Inc. *was*, was a creative collective. Besides, the more buddies you have, the safer you are.

The fourth diplomat, Silverman, had been specifically ordered not to expose himself to space. So early on he asked us to take him out for a walk. Sort of a "they can't tell a fearless SOB like me not to take risks," thing: the order impugned his masculinity. He changed his mind when p-suit plumbing was explained to him, and never brought the subject up again.

But a few weeks before we were to begin deceleration,

Linda came to my room and said, "Chen Ten Li wants to come out for a walk with us."

I winced, and did my Silverman imitation. "It would kill you, first to sit me down and say, 'I have bad news for you'? Like that you tell me?"

"Like that *he* told *me*."

What would DeLaTorre think? Or Bill? Or the others? Or old Wertheimer, who had told me with his eyes that he believed I could be trusted not to fuck up? And as important, why did Chen now want to earn his wings? Not for scenery—he had first-class video, the best Terra could provide, which is *good*. Not for jackass reasons like Silverman.

"What does he *want*, Linda? To see a rehearsal live? To drift and meditate? What?"

"Ask him."

I had never seen the ins. . of Chen's room before. He was playing 3-D chess with the computer. I can barely follow the game, but it was clear that he was losing badly —which surprised me.

"Dr. Chen, I understand you want to come outside with us."

He was dressed in tastefully lavish pajamas, which he had expertly taken in for free fall and velcro'd (Dmirov and DeLaTorre had been forced to ask Raoul for help, and Silverman's clothes looked as though he had backed into a sewing machine). He inclined his shaven head, and replied gravely, "As soon as possible." His voice was like an old cornet, a little feathery.

"That puts me in a difficult position, sir," I said as gravely. "You are under orders not to endanger yourself. DeLaTorre and all the others know it. And if I did bring you outside, and you had a suit malf, or even a nausea attack, the People's Republic of China would ask me some pointed questions. Followed by the Dominion of Canada and the United Nations, not to mention your aged mother."

He smiled politely, with lots of wrinkles. "Is that outcome probable?"

"Do you know Murphy's Law, Dr. Chen? And its corollary?"

His smile widened. "I wish to risk it. You are experienced at introducing neophytes to space."

"I lost two out of seventeen students!"

"How many did you lose in their first three hours, Mr. Armstead? Could I not remain in the Die, wearing a pressure suit for redundancy?"

The Die wasn't cast; it was spot-welded. It was essentially an alloy-framed cube of transparent plastic, outfitted for minimal life support, first aid, and self-locomotion through free space. The crew and all the diplomats except Chen called it the Field Support Module. This disgusted Harry, who had designed and built it. The idea was that one of us Stardancers might blow a gasket in midconference, or want to sit out a piece, or conserve air, or for some other reason need a pressurized cubic with a 360° view. It was currently braced tight against the hull of the big shuttlecraft we called the Limousine, mounted for use, but it could easily be unshipped. And Chen's pressure suit was regulation Space Command armor, as good as or better than even our customized Japanese-made suits. Certainly stronger; better air supply. . . .

"Doctor, I have to know why."

His smile began to slo-o-owly fade, and when I hadn't blanched or retracted by half past, he let it remain there. About a quarter to frowning. "I concede your right to ask the question. I am not certain I can satisfy you at this time." He reflected, and I waited. "I am not accustomed to using an interpreter. I have facility with languages. But there is at least one language I will never acquire. I was once informed that no one could learn to think in Navajo who was not raised a Navajo. Consequently I went to great lengths to accomplish this, and I failed. I can make myself understood to a Navajo, haltingly. I cannot ever learn to think in that language—it is founded on basically different assumptions about reality that my mind cannot enfold.

"I have studied your dance, the 'language' you will speak for us shortly. I have discussed it with Ms. Parsons at great length, exhausted the ship's computer on the subject. I cannot learn to think in that language.

"I wish to try one more time. I theorize that confrontation with naked space, in person, may assist me." He paused, and grinned again. "Ingesting buds of peyote assisted me somewhat in my efforts with Navajo—as my tutor had promised me. I must expose myself to *your* assumptions about reality. I hope they taste better."

It was by far the longest speech I had gotten out of the epigrammatic Chen since the day we met. I looked at him with new respect, and some astonishment. And a growing pleasure: here was a friend I had almost missed making. *My God, suppose old Chen is* Homo novis?

"Dr. Chen," I said, when I could get my breath, "let's go see Commander Cox."

Chen listened with total absorption to eighteen hours' worth of instruction, most of which he already knew, and asked infrequent but highly insightful questions. I'm willing to bet that before the instruction he could have disassembled any subsystem in his suit in the dark. By the end I'd have bet he could *build* 'em in the dark, starting with free-floating components. I have been exposed to a rather high number of extraordinary minds, and he impressed me.

But I *still* wasn't sure I trusted him.

We held the party to three, on the less-to-go-wrong theory—in space, trouble seldom comes in ones. I was the obvious Scoutmaster; I had logged more EVA hours than anyone aboard except Harry. And Linda had been Chen's Alien 101 instructress for the past year; she came along to maintain classroom continuity. And to dance for him, while I played Mother Hen. And, I think, because she was his friend.

The first hour passed without incident, all three of us in the Die, me at the con. We put a few klicks between us and *Siegfried*, trailing a suspenders-*and*-belt safety line, and came to rest, as always, in the exact center of infinity. Chen was reverentially silent rather than awed, impressed rather than intimidated, absorbed rather than isolated. He was, I believe, capable of encompassing that much wonder —it was almost as though he had always known the universe was that big. Still he was speechless for a long time.

So were Linda and I, for that matter. Even at this distance Saturn looked unbelievably beautiful, beyond the power of words to contain. That planet must unquestionably be the damndest tourist attraction in the Solar System, and I had never seen anything so immensely moving in my life.

But we had seen it before in recent days—the whole ship's complement had been glued to the video tanks. We recovered, and Linda told Chen some last thoughts about the way we danced, and then she sealed her hood and went out the airlock to show him some solo work. By prearrangement we were all to remain silent for this period, and Bill too maintained radio silence on our channel. Chen watched with great fascination for three quarters of Linda's first hour. Then he sighed, glanced at me oddly, and kicked himself across the Die to the control panel.

I started to cry out—but what he reached for was only the Die's radio. He switched it off. Then he removed his helmet in one practiced-seeming move, disconnecting his suit's radio. I had my own hood off to save air, and grabbed for it when I saw him kill the radio, but he held a finger to his lips and said, "I would speak with you under the rose." His voice was thin and faint in the low pressure.

I considered the matter. Assuming the wildest paranoid

fantasy, Linda was mobile and could see anything that happened in the transparent cube. "Sure," I called.

"I sense your unease, and understand and respect it. I am going to put my hand in my right pouch and remove an object. It is harmless." He did so, producing one of those microcorders that looks like a fancy button. "I wish there to be truth between us," he added. Was it low pressure stridency alone that gave his voice that edge?

I groped for an appropriate response. Beyond him, Linda was whirling gracefully through space, sublimely pregnant, oblivious. "Sure," I said again.

He thumbnailed the playback niche. Linda's recorded voice said something that I couldn't hear, and I shook my head. He rewound to the same cue and underhanded it gently toward me.

"That's what I mean," Linda's voice repeated. "Their interests and ours may not coincide."

The tape record I spoke of a while ago.

My brain instantly went on computer time, became a hyperefficient thinking machine, ran a thousand consecutive analysis programs in a matter of microseconds, and self-destructed. *Hand in the cookie jar. Halfway down the Mountain and the brakes are gone. I'd have sworn I closed that airlock.* The microcorder hit me in the cheek; instinctively I caught it on the rebound and shut it off as Tom was asking Linda, "Aren't we human?"

And *that* echoed in the Die for a while.

"Only an imbecile would find it difficult to bug an unguarded pressure suit," Chen said tonelessly.

"Yeah," I croaked, and cleared my throat. "Yeah, that was stupid. Who else—?" I broke off and slapped my forehead. "*No*. I don't want to ask any stupid questions. Well, what do *you* think, Chen Ten Li? *Are* we *Homo novis*? Or just gifted acrobats? I'm God damned if I know."

He jaunted cleanly back to me, like an arrow in slow-motion flight. Cats jaunt like that. "*Homo caelestis*, perhaps," he said calmly, and his landing was clean. "Or possibly *Homo ala anima*."

"Allah who? Oh—'winged soul.' Huh. Okay. I'll buy that. Let me try a whammy on *you*, Doc. I'll bet a cookie that you're a 'winged soul' yourself. Potentially, at least."

His reaction astonished me. I had expected a sudden poker face. Instead naked grief splashed his face, stark loss and hopeless yearning, etched by Saturnlight. I never saw such wide-open emotion on his face before or since; it may be that no one but his aged mother and his dead wife ever had. It shocked me to my socks, and it would have shocked him too if he had been remotely aware of it.

"No, Mist' Armstead," he said bleakly, staring at Saturn over my shoulder. His accent slipped for the first and last time, and absurdly reminded me of Fat Humphrey. "No, I am not one of you. Nor can time or my will make it so. I *know* this. I am reconciled to this." As he got this far, his face began relaxing into its customary impassivity, all unconsciously. I marveled at the discipline of his subconscious mind, and interrupted him.

"*I* don't know that you're right. It seems to me that any man who can play three-D chess is a prime candidate for *Homo* Whateverthehell."

"Because you are ignorant of three-D chess," he said, "and of your own nature. Men play three-D chess on Earth. It was designed under one gravity, for a vertical player, and its classic patterns are linear. I have tried to play in free fall, with a set that is not fixed in that relationship to me, and I cannot. I can consistently beat the Martin-Daniels Program at flat chess" (world class) "but in free-fall three-D Mr. Brindle could easily defeat me, if I were unvain enough to play him. I can coordinate myself well enough aboard *Siegfried* or in this most linear of vehicles. But I can never learn to live for any length of time without what you call a 'local vertical.'"

"It comes on slow," I began.

"Five months ago," Li interrupted, "the night light failed in my room. I woke instantly. It took me twenty minutes to locate the light switches. During that entire time I wept with fear and misery, and lost control of my sphincters. The memory offended me, so I spent several weeks devising tests and exercises. I must have a local vertical to live. I am a normal human."

I was silent a long time. Linda had noticed our conversation; I signaled her to keep on dancing and she nodded. After I had thought things through I said, "Do you believe that our interests will fail to coincide with yours?"

He smiled, all diplomat again, and chuckled. "Are you familiar with Murphy's Law, Mr. Armstead?"

I grinned back. "Yeah, but is it *probable*?"

"I don't believe so," he answered seriously. "But I believe that Dmirov would believe so. Possibly Ezequiel. Possibly Commander Cox. Certainly Silverman."

"And we must assume that any of them might also have bugged a suit."

"Tell me: Do you agree that if this conference generates any information of great strategic value, Silverman will attempt to establish sole possession of it?"

Chatting with Chen was like juggling chainsaws. I sighed. We were being honest. "Yeah—if he got a chance to pull it off, sure. But that'd take some doing."

"One person with the right program tapes could bring *Siegfried* close enough to Terra for retrieval," he said, and I noticed that he didn't say "one man."

"Why are you telling me this?"

"I am presently jamming any possible bugs in this vehicle. I believe Silverman will attempt this thing. I smell it. If he does, I will kill him at once. You and your people react quickly in free fall; I want you to understand my motives."

"And they are?"

"Preservation of civilization on Terra. The continued existence of the human race."

I decided to try throwing *him* a hot one. "Will you shoot him with that automatic?"

He registered faint distaste. "I cycled that out the airlock two weeks after departure," he said. "An absurd weapon in free fall, as I should have realized. No, I shall probably break his back."

*Don't give this guy strong serves: his return is murder.*

"Where will you stand in that event, Mr. Armstead?"

"Eh?"

"Silverman is a fellow Caucasian, a fellow North American. You share a cultural matrix. Is that a stronger bond than your bond with *Homo caelestis*?"

"Eh?" I said again.

"Your new species will not survive long if the blue Earth is blown apart," Chen said harshly, "which is what that madman Silverman would have. I don't know *how* your mind works, Mr. Armstead: *what will you do*?"

"I respect your right to ask the question," I said slowly. "I will do what seems right to me at the time. I have no other answer."

He searched my face and nodded. "I would like to go outside now."

"Jesus Christ," I exploded, and he cut me off.

"Yes, I know—I just said I couldn't function in free space, and now I want to try." He gestured with his helmet. "Mr. Armstead, I anticipate that I may die soon. Once before that time I must hang alone in eternity, subject to no acceleration, without right angles for frames, in free space. I have dreamed of space for most of my life, and feared to enter it. Now I *must*. As nearly as I can say it in your language, I must confront my God."

I wanted to say yes. "Do you know how much that can resemble sensory deprivation?" I argued. "How'd you like to lose your ego in a space suit? Or even just your lunch?"

"I have lost my ego before. Someday I will forever. I do not get nauseous." He began putting his helmet on.

"No, dammit, watch out for the nipple. Here, let me do it."

After five minutes he switched his radio back on and said, shakily, "I'm coming in now." After that he didn't say anything until we were unbuttoning in *Siegfried's* shuttlecraft bay. Then he said, very softly, "It is I who am *Homo excastra*. And the others," and those were the last words he said to me until the first day of Second Contact.

What I replied was, "You are always welcome in my home, Doctor," but he made no reply.

Deceleration brought a horde of minor disasters. If you move into a small apartment (and never leave it) by the end of a year your belongings will have tended to *spread out* considerably. Zero gee amplifies the tendency. Storing *everything* for acceleration would have been impossible even if all we'd had to contend with was the twenty-five hours of a hundredth gee. But even the straightest, laser-sighted pipeline has some kinks in it, and our course was one of the longest pipelines ever laid by Man (over a billion klicks). Titan's gravity well was a mighty small target at the end of it, that we had to hit just precisely right. Before Skyfac provided minimicrochip computer crystals the trick would not have been possible, and we had had small course corrections en route. But the moon swam up fast, and we took a couple of one-gee burns that, though mercifully short, made me strongly doubt that we could survive even a two-year return trip. They also scattered wreckage, mostly trivial, all over the ship: Fibber McGee's Closet, indoors. The worst of it, though, appeared to be a ruptured water line to the midships shower bags, and the air conditioning handled it.

Even being forewarned of an earthquake doesn't help much.

On the other hand, cleanup was next to no problem at

all—again, thanks to zero gee. All we had to do was wait, and sooner or later virtually all of the debris collected on the air conditioning grilles of its own accord, just like always. Free-fall housekeeping mostly involves replacing worn-out velcro and grille screens.

(We use sleeping webs and cocoons when we sleep, even though *everything* in a free-fall domicile is *well* padded. It's not as restful—but without any restraints, you keep waking up when you bump into the air grille. One idiot student had wanted to nap in Town Hall, which has no sleeping gear, so he turned off the air conditioning. Fortunately someone came in before he could suffocate in the carbon dioxide sphere of his own exhalations. I paid for an unscheduled elevator and had him dirtside twenty hours later.)

And so nearly at once everyone found time to hang themselves in front of a video monitor and eyeball Titan.

From the *extensive* briefing we all studied, this abstract:

Titan is the sixth of Saturn's nine moons, and quite the largest. I had been expecting something vaguely Luna-sized—but the damned thing has a diameter of almost 5,800 klicks, roughly that of the planet Mercury, or about four tenths that of Earth! At that incredible size its mass is only about .002 that of Earth's. Its orbital inclination is negligible, less than a degree—that is, it orbits almost precisely around the equator of Saturn (as does the Ring), at a mean distance of just over ten planetary diameters. It is tidally locked, so that it always presents the same face to its primary, like Luna, and it takes only about sixteen days to circle Saturn—a speedy moon indeed for its size. (But then Saturn itself has a ten-and-a-quarter-hour day.)

From the time that it had been close enough to eyeball it had looked reddish, and now it looked like Mars on fire, girdled with vast clouds like thunderheads of blood. Through them lunarlike mountains and valleys glowed a slightly cooler red, as though lit by a gobo with a red gel—which, essentially, they were. The overall effect was of hellfire and damnation.

That preternatural red color was one of the principle reasons why Cox and Song went into emergency overdrive the moment we were locked into orbit. The world scientific community had gone into apoplexy when its expensive Saturn probe had been hijacked by the military, for a diplomatic mission, and into double apoplexy when they understood that the scientific complement of the voyage would consist of a single Space Command physicist and an engineer. So Bill and Col. Song spent the twenty-four hours we remained in that orbit working like fishermen when the tide makes, taking the absolute minimum of measurements and recordings that would satisfy *Siegfried*'s original planners. Led by Susan Pha Song, they worked from taped instructions and under the waspish direction of embittered scientists on Terra (with a transmission lag of an hour and a quarter, which improved no one's temper), and they did a good, dogged job. It is a little difficult to imagine the kind of mind that would find chatting with extrasolar plasmoids *less* exciting than studying Saturn's sixth moon, but there are some—and the startling thing is, they're not entirely crazy.

It's that red color. Titan should look sort of blue-greenish. Yet even from Earth it is clearly red. Why? Well, the thing that had professors in a flutter was that Titan's atmosphere (mostly methane) and temperature characteristics made it about the last place in the Solar System where theory grudgingly admitted the possibility of "life as we know it." Experiments with a Titan-normal chamber produced Miller's "primal flash" chemical reactions, a good sign, and the unspoken but dearly beloved theory was that maybe the red cloud-cover was organic matter of some kind—or even conceivably whatever kind of pollution a methane-breather would produce. I couldn't follow even Raoul's popularization of the byplay, and I was only peripherally interested, but I gathered that by the end of twenty-four hours, a pessimist would have said "no" and an optimist "maybe." Raoul mentioned a lot of ambiguous data, stuff that seemed self contradictory— which didn't surprise me in light of how prematurely *Siegfried* had been rushed into commission.

I divided my own attention between Titan and Saturn, which the scientists wouldn't be interested in until after the conference, when they could get a closer look. From where we were it took up about a 6 or 7° piece of sky (for reference, Luna seen from Earth subtends an angle of about half a degree; Earth seen from Luna is about 2° wide. Your fist at arm's length is about 10°.), and the Ring, edge on to us, added another couple of planetary diameters or almost 14°. Call it a total package of 20°, two fists' width. Not cosmic; at home, at the Studio, I've seen Mother Terra take up more than half the sky at perigee. But when Earth *did* take up 20°, we were about 22,000 klicks from its surface. Saturn was 1.2 *million* klicks away.

It's a hellacious big planet—the biggest in the System if you don't call Jupiter a planet (I don't call it at all. It might answer). Its diameter is a little over 116,000 klicks, roughly nine Earths, and it masses a whopping ninety-five Earths. This makes its surface gee of 1.15 Earth normal seem absurdly low—but it must be borne in mind that Saturn is only .69 as dense as a comparable sphere of water (while Earth has more than five times the density of water). Even that low a gee field was more than enough to kill a *Homo caelestis or* a *Homo excastra*, were we silly enough to land on Saturn. And the escape velocity is more than three times that for Earth (a weak gravity well—but a *big* one).

It doesn't exactly *have* a surface, though, as I understand it. Oh, there's probably rock down there somewhere. But long before you got down that far, you'd come to rest, floating on methane, which is what Saturn (and its "atmosphere") mostly is.

Its mighty Ring appears to be a moon that didn't make it, uncountable trillions of orbiting rocks from sand- to boulder-size, covered with water ice.

Together they present an indescribably beautiful appearance. Saturn is a kind of dreamy ocher yellow with wide bands of dark, almost chocolate brown, and it is quite bright as planets go. The Ring, being dirty ice, incorporates literally every color in the visible spectrum, sparkling and shifting as the independent orbits of its component parts change relation. The overall impression is of an immense agate or tiger-eye circled by the shattered remnants of a mighty rainbow. Smaller, literal rainbows come and go randomly within the orbiting mass, like lights seen through wet glasses.

It was a sight I never tired of, will never forget as long as I live, and it alone was worth the trip from Earth and the loss of my heritage. I couldn't decide whether it was more beautiful at the height of our orbit, when we were above the Ring, or at the other end when we were edge-on; both had their points. Raoul spent virtually every minute of his free time glued to the bulkhead across from his video screen, his Musicmaster on his lap, its headphones over his ears, fingers seeking and questioning among its keys. He would not let us put the speakers on—but he gave Harry the auxiliary 'phones. I have subsequently heard the symphony he derived from that working tape, and I would have traded Earth for *that*.

The aliens, of course, were the utter and total center of Bill Cox's attention. Their high-energy emissions nearly overloaded his instruments, though they were too far away to be seen. About a million klicks, give or take a few hundred thousand, waiting with apparent patience at the approximate forward Trojan point for Saturn-Titan. The actual locating of that point was extremely complicated by the presence of eight other moons, and I'm told that no Trojan point would be stable in the long term—even if the O'Neill Colony movement ever gets going at L-5, it'll never spread to Saturn. But what it came down to was that the aliens were waiting about 60° "down the line" of Titan's orbit, at a sensible place for a conference. Which made it even more probable that that was their intention.

So *our* next move was to go say howdy. *Siegfried* and all: that Trojan point was a good four light-seconds away, and lag was not acceptable to any of us.

We dancers also had business of our own to occupy us while Bill and Col. Song were slaving, of course. We didn't spend *all* our time rubbernecking.

The Limousine had been fully supplied and outfitted, field- and board-tested down to the last circuit, and secured long since, in transit. So naturally the first thing we did was to check the supplies and fittings and broad-test down to the last circuit again. If we should buy the emptiest of farms, the next expedition would be two or three years in arriving at the very least—and maybe by then the aliens' Trojan stability would have decayed enough to irritate them and they'd have gone home.

Besides, I wanted personal words with them.

And *that* was the root of the *last* thing we did before blasting for their location, which was to hold the last several hours of a year-long quarrel with the diplomats over choreography.

I finally jaunted right out on them, prepared to float in my room and let *them* dance. I hadn't lost my temper; only my will to argue. DeLaTorre waited a polite interval and then buzzed at my door.

"Come in."

The free-fall haircut spoiled his appearance; he should have had hair like Mark Twain. He had had to shave his beard too—there's no room for one in a helmet—and hating shaving he did it badly; but it actually improved his looks, almost enough to compensate for the big fuzzy skull. His warm brown eyes showed unspeakable fatigue, their lids raisinlike with wrinkles. He stuck himself to the wall, moving with the exaggerated care of the bone-tired, so that he was aligned with the local vertical built into it by its terrestrial designers (when Harry builds his first billion-dollar spaceship, he'll be more imaginative).

DeLaTorre would, at his age, never make a Space Man. Out of respect, I assumed the same orientation. What little anger I had had was gone; my determination remained.

"Charles, an accommodation must be reached."

"Ezequiel, don't tell me you're as blind as the rest of them."

"They only feel that the *first* movement might more properly be respectful, rather than stern; solemn rather than emotional. Once we have established communication, opened relations with these beings in mutual dignity, then would be the time to state our grievances. The third or fourth movement, perhaps."

"Dammit, it doesn't *feel* right that way."

"Charles, forgive me, but—surely you will admit that your emotional judgment might be clouded in this matter?"

I sighed. "Ezequiel, look me in the eye. I have not been in love with Shara Drummond since shortly before she died. I have examined my soul and the dance that came out of it, and I feel no urge for personal vengeance, no thirst for retribution."

"No, your dance is not vengeful," he agreed.

"But I *do* have a grievance—not as a bereaved lover but as a bereaved human being. I want those aliens to know what they cost my race when they wrought the death of Shara Drummond, when they forced her hand and made her into *Homo caelestis* before there was any place or any way for one to live—" I broke off, realizing that I had blundered, but DeLaTorre did not even blink.

"Was she not already *Homo caelestis*, or *ala anima*, when they arrived, Charles?" he asked as blandly as if he was supposed to know those terms. "Would she not have died on her return to Earth in any case, by that point?"

I recognized and accepted the sudden rise in our truth level, distracted by his question. "Perhaps, Ezequiel. Her body must have been on the borderline of permanent adaptation. I have lain awake many nights, thinking about this, talking it over with my wife. I keep thinking: Had Shara visualized what her *Stardance* would do financially, she might have endured a brief wait at Skyfac, might have survived to be a more worthy leader for our Studio. I keep thinking: Had she thought things through, she might not have chosen to burn her wings, so high above her lost planet. I keep thinking: Had she known, she might have lived."

I sucked rotten coffee from a bulb and made a face. "But all the fighting spirit had been sucked out of her, drained into the *Stardance* and hurled at those red fireflies with the last of her strength. All of her life, right up to Carrington, had been slowly draining the will to live out of her, and she threw all that she had left at those things, because that was what it took to scare them back to interstellar space, to frighten them so bad that their nearest subsequent approach was a billion klicks away. There was no will to live left after that, not enough to sustain her.

"I want to convey to those creatures the value of the entity their careless footstep crushed, the enormity of her people's loss. If grief or remorse are in their emotional repertoire, I want to see some. Most of all, I think, I want to forgive them. And so I have to state my complaint *first*. I believe that their reaction will tell us quicker than anything else whether we can *ever* learn to communicate and peacefully coexist with them.

"They *respect* dance, Ezequiel, and they cost us the greatest artist of our time. A race that could open with any other statement is one I don't much want to represent. That'd be Montezuma's Mistake all over again. Norrey and the others agree with me: this is a dealbreaker."

He was silent a long time. The last thing a diplomat will concede is that compromise is impossible. But at last he said, "I follow your thought, Charles. And I admit that it leads me to the same conclusion." He sighed. "You are right. I will make the others accept this." He pushed free and jaunted to me, taking both my shoulders in his wrinkled, mottled hands. "Thank you for explaining to me. Come, let us prepare to go and state our grievance."

He was closeted with the other three for a little over twenty minutes, and emerged with an extremely grudging accord. He was indeed the best man Wertheimer could have chosen. Half an hour later we were on our way.

# Chapter 3

It took the better part of a day to coax *Siegfried* from Titan orbit to the Trojan point, without employing accelerations that would kill us all. Titan is a mighty moon, harder to break free of than Luna. Fortunately we didn't want to break free of it—quite. We essentially widened the circle of our orbit until it intersected the Trojan point—decelerating like hell all the way so that we'd be at rest relative to it when we got there. It had to be at least partly by-guess-and-by-God, because any transit in Saturn's system is a ten-body problem (don't even *think* about the Ring), and Bill was an equal partner with the computer in that astrogating job. He did a world-class job, as I had known he would, wasting no fuel and, more important, no passengers. The worst we had to endure was about fifteen seconds at about .6 gee, mere agony.

Any properly oriented wall will do for an acceleration couch—since everything in a true spaceship is well padded (billion-dollar spaceprobe designers aren't *that* unimaginative). I don't know about all the others, but Norrey and I and anybody sensible customarily underwent acceleration naked. If you've got to lie flat on your back under gravity, you don't want wrinkly clothes and bulky velcro pads between you and the padding.

When we drifted free of the wall and the "acceleration over" horn sounded, we dressed in the same p-suits we had worn on our Last Ride together, a year before. Of the five models of custom-made suits we use, they are the closest to total nudity, resembling abbreviated topless bathing suits with a collared hood. The transparent sections are formfitted and scarcely noticeable; the "trunks" are not for taboo but for sanitary reasons; and the hood-and-collar section is mostly to conceal the unaesthetic amount of hardware that must be built into a p-suit hood. The thrusters are ornate wrist and ankle jewelry; their controls golfing gloves. The group had decided unanimously that we would use these suits for our performance. Perhaps by the overt image of naked humans in space we were unconsciously trying to assert our humanity, to deny the concept of ourselves as *other than human* by displaying the evidence to the contrary. See? Navel. See? Nipples. See? Toes.

"The trouble with these suits, my love," I said as I sealed my own, "is that the sight of you in yours always threatens to dislodge my catheter tube."

She grinned and made an unnecessary adjustment of her left breast. "Steady, boy. Keep your mind on business."

"Especially now that the bloody *weight* is gone. How did you women put up with it for centuries? Having some great heavy clod *lay* on you like that?"

"Stoically," she said, and jaunted for the phone. She diddled its controls, and said, "Linda—how's the baby?"

Linda and Tom appeared on the screen, in the midst of helping each other suit up. "Fine," Linda called happily. "Nary a quiver."

Tom grinned at the phone and said, "What's to worry? She still fits into her p-suit, for crying out loud."

His composure impressed and deeply pleased me. When we left Skyfac I would have predicted that at this pre-curtain moment, with a pregnant wife to worry about,

Tom would be agitated enough to chew pieces off his shoulder blades. But free space, as I have said, is a tranquilizing environment—and more important, he had allowed Linda to teach him much. Not just the dance, and the breathing and meditational exercises for relaxation—we had all learned these things. Not even the extensive spiritual instruction she had given that ex-businessman (which had begun with loud arguments, and calmed down when he finally got it through his head that she had no creed to attack, no brand label to discredit), though that helped of course.

Mostly it was her love and her loving that had finally unsnarled all the knots in Tom's troubled soul. Her love was so transparently genuine and heartfelt that it forced him to take it at face value, forced him therefore to love himself a little more—which is all anyone really needs to relax. Opening up to another frees you at least temporarily of all that armor you've been lugging, and your disposition invariably improves. Sometimes you decide to scrap the armor altogether.

Norrey and I shared all of this in a smile and a glance, and then she said, "That's great, you two. See you at the Garage," and cleared the screen.

She drifted round in space, her lovely breasts majestic in free fall, till she was facing me. "Tom and Linda will be good partners for us," she said, and was silent.

We hung at opposite ends of the room for a few seconds, lost in each other's eyes, and then we kicked off at the same instant and met, hard, at the center of the room. Our embrace was four-limbed and fierce, a spasmodic attempt to break through the boundaries of flesh and bone and plastic and touch hearts.

"I'm not scared," she said in my ear. "I ought to be scared, but I'm not. Not at all. But *oh*, I'd be scared if I were going into this without you!"

I tried to reply and could not, so I hugged tighter.

And then we left to meet the others.

Living in *Siegfried* had been rather like living below-decks in a luxury liner. The shuttlecraft was more like a bus, or a plane. Rows of seats with barely enough room to maneuver above them, a *big* airlock aft, a smaller one in the forward wall, windows on either side, engines in the rear. But from the outside it would have appeared that the bus or plane had rammed a stupendous bubble. The bow of the craft was a transparent sphere about twenty meters in diameter, the observation globe from which the team of diplomats would observe our performance. There was extremely little hardware to spoil the view. The computer itself was in *Siegfried* and the actual terminal was small; the five video monitors were little bigger, and the Limousine's own guidance systems were controlled by another lobe of the same computer. There would be no bad seats.

There had, inevitably, been scores of last-minute messages from Earth, but not even the diplomats had paid any attention to them. Nor was there much conversation on the trip. Everyone's mind was on the coming encounter, and our Master Plan, insofar as we could be said to have one, had been finalized long since.

We had spent a year studying computer analyses of *both* sides of the *Stardance*, and we believed we had gotten enough out of them to prechoreograph an opening statement in four movements. About an hour's worth of dance, sort of a Mandarin's Greeting. By the end of that time we would either have established telepathic rapport or not. If so we would turn the phone over to the diplomats. They would pass their consensus through DeLaTorre, and we would communicate their words to the aliens as best we could. If, for some reason, consensus could not be reached, then we would dance that too. If we could *not* establish rapport, we would watch the aliens' reply to our opening statement and we and the computer would try to agree on a translation. The diplomats would then frame their reply, the computer would feed us choreographic notation, and we'd try it that way. If we got no results by the end of nine hours—two air changes—we'd call it a day, take the Limo back home to *Siegfried* and try again tomorrow. If we got good or promising results, we had enough air cans to stay out for a week—and the Die was stocked with food, water and a stripped-down toilet.

Mostly we all expected to play it by ear. Our ignorance was so total that anything would be a breakthrough, and we all knew it.

There was only one video screen in the passenger compartment, and Cox's face filled it throughout the short journey. He kept us posted on the aliens' status, which was static. At last deceleration ended, and we sank briefly in our seats as the Limousine turned end over end to present the bubble to the aliens, and then we were just finally *there*, at the crossroads. The diplomats unstrapped and went forward to the bubble's airlock; the Stardancers went aft to the big one. The one that had the EXIT light over it.

We hung there together a moment, by unspoken consent, and looked around at each other. No one had a moving, *Casablanca*-ending speech to deliver, no wisecracks or last sentiments to exchange. The last year had forged us into a *family*; we were already beginning to be mutually telepathic after a fashion. We were beyond words. We were ready.

What we did, actually, we smiled big idiotic smiles and joined hands in a snowflake around the airlock.

Then Harry and Raoul let go on either end, kissed each other, seated their hoods, and entered the airlock to go build our set. There was room for four in the airlock; Tom and Linda squeezed in with them. They would deploy the Die and wait for us.

As the door slid closed behind them, Norrey and I shared our own final kiss.

"No words," I said, and she nodded slightly.

"Mr. Armstead," from behind me.

"Yes, Dr. Chen?"

He was half in his airlock, alone. Without facial or vocal expression he said, "Blow a gasket."

I smiled. "Thank you, sir."

And we entered the lock.

There is a kind of familiarity beyond déjà vu, a recall greater than total. It comes on like scales falling from your eyes. Say you haven't taken LSD in a long while, but you sincerely believe that you remember what the experience was like. Then you drop again, and as it comes on you simply say, "Ah yes—reality," and smile indulgently at your foolish shadow memories. Or (if you're too young to remember acid), you discover real true love, at the moment when you are making love with your partner and realize that all of your life together is a single, continuous, and ongoing act of lovemaking, in the course of which you happen to occasionally disengage bodies altogether for hours at a time. It is not something to which you *return*—it is something you suddenly find that you have never really left.

I felt it now as I saw the aliens again.

Red fireflies. Like glowing coals without the coals inside, whirling in something less substantial than a bubble, more immense than *Siegfried*. Ceaselessly whirling, in ceaselessly shifting patterns that drew the eye like the dance of the cobra.

All at once it seemed to me that the whole of my life was the moments I had spent in the presence of these beings—that the intervals between those moments, even the endless hours studying the tapes of the aliens and trying to understand them, had been unreal shadows already fading from my memory. I had always known the aliens. I would always know them, and they me. We went back about a billion years together. Like coming home from school to Mom and Dad, who are unchanging and eternal.

*Hey*, I wanted to tell them, *I've stopped believing I'm a cripple*, as a kid might proudly announce he's passed a difficult Chem test. . . .

I shook my head savagely, and snapped out of it. Looking away helped. Everything about the setting said that something more than confused dreams had occurred since our last meeting. Just past the aliens mighty Saturn shone yellow and brown, ringed with coruscating fire. The Sun behind my back provided only one percent of the illumination it shone on Terra—but the difference was not discernible: the terrestrial eye habitually filters out 99% of available light (it suddenly struck me, the coincidence that this meeting place the aliens had chosen happened to be precisely as far away from the Sun as a human eye could go and still see properly).

We were "above" the Ring. It defied description.

To my "right," Titan was smaller than Luna (under a third of a degree), but clearly visible, nearly three-quarters full from our perspective. Where the terminator faced Saturn the dull red color softened to the hue of a blood-orange, from the reflected Saturnlight. The great moon still looked smoky, like a baleful eye on our proceedings.

And all around me my teammates were floating, staring, hypnotized.

Only Tom was showing signs of self-possession. Like me, he was renewing an old acquaintance; reaffirming strong memories takes less time than making new ones.

We knew them better, this time, even those who were facing them for the first time. At that last confrontation, only Shara had seemed able to understand them to any degree—no matter how hard I had watched them, then, understanding had eluded me. Now my mind was free of terror, my eyes unblinded by need, my heart at peace. I felt as Shara had felt, saw what she had seen, and agreed with her tentative evaluations.

*"There's a flavor of arrogance to them—conviction of superiority. Their dance is a challenging, a dare."*

*". . . biologists studying the antics of a strange, new species. . . ."*

*"They want Earth."*

*". . . in orbits as carefully choreographed as those of electrons. . . ."*

*"Believe me, they can dodge or withstand anything you or Earth can throw at them. I know."*

Cox's voice broke through our reverie. "*Siegfried* to Stardancers. They're the same ones, all right: the signatures match to 3 nines."

We had planned for the possibility that these might have been a *different* group of aliens—say, policemen looking for the others, or possibly even the second batch of suckers to buy a Sol-System Tour on the strength of the brochure. Even low probabilities had been prepared for. As Bill spoke, he, the diplomats and the computer flushed several sheafs of contingency scenarios from their memory banks and confirmed Plan A in their minds.

But *all* of us Stardancers had known already, on sight.

"Roger, *Siegfried*," I acknowledged. "I'm terrible on names, but I never forget a face. 'That's the man, officer.' "

"Initiate your program."

"All right, let's get set up. Harry, Raoul, deploy the set and monitor. Tom and Linda, deploy the Die—about twenty klicks thataway, okay? Norrey, give me a hand with camera placement, we'll all meet at the Die in twenty minutes. Go."

The set was minimal, mostly positional grid markers. Raoul had not taken long to decide that attempting flashy effects in the close vicinity of the Ring would be vain folly. His bank of tracking lasers was low-power, meant only as gobos to color-light us dancers vividly for the camera— and to see how the aliens would react to the presence of lasers, which was their real purpose. I thought it was a damned-fool stupid idea—like Pope Leo picking his teeth with a stiletto as he comes to dicker with Attila—and the whole company, Raoul included, agreed wholeheartedly. We all wanted to stick to conventional lights.

But if you're going to win arguments with diplomats of that stature you've got to make some concessions.

The grid markers were color organs slaved to Raoul's Musicmaster through a system Harry designed. If the aliens responded noticeably to color cues, Raoul would attempt to use his instrument to make visual music, augmenting our communication by making the spectrum dance with us. Just as the sonic range of the Musicmaster exceeded the audible on both ends, the spectral range of the color organs exceeded the visible. If the aliens' language included these subtleties, we would have rich converse indeed. Even the ship's computer might have to stretch itself.

The Musicmaster's audio output would be in circuit with our radios, well below conversational level. We wanted to enhance the possibility of a kind of mutual telepathic resonance, and we were conditioned to Raoul's music that way.

Norrey and I set up five cameras in an open cone facing the aliens, for a proscenium-stage effect, as opposed to the six-camera globe we customarily used at home for 360° coverage. Neither of us felt like traveling around "behind" the aliens to plant the last camera there. This would be the only dance we had ever done that would be shot from every angle *except* the one toward which it was aimed, recorded only "from backstage," as it were.

To tell you the truth, it didn't make that much difference. Artistically it wasn't much of a dance. I wouldn't have released it commercially. The reason's obvious, really: it was never intended for humans.

That had been the real root of our struggle with the diplomats over the last year. They were committed to the belief that what would be understood best by the aliens was precise adherence to a series of computer-generated *movements*. We Stardancers unanimously believed that what the aliens had responded to in Shara had been *not* a series of movements but *art*. The artistic mind behind the movements, the amount of heart and soul that went into them—the very thing an over-rigid choreography destroys in space. If we accepted the diplomats' belief-structure, we were only computer display models. If they had accepted our belief-structure, Dmirov and Silverman at least would have been forced to admit themselves forever deaf to alien speech—and Chen would never have been able to justify siding with us to his superiors.

The result was, of course, compromise that satisfied no one, with provisions to dump whichever scheme didn't seem to be working, *if* consensus could be reached. That was another reason I had had to gamble our lives and our race's fortune on the damned lasers in order to win control of the first movement. The balance would be biased slightly our way: Our very first "utterances" would be —something more than could be expressed mathematically and ballistically.

But even if we had had a totally free hand, our dance would surely have puzzled hell out of anyone but another *Homo caelestis*. Or a computer.

I think Shara would have loved it.

At last all the pieces were in place, the stage was set, and we formed a snowflake around the Die.

"Watch your breathing, Charlie," Norrey warned.

"Right you are, my love." My lungs were taking orders from my hindbrain; it seemed to want me agitated. But *I* didn't. I began forcing measure on my breaths, and soon we were all breathing in unison, in, hold, out, hold, striving to push the interval past five seconds. My agitation began to melt like summer wages, my peripheral vision expanded spherically, and I felt my family as though a literal charge of electricity passed from hand to p-suited hand, completing a circuit that *tuned* us to one another. We became like magnets joined around a monopole, aligned to an imaginary point at the center of our circle. It was an encouraging analogy—however you disperse such magnets in free fall, eventually they will come together again at the pole. We were family; we were one. Not just our shared membership in a hypothetical new genus: we knew each other backstage, a relationship like no other on Earth or off it.

"Mr. Armstead," Silverman growled, "I'm sure you'll be glad to know that for once the world actually *is* waiting for you. Can we get on with the show?"

I just smiled. We all smiled. Bill started to say something, so I cut him off. "Certainly, Mr. Ambassador. At once." We dissolved the snowflake, and I jetted to the Die's external Master Board. "Program locked and . . . *running*, lights *up*, cameras *hot*, hold four three two *curtain!*"

Like a single being, we took our stage.

Feet first, hands high and blasting, we plunged down on the firefly swarm.

Raoul's stage marks pulsed gently with the color analog of the incredible piece he called *Shara's Blues*. Its opening bars are entirely in deep bass register; they translated as all the shades of blue there are, a visual pun. Somehow the incredible splendor of color about us—Saturn, Ring, aliens, Titan, lasers, camera lights, Die, Limousine like a soft red flashlight, and two other moons I didn't know—all only seemed to emphasize the intolerable blackness of the empty space that framed it, the immensity of the sea of black ink through which we all swam, planets and people alike. The literally cosmic perspective it provided was welcome, calming. *What are man or firefly that Thou shouldst be mindful of them?*

It was not detachment. Quite the opposite: I had never

before felt so alive. For the first time in years I was aware
of my p-suit clinging to my skin, aware of the breathing in
my earphones, aware of the smell of my own body and of
canned air, aware of the catheter and telemetry contacts
and the faint sound of my hair rustling against the inside
of my hood. I was perceiving totally, functioning at full
capacity, exhilarated and a little scared. I was completely
happy.

The music swelled suddenly. The far-flung grid pulsed
with color.

We poured on full thrust, all four of us in a tight formation, so that we seemed to fall upon the alien swarm from
a great height. They grew beneath our feet with breathtaking rapidity, but we were more than three klicks away
when I gave the standby command. We stiffened our
bodies, oriented and triggered heel thrusters together on
command, opening out like a Blue Angels flower into four
great loops. We let them close into circles, one of us
spiraling about each of the "compass points" of the alien
sphere, bracketing it with bodies. After three full circles
we broke out in unison and met at the same point where
we had split apart, slowing as we arrived and making a
four-way acrobat's catch. Hard jetting brought us to a
halt; we whirled in space and faced the aliens; pinwheeled
apart into a square fifty meters on a side and waited.

*Here I am again, fireflies*, I thought. *I have hated you
for a long time. I would be done with hating you, however
that may be.*

Lasers turned us red, blue, yellow and aching green, and
Raoul had abandoned known music for new; his spiderlike fingers wove patterns undreamed an hour before,
stitching space with color and our ears with sound. Melan-
choly his melody, minor its wrestling two chords, with a
throbbing undercurrent of dysharmonic bass like a mi-
graine about to happen. It was as though he were pouring
pain into a vessel whose cubic capacity might be inade-
quate.

With that for frame and all space for backdrop, we danced. The mechanical structure of that dance, the "steps" and their interrelation, are forever unknowable to you, and I won't try to describe them. It began slowly, tentatively; as Shara had, we began by defining terms. And so we ourselves gave the choreography less than half our attention.

Perhaps a third. A part of our minds was busy framing computer themes in artistic terms, but an equally large part was straining for any signs of feedback from the aliens, reaching out with eyes ears skin mind for any kind of response, sensitizing to any conceivable touch. And with as large a part of our minds, we felt for each other, strove to connect our awarenesses across meters of black vacuum, to see as the aliens saw, through many eyes at once.

And something began to happen. . . .

It began slowly, subtly, in imperceptible stages. After a year of study, I simply found myself understanding, and accepting the understanding without surprise or wonder. At first I thought the aliens had slowed their speed—but then I noted, again without wonder, that my pulse and everyone's respiration had slowed an equal amount. I was on accelerated time, extracting the maximum of information from each second of life, *be*ing with the whole of my being. Experimentally I accelerated my time sense another increment, saw the aliens' frenzy slow to a speed that anyone could encompass. I was aware that I could make time stop altogether, but I didn't want to yet. I studied them at infinite leisure, and understanding grew. It was clear now that there was a tangible if invisible energy that held them in their tight mutual orbits, as electromagnetism holds electrons in their paths. But this energy boiled furiously at their will, and they surfed its currents like wood chips that magically never collided. They created a never-ending roller coaster before themselves. Slowly, slowly I began to realize that this energy was *more than* analogous to the energy that bound me to my family. What they were surfing on was their mutual awareness of each other, and of the Universe around them.

My own awareness of my family jumped a quantum level. I heard Norrey breathing, could see out her eyes, felt Tom's sprained calf tug at me, felt Linda's baby stir in my womb, watched us all and swore under Harry's breath with him, raced down Raoul's arm to his fingers and back into my own ears. I was a six-brained Snowflake, existing simultaneously in space and time and thought and music and dance and color and something I could not yet name, and all of these things strove toward harmony.

At no point was there any sensation of leaving or losing my *self*, my unique individual identity. It was right there in my body and brain where I had left it, could not be elsewhere, existed as before. It was as though a part of it had always existed independent of brain and body, as though my brain had always known this level but had been unable to *record* the information. Had we six been this close all along, all unawares, like six lonely blind men in the same volume of space? In a way I had always yearned to without knowing it, I touched my selves, and loved them.

We understood entirely that we were being shown this level by the aliens, that they had led us patiently up invisible psychic stairs to this new plane. If any energy detectable by Man had passed between them and us, Bill Cox would have been heating up his laser cannon and screaming for a report, but he was still on conference circuit with the diplomats, letting us dance without distraction.

But communication took place, on levels that even physical instruments could perceive. At first the aliens only echoed portions of our dance, to indicate an emotional or informational connotation they understood, and when they did so we *knew* without question that they had fully grasped whatever nuance we were trying to express. After a time they began more complex responses, began subtly altering the patterns they returned to us, offering variations on a theme, then counterstatements, alternate suggestions. Each time they did so we came to know them better, to grasp the rudiments of their "language" and hence their nature. They agreed with our concept of sphericity, politely disagreed with our concept of mortality, strongly agreed with the notions of pain and joy. When we knew enough "words" to construct a "sentence," we did so.

*We came these billion miles to shame you, and are ashamed.*

The response was at once compassionate and merry. NONSENSE, they might have said, HOW WERE YOU TO KNOW?

*Surely it was obvious that you were wiser than we.*

NO, ONLY THAT WE KNEW MORE. IN POINT OF FACT, WE WERE CULPABLY CLUMSY AND OVEREAGER.

*Overeager?* we echoed interrogatively.

OUR NEED WAS GREAT. All fifty-four aliens suddenly plummeted toward the center of their sphere at varying rates, incredibly failing to collide there even once, saying as plain as day, ONLY RANDOM CHANCE PREVENTED UTTER RUIN.

The nature of the utter ruin eluded us, and we "said" as much. *Our dead sister told us you needed to spawn, on a world like ours. Is this your wish: to come and live with humans?*

Their response was the equivalent of cosmic laughter. It resolved finally into a single, unmistakable "sentence":

ON THE CONTRARY.

Our dance dissolved into confusion for a moment, then recovered.

*We do not understand.*

The aliens hesitated. Something like solicitude emanated from them, something like compassion.

WE CAN—WE MUST—EXPLAIN. BUT UNDERSTANDING WILL BE VERY STRESSFUL. COMPOSE YOURSELVES.

The component of our self that was Linda poured out a flood of maternal warmth, an envelope of calm; she had always been the best of us at prayer. Raoul now played only an *om*-like A-flat that was a warm, golden color. Tom's driving will, Harry's eternal strength, Norrey's quiet acceptance, my own unfailing sense of humor, Linda's infinite caring and Raoul's dogged persistence all heterodyned to produce a kind of peace I had never known, a serene calm based on a sensation of completeness. All fear was gone, all doubt. This was meant to be.

*This was meant to be*, we danced. *Let it be.*

The echo was instantaneous, with a flavor of pleased, almost paternal approval.

NOW!

Their next sending was a relatively short dance, a relatively simple dance. We understood it at once, although it was utterly novel to us, grasped its fullest implications in a single frozen instant. The dance compressed every nanosecond of more than two billion years into a single concept, a single telepathic gestalt.

And that concept was really only the aliens' name.

Terror smashed the Snowflake into six discrete shards. I was alone in my skull in empty space, with a thin film of plastic between me and my death, naked and terribly afraid. I clutched wildly for nonexistent support. Before me, much too close before me, the aliens buzzed like bees. As I watched, they began to gather at the center, forming first a pinhole, then a knothole and then a porthole in the wall of Hell, a single shimmering red coal that raved with furious energy. Its brilliance dwarfed even the Sun; my hood began to polarize automatically.

The barely visible balloon that contained the molten nucleus began to weep red smoke, which spiraled gracefully out to form a kind of Ring. I knew it at once, what it was and what it was for, and I threw back my head and screamed, triggering all thrusters in blind escape reflex.

Five screams echoed mine.

I fainted.

# Chapter 4

I was lying on my back with my knees raised, and I was much too heavy—almost twenty kilos. My ribs were struggling to inflate my chest. I had had a bad dream. . . .

The voices came from above like an old tube amp warming up, intermittent and distorted at first, resolving at last into a kind of clarity. They were near, but they had the trebleless, faraway characteristic of low pressure—and they too were finding the pseudogravity a strain.

"For the last time, tovarisch: *speak to us.* Why are your colleagues all catatonic? How do you continue to function? *What in Lenin's Name happened out there?*"

"Let him be, Ludmilla. He cannot hear you."

"I will have an answer!"

"Will you have him shot? If so, by whom? The man is a hero. If you continue to harass him, I will make full note of it, in our group report and in my own. *Let him be.*" Chen Ten Li's voice was quite composed, exquisitely detached until that last blazing command. It startled me into opening my eyes, which I had been avoiding since I first became aware of the voices.

We were in the Limousine. All ten of us, four Space Command suits and six brightly colored Stardancers, a quorum of bowling pins strapped by twos into a vertical alley. Norrey and I were in the last or bottom row. We were obviously returning to *Siegfried* at full burn, making a good quarter gee. I turned my head at once to Norrey beside me. She seemed to be sleeping peacefully; the stars through the window behind her told me that we had already passed turnover and were decelerating.

I had been out a long time.

Somehow everything had gotten sorted out in my sleep. By definition, I guess: my subconscious had kept me under until I was ready to cope and no longer. A part of my mind boiled in turmoil, but I could encompass that part now and hold it in perspective. The majority of my mind was calm. Nearly all questions were answered now, and the fear dwindled to something that could be borne. I knew for certain that Norrey was all right, that all of us would be all right in time. Not direct knowledge; the telepathic bond was broken. But I knew my family. Our lives were irrevocably changed; into what, we knew not yet—but we would find out together.

At least two more crises would come in rapid succession now, and we would share these fortunes.

Immediate needs first.

"Harry," I called out, "you did a good job. Let go now."

He turned his big crewcut head and looked down past his headrest at me from two rows up. He smiled beatifically. "I almost lost his music box," he said confidentially. "It got away from me when the weight came on." At once he rolled his head up and was asleep, snoring deeply.

I smiled indulgently at myself. I should have expected it, should have known that it would be Harry, great-shouldered great-hearted Harry who would be the strongest of us all, Harry the construction engineer who would prove to have infinite load-bearing capacity. His shoulders had been equal to his heart's need, and his breaking strain was still unknown. He would waken in an hour or so like a giant refreshed.

The diplomats had been yelping at me since I spoke to Harry; now I put my attention on them. "One at a time, please."

By God, not one of the four would yield. Knowing it was foolish they all kept talking at once. They simply couldn't help themselves.

"SHUT UP!" Bill's voice blasted from the phone speaker, overriding the cacophony. They shut up and turned to look at his image. "Charlie," he went on urgently, searching my face in his own screen, "*are you still human?*"

I knew what he was asking. Had the aliens somehow taken me over telepathically? Was I still my own master, or did an aggressive hive-mind live in my skull, working my switches and pulleys? We had discussed the possibility earnestly on the trip out, and I knew that if my answer didn't convince him he would blast us out of space without hesitation. The least of his firepower would vaporize the Limousine instantly.

I grinned. "Only for the last two or three years, Bill. Before that I was semipure bastard."

Later he would be relieved; he was *busy*. "Do I burn them?"

"*Negative*. Hold your fire! Bill, hear me good: If you shot them, and they ever found out about it, they might just take offense. I know you've got a Planet Cracker; forget it: *from here they can turn out the Sun*."

He went pale, and the diplomats held shocked silence, turning with effort to gape at me. "We're nearly home," I went on firmly. "Conference in the exercise room as soon as we're all recovered, call it a couple of hours from now. All hands. We'll answer all your questions then— but until then you'll just have to wait. We've had a hell of a shock; we need time to recover." Norrey was beginning to stir beside me, and Linda was looking about clear-eyed; Tom was shaking his head with great care from side to side. "Now I've got my wife and a pregnant lady to worry about. Get us home and get us to our rooms and we'll see you in two hours."

Bill didn't like it a little bit, but he cleared the screen and got us home. The diplomats, even Dmirov and Silverman, were silent, a little in awe of us.

By the time we were docked everyone had recovered except Harry and Raoul, who slumbered on together. We towed them to their room, washed them gently, strapped them into their hammock so they wouldn't drift against the air grille and drown in carbon dioxide, and dimmed the lights. They held each other automatically in their sleep, breathing to the same rhythm. We left Raoul's Music-master by the door, in case he might ever want it for something, and swam out.

Then the four of us went back to our respective rooms, showered, and made love for two hours.

The exercise room was the only one in *Siegfried* with enough cubic to contain the entire ship's complement comfortably. We could all have squeezed into the dining room; we often did for dinner. But it was cramped, and I did not want close quarters. The exercise room was a cube perhaps thirty meters on a side. One wall was studded with various rigs and harnesses for whole-body workout in free fall. Retaining racks on another held duckpins, Frisbees, hula hoops, and handballs. Two opposing walls were trampolines. It offered elbow room, visibility, and marvelous maneuverability.

And it was the only room in the ship arranged with no particular local vertical.

The diplomats, of course, arbitrarily selected one, taping velcro strips to the bare handball wall so that the opposed trampolines were their "ceiling" and "floor." We Star-dancers aligned ourselves against the far wall, among the exercise rigs, holding on to them with a hand or foot rather than velcroing ourselves to the wall between them. Bill and Col. Song took the wall to our left.

"Let's begin," I said as soon as we had all settled ourselves.

"First, Mr. Armstrong," Silverman said aggrievedly, "I would like to protest the high-handed manner in which you have withheld information from this body to suit your convenience."

"Sheldon," DeLaTorre began wearily.

"No sir," Silverman cut him off, "I vigorously protest. Are we children, to be kept twiddling our thumbs for two hours? Are all the people of Earth insignificant, that they should wait in suspense for three and a quarter hours while these—*artists* have an orgy?"

"Sounds like you've been twiddling volume controls," Tom said cheerily. "You know, Silverman, I knew you were listening the whole time. I didn't mind. I knew how much it must be bugging you."

His face turned bright red, unusual in free fall; his feet must be just as red.

"No," Linda said judiciously, "I rather think he was monitoring Raoul and Harry's room."

He went paler than he had started and his pupils contracted with hatred. Bullseye.

"All right, can it," Bill rapped. "You too, Mr. Ambassador. Snipe on your own time—as you say, all Terra is waiting."

"Yes, Sheldon," DeLaTorre said forcefully. "Let Mr. Armstead speak."

He nodded, white-lipped. "So speak."

I relaxed my grip on an exercise bike and spread my arms. "First tell me what happened from your perspective. What did you see and hear?"

Chen took it, his features masklike, almost waxen. "You began your dance. The music became progressively stranger. Your dance began to deviate radically from the computer pattern, and you were apparently answered with other patterns of which the computer could make nothing. The speed of your movements increased drastically with time, to a rate I would not have believed if I had not witnessed it with my unaided eyes. The music increased in tempo accordingly. There were muffled grunts, exclamations, nothing intelligible. The aliens united to form a single entity in the center of their envelope, which began to emit quantities of what we are told is organic matter. You all screamed.

"We tried to raise you without success. Mr. Stein would not answer our calls, but he retrieved all five of you with extreme efficiency, lashed you together, and towed you all back to the shuttlecraft in one trip."

I pictured the load that five of us, massing over three hundred kilos, must have been when the thrust came on, and acquired new respect for Harry's arms and shoulders. Brute muscle was usually so superfluous in space—but another man's muscles might have parted under that terrible strain.

"As soon as the airlock had cycled he brought you all inboard, strapped you in place, and said the single word 'Go.' Then he very carefully stowed Mr. Brindle's musical instrument and—just sat down and stared at nothing. We were abandoning the task of communicating with him when you awoke."

"Okay," I said. "Let me cover the high spots. First, as you must have guessed, we achieved rapport with the aliens."

"And are they a threat to us?" Dmirov interrupted. "Did they harm you?"

"No. And no."

"But you screamed, like ones sure to die. And Shara Drummond clearly stated before she died—"

"That the aliens were aggressive and arrogant, that they wanted Earth for a spawning ground, I know," I agreed. "Translation error, subtle and in retrospect almost inevitable. Shara had only been in space a few months; she said herself she was getting about one concept in three."

"What is the correct translation?" Chen asked.

"Earth *is* their spawning ground," I said. "So is Titan. So are a lot of places, outside this system."

"What do you mean?" Silverman barked.

"The aliens' last sending was what kicked us over the deep end. It was stunningly simple, really, considering how much it explained. You could render it as a single word. All they really did was tell us their collective name."

Dmirov scowled. "And that is?"

"Starseeder."

Stunned silence at first. I think Chen was the first to begin to grasp it, and maybe Bill was nearly as fast.

"That's their name," I went on, "their occupation, the thing they do to be fulfilled. They farm stars. Their lifetime spans billions of years, and they spend them much as we do, trying to reproduce a good part of the time. They seed stars with organic life. They seeded *this* solar system, a long time ago.

"They are our race's creator, and its remotest ancestor."

"Ridiculous," Silverman burst out. "They're nothing like us, *in no way* are they like us."

"In how many ways are you like an amoeba?" I asked. "Or a paramecium or a plant or a fish or an amphibian or any of your evolutionary forebears? The aliens are at least one or two and possibly three evolutionary stages beyond us. The wonder is that they can make themselves understood to us at all. I believe the next level beyond them has no physical existence in space or time."

Silverman shut up. DeLaTorre and Song crossed themselves. Chen's eyes were very wide.

"Picture the planet Earth as a single, stupendous womb," I went on quietly, "fecund and perpetually pregnant. Ideally designed to host a maximum of organic life, commanded by a kind of super-DNA to constantly grow and shuffle progressively more complex life forms into literally billions of different combinations, in search of one complex enough to survive outside the womb, curious enough to try.

"I nearly had a brother once. He was born dead. He was three weeks past term by then; he had stayed in the womb past his birthing time, by God knows what subtle biological error. His waste products exceeded the ability of the placenta to absorb and carry them away; the placenta began to die, to decay around him, polluted by his wastes. His life support eroded away and he died. He very nearly killed my mother.

"Picture your race as a gestalt, a single organism with a subtle flaw in its genetic coding. An overstrong cell wall, so that at the moment when it is complex enough that it ought to have a united planetary consciousness, each separate cell continues to function most often as an individual. The thick cell wall impedes information exchange, allows the organism to form only the most rudimentary approximation of a central nervous system, a network that transmits only aches and pains and shared nightmares. The news and entertainment media.

"The organism is not hopelessly deformed. It trembles on the verge of birthing, yearns to live even as it feels itself dying. It may yet succeed. On the verge of extinction, Man gropes for the stars, and now less than a century after the first man left the surface of Earth in powered flight, we gather here in the orbit of Saturn to decide whether our race's destiny should now be extended or cut short.

"Our womb is nearly filled with our poisonous by-products. The question before us is: Are we or are we not going to outgrow our neurotic dependence on planets—before it destroys us?"

"What is this crap," Silverman snarled, "some more of your *Homo caelestis* horseshit? Is that your next evolutionary step? McGillicuddy was right, it's a goddam evolutionary *dead end*! You couldn't be self-supporting in fifty years from a standing start, the speed you recruit. If the Earth and Moon blew up tomorrow, God forbid, you would be dead within two or three years at the outside. You're parasites on your evolutionary inferiors, Armstead, exiled parasites at that. You can't live in your new environment without cell walls of steel and slashproof plastic, essential artifacts that are manufactured *only back there in the womb*."

"I was wrong," Tom said softly. "We're not an evolutionary dead end. I couldn't see the whole picture."

"*What did you miss?*" Silverman screamed.

"We have to change the analogy now," Linda spoke up. "It starts to break down." Her warm contralto was measured and soothing; I saw Silverman begin to relax as the magic worked on him. "Think of us now not as sextuplets, or even as a kind of six-personed fetus. Think of the Earth not as a uterus but as an ovary—and the six of us as a single ovum. Together we carry *half* of the genes for a new kind of being.

"The most awesome and miraculous moment of all creation is the instant of syngamy, the instant at which two things come together to form so infinitely much more than the sum or even the product of their parts: the moment of conception. That is the crossroads, with phylogeny behind and ontogeny ahead, and that is the crossroads at which we are poised now."

"What is the sperm cell for your ovum?" Chen asked. "The alien swarm, I presume?"

"Oh, no," Norrey said. "They're something more like the yin/yang, male/female overmind that produces the syngamy, in response to needs of its own. Change the analogy again: Think of them as the bees they so resemble, the pollinators of a gigantic monoclinous flower we call the Solar System. It is a true hermaphrodite, containing both pistil and stamen within itself. Call Earth the pistil, if you will, and we Stardancers are its combined ovule and stigma."

"And the stamen?" Chen insisted, "The pollen?"

"The stamen is Titan," Norrey said simply. "That red organic matter the aliens' balloon gave off was some of its pollen."

Another stunned silence.

"Can you explain its nature to us?" DeLaTorre asked at last. "I confess my incomprehension."

Raoul spoke now, tugging his glasses out from the bridge of his nose and letting the elastic pull them back. "The stuff is essentially a kind of superplant itself. The aliens have been growing it in Titan's upper atmosphere for millennia, staining the planetoid red. Upon contact with a human body, a kind of mutual interaction takes place that can't be described. Energy from another . . . from another plane infuses both sides. Syngamy takes place, and perfect metabolism begins."

"*Perfect* metabolism?" DeLaTorre echoed uncertainly.

"The substance is a perfect symbiotic complement to the human organism."

"But—but . . . but *how*—?"

"You wear it like a second skin, and you live naked in space," he said flatly. "It enters the body at mouth and nostrils, spreads a million microtendrils throughout the system, emerges to rejoin itself at the anus. It covers you inside and out, becomes a part of you, in total metabolic balance."

Chen Ten Li looked poleaxed. "A *perfect* symbiote. . . ." he breathed.

"Right down to the trace elements," Raoul agreed. "Planned that way a billion years ago. It is our Other Half."

"How is it done?" he whispered.

"Just enter a cloud of the stuff and open your hood. The escaping air is their chemical cue: they home in, swim upstream and spawn. From the moment they first contact bare flesh until the point of total absorption and adsorption, complete synthesis, is maybe three seconds. About a second and a half in, you cease being human, forever." He shivered. "Do you understand why we screamed?"

"No," Silverman cried. "No, I do *not*. None of this makes sense! So the red crap is a living spacesuit, a biologically tailored what you said, you give it carbon dioxide it gives you oxygen, you give it shit it gives you strawberry jam. Very lovely: you've just eliminated all your overhead except for fuel and leisure aids. Very nice fellows, these aliens. How does it make you inhuman? Does the crap take over your mind or what?"

"It has no 'mind' of its own," Raoul told him. "Oh, it's remarkably sophisticated for a plant, with awareness above the vegetable. There are some remarkably complex tropisms, but you couldn't call it sentient. It sort of sets up partnership with the medulla, and rarely gets even as preconscious as a reflex. It just performs its function, in accordance with its biological programming."

"What would make you inhuman then?"

My voice sounded funny, even to me. "You don't understand," I said. "You don't *know*. We would never die, Silverman. We would never again hunger or thirst, never need a place to dispose of our wastes. We would never again fear heat or cold, never fear vacuum, Silverman; we would never fear anything again. We would acquire instant and complete control of our autonomic nervous systems, gain access to the sensorium keyboard of the hypothalamus itself. We would attain symphysis, telepathic communion, become a single mind in six immortal bodies, endlessly dreaming and never asleep. Individually and together we would become no more like a human than a human is like a chimpanzee. I don't mind telling you that all six of us used our diapers out there. I'm still a little scared."

"But you are ready. . . ." Chen said softly.

"Not yet," Linda said for all of us. "But we will be soon. That much we know."

"This telepathy business," Silverman said tentatively. "This 'single mind' stuff—is that for sure?"

"Oh, it's not dependent on the aliens," Linda assured him. "They showed us how to find that plane—but the capacity was always there, in every human that ever lived. Every holy man that ever got enlightened came down off the mountain saying, 'We're all one'—and every damn time the people decided it must be a metaphor. The symbiote helps us *some*, but—"

"How does it help?" Silverman interrupted.

"Well, the distraction factor, mostly. I mean, most people have flashes of telepathic ability, but there are so many *distractions*. It's worse for a planetdweller, of course, but even in the Studio we got hungry, we got thirsty and horny and bored and tired and sore and angry and afraid. 'Being in our heads,' we called it. The animal part of us impeding the progress of the angel. The symbiote frees you from all animal needs—you can experience them, at whim, but never again are you subject to their arbitrary command. The symbiote does act as a kind of mild amplifier of the telepathic 'wave band,' but it helps much more by improving the "signal-to-noise ratio' at the point of origin."

"What I mean," Silverman said, "if God forbid *I* were to let this fungus infest me, *I* would become at least mildly telepathic? As well as immortal and beyond having to go to the bathroom?"

"No sir," she said politely but firmly. "If you were *already* mildly telepathic before you entered symbiotic partnership, you would become significantly more so. If, at that time, you happened to be in the field of a fully functioning telepath, you would become exponentially more so."

"But if I took, say, the average man in the street and put him in a symbiote suit—"

"—you'd get an average immortal who never needed to

go to the bathroom and was more empathic than he used to be," I finished.

"Empathy is sort of telepathy's kid brother," Linda said.

"More like its larval stage," I corrected.

"But two average guys in symbiote suits wouldn't necessarily be able to read each other's minds?"

"Not unless they worked long and hard at learning how that's done," I told him, "which they would almost certainly do. It's *lonely* in space."

He fell silent, and there was a pause while the rest of them sorted out their opinions and emotions. It took a while.

I had things to sort out myself. I was still possessed of that same internal *certainty* that I had felt since I woke up in the Limousine, feeling that almost prescient sense of inevitability, but the cusp was approaching quickly now. *What if you should die, at this moment of moments?* whispered an animal voice from the back of my skull.

As I had at the moment I confronted the aliens, I felt totally alive.

"Mr. Armstead," DeLaTorre said, shaking his head and frowning mightily, "it seems to me that you are saying that all human want is coming to an end?"

"Oh no," I said hastily. "I'm very sorry if we accidentally implied that. The symbiote cannot live in a terrestrial environment. Anything like that kind of gravity and atmosphere would kill it. No, the symbiote will not bring Heaven to Earth. *Nothing* can. Mohammed must go to the mountain—and many will refuse."

"Perhaps," Chen suggested delicately, "terrestrial scientists might be able to genetically modify the aliens' gift?"

"No," Harry said flatly. "There is no *way* you can give symphonies and sunsets to a fetus that insists on staying in the womb. That cloud of symbiote over Titan is every person's birthright—but first they gotta earn it, by consenting to be born."

"And to do that," Raoul agreed, "they have to cut loose of Earth forever."

"There is an appealing symmetry to the concept," Chen said thoughtfully.

"Hell, yes," Raoul said. "We should have expected something like it. The whole business of adaptation to free fall being possible but irreversible . . . look, at the moment of your birth, a very heavy miracle happened, in a single instant. One minute you were essentially a fish, with a fish's two-valved circulatory system, parasitic on the womb. Then, all at once, a switch slammed shut. Zippo-bang, you were a mammal, just like that. Four-valved heart, self-contained—*you made a major, irreversible physiological leap, into a new plane of evolution.* It was accompanied by pain, trauma, and a flood of data from senses you hadn't known you possessed. Nearly at once a whole bunch of infinitely more advanced beings in the same predicament began trying to teach you how to communicate. 'Appealing'? The fucking symmetry is overwhelming! *Now* do you begin to understand why we screamed? We're in the very midst of the same process—and all babies scream."

"I don't understand," Dmirov complained. "You would be able to live naked in space—but how could you *go* anywhere?"

"Light pressure?" Chen suggested.

"The symbiote can deploy itself as a light sail," I agreed, "but there are other forces we will use to carry us where we want to go."

"Gravity gradients?"

"No. Nothing you could detect or measure."

"Preposterous," Dmirov snorted.

"How did the aliens get here?" I asked gently, and she reddened.

"The thing that makes it so difficult for me to credit your story," Chen said, "is the improbability factor. So much of your coming here was random chance."

"Dr. Chen," I cut him off, "are you familiar with the proverb that says there is a destiny which shapes our ends, rough-hew them how we will?"

"But any of a thousand things might have conspired to prevent any of this from occurring."

"Fifty-four things conspired to make it all occur. Superthings. Or did you think that the aliens just happened to appear in this system at the time that Shara Drummond began working at Skyfac? That they just happened to jump to Saturn when she returned to Skyfac to dance? That they just happened to appear outside Skyfac at the moment that Shara was about to return to Earth forever, a failure? Or that this whole trip to Saturn just happened to be feasible in the first place? Me, I wonder what they were doing out Neptune way, that first time they appeared." I considered it. "I'll have to go see."

"You don't understand," Chen said urgently, and then controlled himself. "It is not generally known, but six years ago our planet was nearly destroyed by nuclear holocaust. Chance and good fortune saved us—there were no aliens in our skies then."

Harry spoke up. "Know what a pregnant rabbit does if conditions aren't favorable for birth? Reabsorbs the fetuses into the womb. Just reverses the process, recycles the ingredients and tries again when conditions are better."

"I don't follow."

"Have you ever heard of Atlantis?"

Chen's face went the color of meerschaum, and everyone else gaped or gasped.

"It comes in cycles," I said, "like labor pains building to a peak. They come as close together as four or five thousand years—the Pyramids were built that far back—and as far apart as twenty thousand."

"Sometimes they get pretty rough," Harry added. "There used to be a planet between Mars and Jupiter."

"*Bojemoi*," Dmirov breathed. "The Asteroid Belt. . . ."

"And Venus is handy in case *we* screw up altogether,"

I agreed, "reducing atmosphere all ready to go, just seed with algae and wait. *God*, they must be patient."

Another extensive stunned silence. They believed now, all of them, or were beginning to. Therefore they had to rearrange literally everything they had ever known, recast all of existence in the light of this new information and try to determine just who, in relation to this confusion, they themselves might be. They were advanced in years for this kind of uprooting, their beliefs and opinions deeply ingrained by time; that they were able to accept the information and think at all said clearly that every one of them possessed a strong and flexible mind. Wertheimer had chosen well; none of them cracked, rejected the truth and went catatonic as we had. Of course, they were not out in free space, thinking seriously of removing their p-suits. But then, they had pressures *we* lacked: they represented a planet.

"Your intention, then," Silverman said slowly, "is to do this thing?"

Six voices chorused, "Yes."

"At once," I added.

"And you are sure that all you have told us is true, that the aliens have told no lies, held out nothing?" Ever so casually he had been separating himself from the other diplomats.

"We're certain," I said, tensing my thighs again.

"But where will you go?" DeLaTorre cried. "What will you *do*?"

"What all newborns do. We'll examine our nursery. The Solar System."

Silverman kicked off suddenly, jaunting to the empty fourth wall. "I'm very sorry," he said mournfully. "You'll do nothing of the kind."

There was a small Beretta in his hand.

# Chapter 5

There was a calculator in his other hand. At least, it looked like one. All at once I knew better, and feared it more than the gun.

"This," he said, confirming my guess, "is a short-range transmitter. If anyone approaches me suddenly, I will use it to trigger radio-controlled explosives, which I placed during the trip here. They will cripple the ship's computer."

"Sheldon," DeLaTorre cried, "are you mad? The computer oversees *life support*."

"I would rather not use this," Silverman said calmly. "But I am utterly determined that the information we have heard will be the exclusive possession of the United States of America—or of no one."

I watched diplomats and soldiers carefully for signs of suicidal bravery, and relaxed slightly. None of them was the kind of fool who jumps a gunman; their common expression was intense disgust. Disgust at Silverman's treachery, and disgust at themselves for not having expected it. I looked most closely at Chen Ten Li, who *had* expected it and had promised to kill Silverman with his hands—but he was totally relaxed, a gentle, mocking smile beginning at the corners of his lips. Interesting.

"Mr. Silverman," Susan Pha Song said, "you have not thought this thing through."

"Colonel," he said ironically, "I have had the better part of a year in which to do little else."

"Nevertheless, you have overlooked something," she insisted.

"Pray enlighten me."

"If we were all to rush you now," she said evenly, "you might shoot perhaps two or three of us before you were overwhelmed. If we do not, you will certainly kill us all. Or had you planned to hold a gun on us for two years?"

"If you rush me," Silverman promised, "I will kill the computer, and you will all die anyway."

"So either we die and you return to Earth with your secret, or we die and you do not." She put a hand on the wall on either side of her.

"Wrong," Silverman said hurriedly. "I do not intend to kill you all. I don't have to. I will leave you all in this room. My pressure suit just so happens to be in the next room—I will put it on and instruct the computer to evacuate all the compartments adjacent to this one. I will of course have disabled your own terminal here. Air pressure and the safety interlocks will prevent you from opening a door to vacuum: a foolproof prison. And so long as I detect no attempts to escape on the phone, I will continue to permit food, air and water systems to operate in here. I have the necessary program tapes to bring us back to Earth, where you will all be treated as prisoners of war under international conventions."

"What war?"

"The one that just started and ended. Have you heard? America won."

"Sheldon, Sheldon," DeLaTorre insisted, "what can you hope to accomplish by this insane expedient?"

"Are you kidding?" Silverman snorted. "The biggest component of capital investment in space exploitation is life support. This moon full of fungus is a free ticket to the whole Solar System—with immortality thrown in! And the United States is going to have it, that I promise you." He turned to Li and Dmirov and said, with utter sincerity, the most incredible sentence I have ever heard in my life: "I am not going to allow you to export your godless way of life to the stars."

Chen actually laughed out loud, and I joined him.

"One of those Canuck socialists, eh, Armstrong?" Silverman snarled.

"That's the thing that bugs you the most, isn't it, Silverman?" I grinned. "A *Homo caelestis* in symbiosis has no wants, no needs: *there's nothing you can sell him.* And he submerges himself in a group: a natural Commie. Men without self-interest scare you silly, don't they?"

"Pseudophilosophical bullshit," Silverman barked. "I'm taking possession of the most stupendous military intelligence of the century."

"Oh my God," Raoul drawled disgustedly, "Hi Yo Silverman, the John Wayne of the Spaceways. You're actually visualizing soldiers in symbiote suits, aren't you? The Space Infantry."

"I like the idea," Silverman admitted. "It seems to me that a naked man with a symbiote would evade most detection devices. No metals, low albedo—and if it's a perfect symbiosis there'd be no waste heat. What a saboteur! No support or supplies required . . . by God, we could *use infantry to interdict Titan.*"

"Silverman," I said gently, "you're an imbecile. Assume for a moment that you can bludgeon GI Joe into letting what you call a fungus crawl up his nose and down his throat. Fine. You now have an *extremely* mobile infantryman. He has no wants or needs whatsoever, he knows that he will be immortal if he can avoid getting killed, and his empathic faculty is at a maximum. *What's going to keep him from deserting?* Loyalty to a country he'll never see again? Relatives in Hoboken, who live in a gravity field that'd kill him?"

"Laser beams if necessary," he began.

"Remember how fast we were dancing there before the end? Go ask the computer whether we could have danced around a laser beam—even a computer-operated one. You said yourself we'd be bloody hard to track."

"Your military secret is worthless, Silverman," Tom said.

"Better minds than mine will work out the practical details," he insisted. "I know a military edge when I see one. Commander Cox," he said suddenly, "you are an American. Are you with me?"

"There are three other Americans aboard," Cox answered obliquely. Tom, Harry, and Raoul stiffened.

"Yeah. One's got a pregnant Canadian wife, two are perverts, and all three are under the influence of those alien creatures. Are you with me?"

Bill seemed to be thinking hard. "Yeah. You're right. I hate to admit it, but only the United States can be trusted with this much power."

Silverman was studying him intently. "No," he decided, "no, Commander, I'm afraid I don't believe you. Your oath of allegiance is to the United Nations. If you had said no, or answered ambiguously, in a few days I might have believed a yes. But you are lying." He shook his head regretfully. "All right, ladies and gentlemen, here is how we shall proceed. No one will make a move until I say so. Then, one at a time, on command, you will all jump to that wall there with the dancers, farthest from the forward door. I will then back out this door, and—"

"Mr. Silverman," Chen interrupted gently, "there is something everyone in this room should know first."

"So speak."

"The installations that you made at Conduits 364-B and 1117-A, *and* at the central core, were removed and thrown out the airlock some twenty minutes after you completed them. You are a clumsy fool, Silverman, and an utterly predictable one. Your transmitter is useless."

"You're lying," Silverman snarled, and Chen didn't bother to answer. His mocking smile was answer enough.

Right there Silverman proved himself a chump. If he'd had the quickness to bluff, to claim *other* installations Chen didn't know about, he might even then have salvaged something. I'm sure he never thought of it.

Bill and Colonel Song made their decisions at the same instant and sprang.

Silverman pressed a button on the transmitter, and the lights and air conditioning *didn't* go out. Crying with rage, he stuck up his silly gun and fired.

Ian Fleming to the contrary, the small Beretta is a miserable weapon, best suited to use across a desk. But the Law of Chaos worked with Silverman: The slug he aimed at Bill neatly nicked open Colonel Song's jugular, ricocheted off the wall behind her—the wall opposite Silverman—and smacked into Bill from behind, tumbling him and adding acceleration.

Silverman was not a complete idiot—he had expected greater recoil in free fall and braced for it. But he wasn't expecting his own slug to bring Bill to him quicker—before he could reaim, Bill smacked into him. Still he retained his grip on the pistol, and everyone in the room jumped for cover.

But by that time I was across the room. I slapped switches, and the lights and air conditioning *did* go out.

It was simple, then. We had only to wait.

Silverman began to scream first, followed by Dmirov and DeLaTorre. Most humans go a little crazy in total darkness, and free fall makes it *much* worse. Without a local vertical, as Chen Ten Li had learned when his bedroom lights failed, you are *lost*. The distress is primeval and quite hard to override.

Silverman hadn't learned enough about free fall—or else he hadn't heard the air conditioning quit. He was the only one in the room still velcro'd to a wall, and he was too terrified to move. After a time his screams diminished, became gasps, then one last scream and silence. I waited just a moment to be sure—Song was certainly dead already, but Bill's condition was unknown—then jaunted back to the switches and cut in lights and air again. Silverman was stuck like a fly to the wall, dying of oxygen lack in a room full of air, an invisible bubble of his own exhalations around his head. The gun drifted a half meter from his outstretched hand.

I pointed, and Harry collected it. "Secure him before he wakes up," I said, and jaunted to Bill. Linda and Raoul were already with him, examining the wound. Across the room Susan Pha Song drifted limply, and her throat had stopped pumping blood. I had lived with that lady for over a year, and I did not know her at all; and while that had been at least half her idea, I was ashamed. As I watched, eight or ten red softballs met at the air grille and vanished with a wet sucking sound.

"How is he?"

"I don't think it's critical," Linda reported. "Grazed a rib and exited. Cracked it, maybe."

"I have medical training," Dmirov, of all people, said. "I have never practiced in free fall—but I have treated bullet wounds before."

Linda took him to the first aid compartment over by the duckpins and Frisbees. Bill trailed a string of red beads that drifted in a lazy arc toward the grille. Dmirov followed Linda, shaking with rage or reaction or both.

Harry and Tom had efficiently trussed Silverman with weighted jump ropes. It appeared superfluous—a man his age takes anoxia hard; he was sleeping soundly. Chen was hovering near the computer terminal, programming something, and Norrey and DeLaTorre were preparing to tow Song's body to the dispensary, where grim forethought had placed supplies of embalming fluid.

But when they reached the door, it would not open for them. Norrey checked the indicator, which showed pressure on the other side, frowned, hit the manual override and frowned again when it failed to work.

"I am deeply sorry, Ms. Armstead," Chen said with sincere regret. "I have instructed the computer to seal off this room. No one may leave." From behind the terminal he produced a portable laser. "This is a recoilless weapon, and can kill you all in a single sweep. If anyone threatens me, I will use it at once."

"Why should anyone threaten you, Li?" I asked softly.

"I have come all this way to negotiate a treaty with aliens. I have not yet done so." He looked me right in the eye.

DeLaTorre looked startled. "Madre de Dios, the aliens—what are they doing while we fight among ourselves?"

"That is not what I mean, Ezequiel," Chen said. "I believe that Mr. Armstead lied when Commander Cox asked him if he was still human. We have yet to negotiate terms of mutual coexistence between his new species and our own. Both lay claim to the same territory."

"*How?*" Raoul asked. "We have no interests in common."

"We both propose to eventually populate what is known as human space."

"But you're welcome to any of it that's of any conceivable human value," Tom insisted. "Planets are no use to us, the asteroids are no use to us—all we need is cubic and sunshine. You're not begrudging us *cubic*, are you? Even *our* scale isn't that big."

"If ever Cro-Magnon and Neanderthal lived in peace in the same valley, it took an extraordinary social contract to enforce it," he insisted. "Precisely because you will need nothing that we need, you will be difficult to live with. As I speak I realize that you will be *impossible* to live with. Looking down godlike on our frantic scurrying, amused by our terrible urgency—how I hate you already! Your very existence makes nearly every living human a failure; and only those with a peculiar acrobat's knack for functioning spherically—and the resources to get to Titan!—can hope to strive for success. If you are not an evolutionary dead end, then most of the human race *is*. No, Stardancers: I do not believe we could ever share the same volume of space with you."

He had been programming the computer as he spoke, by touch, never taking his full attention from us.

"The world we left behind us was poised on a knife edge. It has been a truism for a long time that if we did not blow ourselves up by the year 2010, the world would be past the crisis point, and an age of plenty would follow. But at the time that we left Earth, the chances of surviving that long were slim, I think you will all agree.

"Our planet is wound to the bursting point with need," he said sadly. "Nothing could push it more certainly over the edge than the erosion of planetary morale which your existence would precipitate—than the knowledge that there *are* gods, who have no more heed for Man than Man has for the billions and trillions of sperm and eggs that failed to become gametes. That salvation and eternal life are only for a few."

Ezequiel was glowering thoughtfully, and so was Dmirov, who had just finished bandaging Bill. I began to reply, but Chen cut me off.

"Please, Charles. I recognize that you must act to preserve your species. Surely you can understand that I must protect my own?"

In that moment he was the most dangerous man I had ever known, and the most noble. With love and deep respect I inclined my head. "Li," I said, "I concede and admire your logic. But you are in error."

"Perhaps," he agreed. "But I am certain."

"Your intentions?" I knew already; I wanted to hear him state them.

He gestured to the computer terminal. "This vessel was equipped with the finest computer made. Made in Peking. I have set up a program prepared for me before we left, by its designers. A tapeworm program. When I touch the "Execute" key, it will begin to disembowel the computer's memory banks, requiring only fifteen minutes to complete a total core dump."

"You would kill us all, like Silverman?" DeLaTorre demanded.

"Not like Silverman!" Chen blazed, reddening with anger. At once he recovered, and half-smiled. "More efficiently, at the very least. And *for different reasons*. He wished this news communicated only to his own country. I wish it communicated to no one. I propose to disable this ship's deep-space communications lasers, empty its memory banks, and leave it derelict. Then I shall kill you all, quickly and mercifully. The bomb you call the Planet Cracker has its own guidance system; I can open the bomb-bay doors manually. I do not believe I will bring my pressure suit." His voice was terrifying calm. "Perhaps the next Earth ship will find the aliens still here, four or five years hence. But Saturn will have eight moons and two Rings."

Linda was shaking her head. "So wrong, Li, so wrong, you're a Confucian Legalist looking at the Tao—"

"I'm part of a terrified womb," Chen said firmly, "and it is my judgment that birth now would kill the mother. I have decided that the womb must reabsorb the fetus of *Homo caelestis*. Perhaps at the peak of the *next* cycle the human race will be mature enough to survive parturition— it is not now. *My* responsibility must be to the womb—for it is all the world I know or can know."

It had begun at the instant that I asked him his intentions, knowing them already.

It had happened before, briefly and too late, at the moment of showdown with Silverman. It had faded again unnoticed by the humans in the room. There had been nothing visible to notice: our only action had been to darken the room. We had been afraid then—and a person had died.

But this threat was not to our freedom but to our existence as a species. For the second time in fifteen minutes, my family entered rapport.

Time spiraled down like an unwound Victrola. Six viewpoints melded into one. More than six camera angles: the 360° visual integration was merely useful. Six *viewpoints* combined, six lifetimes' worth of perceptions, opinions, skills, and insights impinged upon each other and coalesced like droplets of mercury into a single entity. Since the part of us that was Linda knew Li best, we used her eyes and ears to monitor his words and his energy in realtime, while beneath and around them, we contemplated how best to bring tranquility to our cousin. At his only pause for breath, we used Linda's words to try and divert his energies, but were unsurprised to fail. He was too blind with pain. By the time the monitor fragment of her awareness reported that his finger was tensing to reach for the "Execute" key, the whole of us was more than ready with our plan.

All six of us contributed choreography to that dance, and polished it mentally until it filled our dancers' souls with joy. The first priority was the tapeworm program; the second was the laser. It was Tom the martial-arts expert who knew precisely where and how to strike so as to cause Chen's muscles to spasm involuntarily. It was Raoul the visual-effects specialist who knew where Chen's optical "blind spot" was, and knew that Norrey would be in it at the critical instant. Norrey *knew* the position of the racked Frisbees behind her because Harry and I could see them peripherally from where we were. And it was Linda who supplied me with the only words that might have captured Chen's attention in that moment, fixing his gaze on me and his blind spot on Norrey.

"And what of your grandchildren, Chen Ten Li?"

His tortured eyes focused on me and widened. Norrey reached behind her with both arms, and surrendered control of them. Harry, who was our best shot, used her right arm to throw the Frisbee that yanked Chen's right hand away from the terminal in uncontrollable pain reflex. Raoul, who was left-handed, used her left arm to throw the Frisbee that ruined the laser and smashed it out of the crook of Chen's left arm. Both missiles arrived before he knew they had been launched; even as they struck, Tom had kicked Song's corpse between Linda and the line of fire in case of a miss, and Norrey had grabbed two more Frisbees on the same chance. And I was already halfway to Chen myself: I was intuitively sure that he knew one of the ways to suicide barehanded.

It was over in less than a second of realtime. To the eyes of DeLaTorre and Dmirov we must have seemed to . . . *flicker* and then reappear in new relative positions, like a frightened school of fish. Chen was crying out in pain and rage and shame, and I was holding him in a four-limbed hammerlock, conspicuously not hurting him. Harry was waiting for the ricocheting Frisbees, retrieving them lazily; Raoul was by the computer, wiping Chen's program.

The dance was finished. And correctly this time: no blood had been spilled. We knew with a guiltless regret that if we had yielded to rapport more freely the first time, Song would not be dead and Bill wounded. We had been afraid, then, yielded only tentatively and too late. Now the last trace of fear was gone; our hearts were sure. We were ready to be responsible.

"Dr. Chen," I said formally, "do I have your parole?"

He stiffened in my grip, and then relaxed totally. "Yes," he said, his voice gone empty. I released him, and was stunned by how *old* he looked. His calendar age was fifty-six.

"Sir," I said urgently, trying to hold him with my eyes, "your fears are groundless. Your pain is needless. *Listen to me*: you are *not* a useless by-product of *Homo caelestis*. You are not a failed gamete. You are one of the people who personally held our planet Earth together, with your bare hands, until it could birth the next stage. Does that rob your life of meaning, diminish your dignity? You are one of the few living statesmen who can help ease Earth through the coming transition—do you lack the self-confidence, or the courage? You helped open up space, and you have grandchildren—didn't you mean for them to have the stars? Would you deny them now? Will you listen to what *we* think will happen? Can happen? Must happen?"

Chen shook his head like a twitching cat, absently massaging his right arm. "I will listen."

"In the first place, stop tripping over analogies and metaphors. You're not a failed gamete, or anything of the kind, *unless you choose to be*. The whole human race can be *Homo caelestis* if it wants to. Many of 'em won't, but the choice is theirs. And yours."

"But the vast majority of us cannot perceive spherically," Chen shouted.

I smiled. "Doctor, when one of my failed students left for Earth he said to me, 'I couldn't learn to see the way you do if I tried for a hundred years.'"

"Exactly. I have been in free space, and I agree."

"Suppose you had *two* hundred years?"

"*Eh?*"

"Suppose you entered symbiosis, right now. You'd have to have a tailored environment of right angles to stay sane, at first. But *you'd be immortal*. With absolutely nothing better to do, could you not unlearn your gravitic bias in time?"

"There's more," Linda said. "Children born in free space will think spherically from infancy. They won't have to unlearn a lifetime of essentially false, purely local information about how reality works. Li, in free fall you are not too old to sire more children. You can learn with them, telepathically—and inherit the stars together!"

"All mankind," I went on, "all that wants to, can begin preparing at once, by moving to Trojan-point O'Neill

Colonies and entering symbiosis. The colonization of space can begin with this generation."

"But how is such a migration to be financed?" he cried.

"Li, Li," Linda said, as one explaining to a child, "the human race is *rich*, as of now. The total resources of the System are now available to all, for free. Why haven't L-5 colonies gotten off the ground, or the asteroid mining that would support them? Silverman said it ten minutes ago: The biggest single component of expense has always been life support, and elaborate attempts to prevent the crew from adapting to free fall by simulating gravity. If all you need is a set of right angles that will last for a few centuries, you can build cities out of aluminum foil, haul enormous quantities of symbiote from Titan to Terra."

"Imagine a telepathic construction gang," Harry said, "who never have to eat or rest."

"Imagine an explosion of art and music," Raoul said, "raining down on Earth from the heavens, drawing every heart that ever yearned for the stars."

"Imagine an Earth," Tom said, "filled with only those who want to be there."

"And imagine your children-to-be," Norrey said. "The first children in all history to be raised free of the bitter intergenerational resentments that arise from a child's utter dependence on his parents. In space, children and parents will relate at eyelevel, in every sense. Perhaps they need not be natural enemies after all."

"But you are not human!" Chen Ten Li cried. "Why should you give us all this time and energy? What is Man, that you should be mindful of him?"

"Li," Linda said compassionately, "were we not born of man and woman? Does not the child remember the womb, and yearn for it all his life? Do you not honor your mother, although you may never be part of her again? We would preserve and cherish the Earth, our womb, that it may remain alive and fruitful and bear multiple births to its capacity."

"That is our only defense," I said quietly, "against the immense loneliness of being even *Homo caelestis* in empty space. Six minds isn't enough—when we have six billion united in undisturbed thought, then, perhaps, we will learn some things. All mankind is our genetic heritage."

"Besides," Raoul added cheerfully, "what's a few centuries of our time? *We're in no hurry*."

"Li," I went on, "to be human is to stand between ape and angel. To be angel, as are my family and I, is to float between man and the gods, *partaking fully of both*. Without gravity or a local vertical there can be no false concept of the 'high' and the 'low': how could we act other than ethically? Immortal, needing nothing, how could we be evil?"

"As a species," Tom picked up, "we naturally will deal only through the United Nations. Dr. Chen, believe me: we've studied this on something faster than computer-time. There is no way for our plans to be subverted, for the symbiote to be hijacked. All the evil men and women on Earth will not stop us, and the days of evil are numbered."

"But," I finished, "we need the help and cooperation of you and every man like you, on the globe or off it. Are you up to it, Chen Ten Li?"

He drifted freely, in the partial crouch of complete relaxation, his face slack with thought and his eyes rolled up into his head. At long last his pupils reappeared, and life returned to his features. He met my eyes, and a gentle slight smile tugged at his mouth.

"You remind me greatly," he said, "of a *man* I once knew, named Charles Armstead."

"Dr. Chen," I said, feeling tension drain away, "Li my friend, I *am* that man. I am also something else, and you have rightly deduced that I am maintaining my six discrete conversational *personas* only as a courtesy to you, in the same way that I adapt my bodies to your local vertical. It demonstrates clearly that telepathic communion does not involve what you would call ego loss." Shifting *persona* as I spoke, so that each of us uttered a single word, I/we said:

"I'm"

"more"

"than"

"human"

"not"

"less."

"Very well," Li said, shaking his head. "Together we will bring the millennium to our weary planet."

"I am with you," DeLaTorre said simply.

"I too," Dmirov said.

"Let's get Bill and Col. Song's body to sickbay," six voices said.

And an hour later we six departed for the Starseeders' location. We didn't bother with the shuttlecraft, this time. Our suit thrusters held enough for a one-way trip . . .

# 4

## *Syngamy....*

# Chapter 1

Saturn burned ocher and brown against an aching blackness so vast it was barely interrupted by the cold light of a billion billion suns.

We danced as we jetted through that blackness, almost without thinking about it. We were leaving human life behind, and we danced our leaving of it. Essentially each of us created our own *Stardance*, and the great empty cosmic hall rang with Raoul's last symphony. Each dance was individual and self-complete; each happened to mesh with the other three and with the music, in a kind of second-level statement; and although all of these were conceived without any perceived constraints of time or distance, Harry's overawareness saw to it that all five works of art happened to end, together, before the aliens. It was always Harry who made us meet our deadlines.

None of this was taped. Unlike Shara's *Stardance*, this was not meant to be witnessed. It was meant to be shared, to be danced.

But it was witnessed. The Starseeders (aliens they were *not*) writhed in something analogous to applause as we hung before them, gasping for breath, savoring the feel of the last sweat we would ever know.

We were no longer afraid of them.

YOU HAVE MADE YOUR CHOICE?

*Yes.*

IT WILL BE A FINE BIRTHING.

Raoul hurled his Musicmaster into deep space. *Let it begin without delay.*

AT ONCE:

There was an excitement in their dance, now, an elemental energy that somehow seemed to contain an element of humor, of suppressed mirth. They began a pattern that we had never seen before, yet seemed to *know* in some cellular fashion, a pattern that alternated between the simple and the complex, without ever resolving. The Harry part of our mind called it "the naming of pi," and all of us raptly watched it unfold. It was the most hypnotic pattern ever dreamed, the dance of creation itself, the most essential expression of the Tao, and the stars themselves seemed to pay attention.

And as we stared, transfixed, the semivisible sphere around the Starseeders began for the second time to weep bloody tears.

They coalesced into a thin crimson ring about the immense sphere, then contracted into six orbiting bubbles.

Without hesitation we each jetted to a bubble and plunged inside. Once we were in, we skinned out of our p-suits and flung them at the walls of our bubbles, which passed them out into space. Raoul added his glasses. Then the bubbles contracted around and into and through us.

Things happened on a thousand different levels, then, to all six of me; but it is Charlie Armstead who is telling you this. I felt something cool slide down my throat and up my nostrils, suppressed gag reflex with free-fall training, thought briefly of Chen Ten Li and the ancient Chinese legends of edible gold that brings immortality—felt suddenly and forever a total awareness, knowledge, and control of my entire body and brain. In a frozen instant of timelessness I scanned my life's accumulation of memories, savored them, transmitted them in a single sending to my family, and savored theirs. Simultaneously I was employing eyes that now registered a wider spectrum to see the universe in greater depth, and simultaneously I was playing the keys of my own internal sensorium, tasting crisp bacon and Norrey's breast and the sweet taste of courage, smelling woodsmoke and Norrey's loins and the sweet smell of caring, hearing Raoul's music and Norrey's voice and the sweet sound of silence. Almost absentmindedly I healed the damage to my hip, felt complete function return as if it had never been gone.

As to happenings on a group level, there is not much I can tell you that will mean anything. We made love, again almost absentmindedly, and we all felt together the yearnings toward life in Linda's belly, felt the symbiote that shielded her body make the same perception and begin preparing its own mitosis. Quite consciously and deliberately, Norrey and I conceived a child of our own. These things were only incidentals, but what can I tell you of the essentials? On one major level we shared each other's every memory and forgave each other the shameful parts and rejoiced in all the proud parts. On another major level we began what would become an ongoing lifespan symposium on the meaning of beauty. On another we began planning the last details of the migration of Man into space.

A significant part of us was pure-plant consciousness, a six-petaled flower basking mindlessly in the sunlight.

We were less than a kilometer from the Starseeders, and we had forgotten their very existence.

We were startled into full awareness of our surroundings as the Starseeders once again collapsed into a single molten ball of intolerable brilliance—and vanished without a good-bye or a final sending.

They will be back, in a mere few centuries of realtime, to see whether anybody feels ready to become a firefly.

In stunned surprise we hovered, and, our attention now focused on the external universe, saw what we had missed.

A crimson-winged angel was approaching us from the direction of Saturn's great Ring. On twin spans of thin red lightsail, an impossible figure came nearer.

*Hello, Norrey, Charlie,* the familiar voice said in our skulls. *Hi Tom, Harry. Linda and Raoul, I don't know you yet, but you love my loved ones—hello.*

*Shara!* screamed six voiceless brains.

*Sometimes fireflies pick up a hitchhiker.*

*But how—?*

*I was more like an incubator baby, actually, but they got me to Titan alive. That was my suit and tanks you saw burning up. They were desperate and overeager, just as they said. I've . . . I've been waiting in the Ring for you to make your decision. I didn't want to influence its outcome.*

The Snowflake that was me groped for "words."

*You have made a good marriage,* she said, *you six.*

*Marry us!* we cried.

*I thought you'd never ask.*

And my sister swarmed into me and we are one.

That is essentially the whole of this story.

I—the Charlie Armstead component of "I"—began this work long ago, as an article for magazine and computer-fax sale. So much nonsense had been talked and written about Shara that I was angry, and determined to set the record straight. In that incarnation, this manuscript ended with Shara's death.

But when I was done, I no longer needed to publish the

article. I found that I had written it only to clarify things in my own mind. I withheld it, and hung on to the manuscript with the vague idea of someday using it as a seed for my eventual memoirs (in the same spirit in which Harry had begun his Book: because someone had to and who else was there?). From time to time, over the next three years, I added to it with that purpose in mind, "novelizing" rather than "diarizing" to spare the trouble of altering the manuscript later. I spent a lot of the year of *Siegfried*'s outward flight in writing and revising the total, bringing the history up to the point where Chen Ten Li took his first space walk, a few weeks out of Saturn.

All of the subsequent material has been written in a single half-day "sitting," here at the Die's computer terminal. I have been limited only by the physical speed at which the terminal's heat-sensitive "keys" can disengage. As I write, other parts of me drift through eternity. We make love. We worship. We sing. We dance. Endlessly we are each other, yet are ourselves. I know it does not seem that this could be: that is why I have chosen to tell my story by completing Charlie's memoirs (while Shara, approving, reads over my shoulder from a hundred klicks away). I want you to know that Charles Armstead has not been dissolved or diluted into something alien. In *no* sense have I died. I never will. It would be more accurate to say that I am Charlie Armstead to the seventh power. At long last I have managed to destroy the phone company, and great is my glee. I still choreograph dances with Norrey and Shara and the others, still swap abominable multilevel puns with Raoul (right now he's singing an old '40's love song, "I May Never Come Back to Earth Again"), still taste in my mind (where I always did) the smell of fine coffee, the bite of strong drink, the flavor of good grass. The distance between me and you is only time and changes. Once I was a bitter, twisted cripple, poisoning the air around me; now I know no evil because I know no fear.

I have spent the minuscule fraction of energy to complete this manuscript because Bill Cox is preparing to blast for Terra (he'll be back) and it must go now if ever.

This news will not fit into any diplomat's laser message, nor will even those extraordinary men and women be able to express it as I can.

I am Charlie Armstead, and my message to you is: The stars can be even yours.